D1580472

00401205194

THE LOST AND
THE DAMNED

OLIVIER NOREK

THE LOST AND
THE DAMNED

Translated from the French by
Nick Caistor

MACLEHOSE PRESS
QUERCUS · LONDON

First published in the French language by Michel Lafon, Paris, 2013
First published in Great Britain by

MacLehose Press
An imprint of Quercus Publishing Ltd
Carmelite House
50 Victoria Embankment
London EC4Y 0DZ

An Hachette UK company

A CIP catalogue record for this book is available
from the British Library.

ISBN (HB) 978 0 85705 962 8
ISBN (TPB) 978 0 85705 961 1
ISBN (Ebook) 978 0 85705 963 5

10 9 8 7 6 5 4 3 2 1

Designed and typeset in Garamond by Libanus Press
Printed and bound in Great Britain by Clays Ltd, Elcograf S.p.A.

To my family, who keep me in line:
Martine, Claude, Victor, Corinne and Bruno

TRANSLATOR'S NO[TE]

Administratively, France is divided into 96 *départ*[emen]*ts*, where the central government is represented by the *préfe*[t,] prefect. The *départements* are numbered alphabetically: Ain No. 1, Paris No. 75. In the 1960s, as Paris spread outwards into the *banlieues* (suburbs or outskirts) separated from the inner city by the *Périphérique* or ring road, three new *départements* were created: 92 Hauts-de-Seine, 93 Seine-Saint-Denis, 94 Val de Marne. The action of the novel takes place in Seine-Saint-Denis, formerly an area of heavy industry, but more recently one with a high proportion of tower blocks and a substantial immigrant population.

PROLOGUE

March 2011

The height could be a match. The age certainly was. As for the physique, it was hard to be sure. Old Simon picked up his telephone and, taking care not to raise too many hopes, announced:

"I may have a lead."

At the far end of the line, the old lady's voice was little more than a breath.

"Camille?"

"I'm not sure, madame."

Before hanging up, Simon told her the time and place they should meet: the mortuary at the Institut médico-légal de Paris.

Found lifeless, half-naked and with no proof of identity in a squat in the Les Lilas neighbourhood of Seine-Saint-Denis, she must have been around twenty. For the autopsy, Dr Léa Marquant, the forensic pathologist at the Institut médico-légal, the Paris forensics institute, had slit from the base of her neck down to her pubis with a single stroke of her scalpel, as gently as a caress. The girl's interior betrayed the effects of an abusive consumption of drugs and alcohol, as well as of violent sexual relations no-one could have imagined to be consensual. Never before in her career as a forensics expert had Dr Marquant used the expression "massive destruction of the perineum". How on earth had it come to that? What savagery had been inflicted on

9

the victim for there to be literally no wall between her vagina and anus?

Dr Marquant had taken the corpse's dirty hands in her own, stroked her hair, and then traced with her fingers the wounds on her face. First, though, she looked all around: things like that weren't done. She had removed her latex gloves and run her hands over the face once more. She had succumbed to the worst emotion known to her profession: empathy.

And so when a few days later she read by chance in the Institute diary that family members were coming to identify the corpse, Léa Marquant had wanted to be there. It was not an obligation, but she wanted to be there. For her own sake. And for *hers*.

When the sheet is pulled off, people react differently, unpredictably. Mute suffering that sinks in and robs a person of all their strength as they desperately try not to see the ground opening beneath their feet. Vengeful anger that will not accept the verdict and searches for a suitable target. Tearful sorrow that is so loud it ends up getting on your nerves. Impassive calm that is the harbinger of huge storms.

Dr Marquant saw three visitors arrive. She did not recognise any of them, but deduced that the one who was a head and a half taller than the other two and looked like a retired wrestler must be the police officer. His greeting was terse.

"Lieutenant Mathias Aubin."

"Good morning, lieutenant. Dr Marquant. Doesn't Capitaine Coste like us anymore, or are you being punished?"

"It's just something I'd like to see through. The capitaine said to say hello."

She would cope. Shame though, she preferred Coste, who was more discreet, with those sad blue eyes of his.

She introduced herself to the family. First of all to the old lady in the wheelchair, then to the young man pushing her. She invited them to follow her to the mortuary. The policeman fell into step with them, silent as a shadow.

They made their way through the basement. She opened the door to a large space like a deposit box vault, the walls lined with square doors about seventy centimetres wide. Each of them the portal to a life, a story, an ending. The neon lights clicked on, lighting up the mortuary. Dr Marquant checked the file number and from among the 450 cold chambers opened the one containing corpse number 11-1237. She pulled the drawer out, revealing the shape of a body beneath a white sheet.

Glancing enquiringly at the family members, she thought she caught a flicker of apprehension in their eyes. She paused for a moment, her hand on the sheet, then gently drew it down so that only the ruined face was visible.

A few minutes earlier, the massive policeman had tried to warn them. The body they were about to see was that of an addict who may once have been their daughter and sister, but who had no doubt changed, aged, and become scarred by her life in the margins. He had deliberately chosen not to mention the sexual abuse: such details were not necessary until the body had been formally identified. Yet no warning or preparation could have prevented their revulsion when the face appeared.

A prisoner in her wheelchair, the old lady pushed on its arms. Struggled to her feet as best she could to gain some height. Authoritatively, but audibly shocked, she declared it was not her daughter. The son did not utter a sound. The face was so swollen there could easily be a mistake. The forensic expert lowered the sheet completely to reveal a corpse speckled with bruises, scratches, raw wounds with brown scabs, and traces of a thousand syringe marks in blackened, infected craters. The old woman clasped her son's hand and in a firmer voice again insisted that the person stretched out in front of them was not their Camille. Next to her, the son had half-opened his mouth, but the words he was trying to say came out as nothing more than a sigh.

Léa Marquant knew there could be an infinite array of reactions to the sight of a corpse. Yet she could not stop herself quickly covering up the naked body, troubled by the unhealthy way the young man was staring at it. Especially since he too had said he did not recognise the girl.

As they were leaving, the police officer produced a form from his briefcase, crossed the box RECOGNITION NEGATIVE, and got the two visitors to sign it. His hopes of giving this anonymous figure a family were dashed. He offered to accompany them home, but they politely refused.

In the taxi taking them back to their residence in the heights of Saint-Cloud, they did not exchange a word. The mother refused to accept any feeling of guilt. She had acted for the good of the family, ready and willing to pay for it with her soul if one day God reproached her for it.

Huddled in his corner, her son concentrated on trying to breathe steadily. Whenever the taxi took a bend, he was afraid he would throw up onto the leather seats. Heart in his mouth, he could feel all the strength draining out of him, the extremities of his body tingling in a way that was a precursor to being seriously ill. For a second his mind was elsewhere, and it took him some time to remember where he was and what he was doing.

Camille. He had recognised her as well. His Camille, his almost sister. He had recognised her and not said so.

PART ONE

This isn't Hollywood, it's Seine-Saint-Denis.
Commandant M.C. Damiani

I

Coste opened one eye. His mobile went on vibrating on the pillow he did not use. He screwed up his face to read the time. Four-thirty. Even before he picked it up, he knew that someone, somewhere, had been taken out. There was no other reason in Coste's life for him to be woken in the middle of the night.

Grimacing, he swallowed a cup of bitter coffee, leaning against the fridge where a Post-it reading BUY SUGAR was coming unstuck. From the silence of his kitchen, he stared out at the sleeping buildings. His was the only light on in the neighbourhood; I'm the town's wake-up call this morning, he told himself. Checking the gun at his waist, he pulled on a sweater and a baggy black coat, then pocketed his keys. The police Peugeot 306 did not like the cold and refused to start. At this early hour, Victor Coste and his vehicle were in the same mood. He waited a while, lit a cigarette, coughed, tried again. After a few hiccups, the engine came to life. The empty streets offered him an avenue of red traffic lights which he drove through cautiously until he came out on Route Nationale 3.

Four endless grey lanes thrusting like a lance into the heart of the Paris outskirts. As he drove, the houses turned into high-rise buildings and then tower blocks. He looked the other way as he passed the Roma camps. Lines of caravans pressed up against each other next to the R.E.R. railway lines. Washing hung out to dry on the metal fences cordoning off this part of the city no-one was sure whether they loved or hated. He closed his car window as he passed through the stench of the municipal rubbish dump, just a few yards from the first dwellings. This showed how far *Département* 93 and its citizens were respected: as far as sticking mountains of garbage under their noses. An idea that ought to be suggested to the people living in the city of Paris itself, just to see how they liked it. Unless of course the poor and immigrants had a less keenly developed sense of smell . . . Past row upon row of construction firms and a quick hello to the black-economy workers waiting in a huddle for the gangmaster's van. Trying to arrive without feeling too depressed as a new day dawned.

2

Pantin, 5.15 a.m.

Derelict warehouses on the banks of the Canal de l'Ourcq. Stretching for thousands of square metres like an abandoned village, despite the yearly promise that they would be pulled down. A succession of empty buildings where, back in the 1930s, canal barges unloaded their cargoes. All that remained from those days was a rusty iron carcass, its doors boarded up, windows smashed.

A fine drizzle only added to the inhospitable appearance of the surroundings.

Coste lifted the yellow POLICE tape marking the security perimeter designed to keep away any unlikely onlookers at this time of the morning. He took out his I.D. and flashed it at the uniforms on duty. Ronan, the motorbike rider in his team, crushed his cigarette and greeted him, handing him a Maglite torch. Growling a "Good morning" in response, Coste pointed the beam of light at the rusty iron door separating them from the crime scene.

They pushed at it several times until finally, with a prolonged screech, it gave way. Coste went in first, followed by his colleague. He climbed a staircase steep enough to remind him he would soon turn forty, and found himself in a room that seemed vast in the darkness. He shone his torch, which revealed nothing but dancing dust particles. A uniform appeared out of nowhere.

"You two from the Police Judiciaire?"

"Capitaine Coste. What have you got for me?"

Lighting the way for him, the policeman began:

"It's the security guard, or rather his dog, that raised the alarm. The guy got off his backside and went to take a look."

He stepped to one side.

"Be careful! There's a hole there. So he went to see and found him here. Dead."

Ronan muttered what a wonderfully informative summary this was. The uniform took this badly and vanished. Coste and his colleague found themselves alone, staring down at a black giant. Slumped on the floor as if he had collapsed on top of himself, arms hanging from a body that must have measured almost two metres. His head was down on his chest. In the centre of his chest, on a startlingly white sweater, were three gaping holes ringed with blackened bloodstains.

The two men stayed silent for a moment in front of the corpse. Somehow it gave them a strange feeling of being more alive than usual.

"Ronan, go and find that officer you managed to upset so much. Make sure he gives you a more detailed report and then get on the radio and tell them we need the forensic people and a doctor. Ask them for some floodlights. Powerful ones."

3

A seemingly endless extension lead snaked through the warehouse to power the two halogen lamps trained on the inert body. Sam Dorfrey, the newest recruit to Coste's team, was fiddling with them, adjusting the height. A little too skinny and fragile-looking, Sam gave the impression of having become a police officer by accident. Or by chance. Perched high on two uselessly long legs, he was looking all around. Except, that is, at the inordinately large body in the bloodstained sweater spot-lit like a rock star.

"What's wrong, Sam? You don't look too good."

"Go fuck yourself, Ronan, go fuck yourself and I'm going to throw up. Seriously, Coste, you know I don't like this kind of thing. Can't I go and see if there's any C.C.T.V. footage somewhere, or knock on doors in the neighbourhood, get some coffees? I don't care, anything."

"The C.C.T.V. is a good idea. Stick to the neighbouring streets. Ronan, take your bike and go with him. We'll start from the usual principle that the perpetrators of the crime have tried to be clever and not knocked him off near where they live. Search for all possible entry points. We're looking for a car. You don't carry a guy this size on your back, so we're looking for a car, a van, any kind of vehicle."

Coste took out his walkie-talkie.

"Aubin, where have you got to?"

The immense iron building made reception almost impossible, and a cracked voice croaked an inaudible reply. Coste stared at his radio, trying to remember a day when it had worked properly. He took out his mobile.

"Aubin, where have you got to?"

"I'm on the road with the duty medic. We're three minutes away; he's dreaming sweet dreams alongside me."

The forensic team had cordoned off the crime scene. As their flashes went off round the corpse, the room was lit up in Technicolor. Biological samples, sealed bags of cigarette butts, bottles and other flotsam typical of a disused warehouse. Routine stuff. In their white sterile gear, mouths and hair covered to avoid contaminating anything with their own D.N.A., the crime scene experts from the C.S.U. performed a well-rehearsed ballet, ignoring the giant at the centre of their efforts and the reasons why he had been gunned down this January morning.

One of them switched off the two halogen lamps and checked the outlines of the scene with the Crimescope. Searching for any traces of blood or other biological fluids, he ran the bluish light over every square centimetre. Then he sprayed BlueStar developer on a narrow area round the body, but it stayed dark. The head of the C.S.U. was a man with a bushy beard who looked like an old-fashioned professor. His colleagues called him "Can't Touch This". He reported the findings to Coste.

"No luminescent traces, no blood. Your guy wasn't killed here, this is where they dumped him. You can go ahead now and trample on everything, we're done."

*

While the forensic team were stowing their equipment, Aubin was parking his car outside the warehouse. He woke up the doctor, who was snoring now, mouth open wide.

"We're there, Doc."

Without even opening his eyes, his passenger started to complain.

"All this fuss just to check a fucking cadaver. You lot are taking the piss."

"You're as foul-mouthed as one of us, Doc."

When he saw Mathias Aubin approaching, Coste thought at first he must have somehow lost the doctor on the way, until finally he spotted him hidden behind his colleague. Aubin would eclipse anyone. Built like a Normandy wardrobe, topped by a rugged, weary-looking face that gave him the appearance of Lino Ventura when he grew angry. At their first meeting, Coste would never have dreamed this man would become one of the few people he could trust. He had been in the 93 Police Judiciaire for ten years, with all the crap that implied.

Aubin greeted Coste in his gravelly voice:

"Morning, Victor."

"Morning, Mathias. Morning, Doc."

"So where is this fellow of yours?"

"He's the only dead guy in the room: we put halogen lamps round him so you wouldn't miss him."

The doctor bent down in front of the corpse and realised that, even slumped on the floor, the giant was taller than he was.

"Big, isn't he?"

"We couldn't give a damn about that, we want to know if he's dead."

The medic reassumed a professional tone.

"Well, yes, he is. Really and truly dead. Indications of bullet wounds on his sweater, so he doesn't appear to have died of natural causes. I'll draw up a medico-legal certificate so that you can go and chop him up in an autopsy. There's no way I'm going to touch him, it's far too early for that. I'm going back to bed. Send the judicial paperwork to my department."

With that he turned to go, only to find Aubin blocking his way.

"You're going to check his pulse though, aren't you, just to be sure?"

"Shit, there are three gaping holes in a bloodstained sweater, and he hasn't moved since we got here. Isn't that enough for you?"

Aubin did not budge: that was persuasion enough. The doctor pulled on a pair of latex gloves and pressed two fingers against the dead man's neck.

"Nothing. No discernible pulse. Can I go now, or would you like me to check if he's had all his jabs?"

Aubin accompanied him back outside the building while Coste dialled the number of the justice department to brief the night-duty investigating magistrate.

"No I.D. on him, discovered at three o'clock this morning by the security guard, probably shot with a handgun. The doctor has given us a certificate, all you have to do is authorise an autopsy . . . thanks . . . we'll let you know if there's anything new."

Coste ended the call, watching as the undertakers struggled to zip the giant's body up in a black bag that was too small for him. Coste had seen so many stiffs he could have eaten an ice cream while observing any sort of autopsy, and felt no great emotion as he watched his new case being carted off to the morgue.

4

Léa Marquant remained a mystery to Coste. The daughter of the director of a private clinic in Paris, she preferred to live with the dead than to have to listen to the lamentations of the living. Coste had only ever seen her in her white coat, auburn hair scraped back, pale green eyes behind a pair of rectangular glasses. Her face was innocent and smiling, a complete contrast to her ability to saw open a skull in less than a minute, or plunge her hands into someone's intestines. He often wondered what she would look like with her hair loose and a little less blood on her clothes.

The strange nature of their relationship meant they only met as a result of a suspicious death. This time, Coste took advantage of their encounter to discreetly observe the absence of any ring on her fingers.

They were walking down one of the Institute's long corridors.

"Does your client have a story?"

"Yeah, the story of a guy found dead this morning in a warehouse with three bullets in his chest."

"A settling of scores?"

"Why not? The rest is for you to tell me."

The pathologist slid her security badge over the magnetic lock to the autopsy room.

*

Under the cold neon light, the giant's body had taken on a greyish hue. His feet stuck out over the end of the operating table. Dr Marquant pulled up her surgical mask, stood silent for a few seconds, then took a series of photographs.

"O.K., let's start by cutting his clothes off so we can see what damage the bullets did."

She lifted the bottom of the blood-soaked sweater and cut it up to the neck. Watching her closely, Coste took out his tiger balm and rubbed some on his top lip. Within ten minutes, it would be impossible to breathe in the room.

The garment came away easily. Incredulous, the pathologist ran her hand over the dead man's intact torso. No bullet impacts of any kind. Not a single wound.

"Your guy recovers quickly."

Coste went over to her. Checked what she had said. Gave a big sigh. What a mess. So he did as he always did: he kept things as simple as possible.

"Three holes in the sweater, but no corresponding wounds. That means somebody put it on him . . ."

He continued with his reasoning in silence.

"I hate that," Léa Marquant grumbled.

"What?"

"I hate it when you start with a hypothesis then finish it in your own mind."

"Sorry. I was thinking that if this unknown individual wasn't shot, you're going to have to find another explanation for his death . . . and I'm going to have to investigate a sweater."

She finished removing the man's clothes and took another series of photographs.

Lying there with his eyes closed, stark naked, he looked peaceful.

And yet it cannot have been a peaceful night for him. The

base of his penis was wrapped more than a hundred times with string, and looked like a black, withered vegetable. The pathologist paused, bent over the body, readjusted her protective eyewear.

"Victor, I think he's lost his balls."

Instantly recovering her composure, she continued in a more appropriate register.

"A surgical intervention, ablation of the testicles after ligature. That can't have been pleasant, the wounds are pre-mortem. This is confirmed by the use of what appears to me to be string for Sunday roast at the base of the penis, as a garrotte."

"That doesn't confirm anything, it narrows it down."

"Meaning what, Sherlock?"

"That not only did somebody want him to be alive while they chopped them off, but that they wanted him to live afterwards. That narrows things down."

A corner of the pathologist's lip rose in a slight smile: she liked the capitaine's alert mind. She went on inspecting every square centimetre of the body, then with Coste's help turned him over.

"Rigor mortis has set in all over the body, although it's still quite supple; death must have occurred no more than six hours ago. Post-mortem decay; the body temperature is low. No visible wounds or other injuries. I'll look for any subcutaneous bruising."

She pulled the instrument table towards her and chose a scalpel. Grasping the left calf, she made a deep incision into the skin and flesh all the way up to the knee. The muscle bloomed like a red flower.

Unseen by the other two, the giant, his face crushed against the operating table, opened one eye wide.

"I can't see anything special: no sign of any blows."

The pathologist bent over, grasped the other calf and made a second precise incision.

With a deafening shriek, the dead man raised himself onto his elbows. Coste and the pathologist froze. The giant twisted his neck backwards and stared at his two sliced-open calves, then swivelled round to look at the man and woman standing there thunderstruck. He tried to get up, but succeeded only in collapsing to the floor, knocking over the tables laden with instruments and jars in a deafening crash of metal and shattered glass. He grabbed the scalpel nearest to him and brandished it. Coste took out his gun, moved in front of the pathologist, and pointed it at the man's shoulder.

Unable to stand, the giant pushed himself painfully backwards over the white, blood-smeared tiles until he was stuck in a corner, still waving the scalpel. He was trembling, his empty eyes flitting around the room. Coste felt ridiculous aiming at a man in such a state of shock, and returned his gun to its holster.

"Shit, your guy really does recover quickly, Coste."

5

Quai de la Rapée métro station on the banks of the Seine,
a few metres from the Institut médico-légal

The métro carries its mass of passengers alive and kicking past the red-brick building. None of them are aware of the corpses waiting in the mortuary to confide their secrets one last time. Occasionally a strange smell lingers in the air at this métro station. Only the police and doctors know enough to identify it. The smell of death. Stored in the memory like a warning. The changes death inevitably brings. Cooling, rigidity, dehydration, lividity, decomposition.

From birth, certain animals flatten themselves on the ground, hiding in the grass to avoid being targeted by a predator. The survival instinct is innate. When we breathe in the smell of rotten meat mixed with blood and excrement, our unconscious immediately identifies an unavoidable, unforgettable stench. It's innate: the death instinct.

Leaning on the stone balustrade of the Pont Morland opposite the Institut médico-légal, Coste gazed absent-mindedly at the Seine's dirty green waters. Filthy seagulls were fighting over bits of rubbish bobbing along the river. He was thinking about the scene he had witnessed out at Pantin, and all the trouble a sick mind had gone to, someone so twisted as to castrate his victim before dressing him up in a bullet-holed sweater and having him sent to be cut up in an autopsy.

A murder means a stabbing, a gunshot, or a hearty swing of an iron bar. Something spontaneous, done in a rush, with a minimum of premeditation. A murder is often a botched job. Never a piece of theatre.

Coste could sense his problems mounting.

An ambulance reversed swiftly to park with its rear doors facing the Institute entrance. For a second time, the body of the giant passed in front of Coste, a little less dead, a little more drugged, as it was taken to the secure police unit at the Jean-Verdier hospital in Bondy. He tossed away his cigarette, watching it turn slow-motion cartwheels before being extinguished as it hit the water. He took out his mobile and brought Aubin up to speed on the strange turn the investigation had taken.

"Get a guard put on duty outside his room until he wakes up. I'm taking his clothes and samples and sending everything for a D.N.A. test. I'm not very hopeful, but I don't think the blood on the sweater is his."

"A second victim?"

"A great start to the year."

Coste climbed into his car. Through the Institute's glass doors he caught a glimpse of the pathologist, coffee cup in one hand. In the other, coins she was stuffing nervously into the confectionery vending machine. She had just sliced into a living being: that has to be a shock to your system. She was bound to have a hard time explaining it to herself.

He should have gone over to her. To talk to her. To apologise.

But what for?

He sighed and drove off.

6

Bobigny police headquarters

A two-storey rectangular glass and metal labyrinth, with a long roofed-in garden at its centre. On the ground floor, the uniformed police handle routine cases of everyday crime. On the first floor, the local detectives are in charge of more serious infractions. Those on the top floor deal with the worst crimes of all.

The departmental headquarters for Seine-Saint-Denis, S.D.P.J. 93.

In the north wing, the Groupes Stups offices, with their constant smell of cannabis seized in the latest raids. On call at all hours of the day and night, weary faces, so similar in appearance to rough sleepers' it's impossible to distinguish between the officer and his snitch. Further on, the Finance team, a little softer, a little classier, the only place you'll find tea. Its walls lined with volumes containing thousands of pages outlining fiscal misdemeanours. Beyond them, the investigation and research department, always a hive of activity. Their speciality: rape and abductions. As soon as one case is closed, two more are opened.

In the south wing, the unit combating organised crime, with their skull and crossbones flag. Robberies here mean assault rifles or rocket launchers. You have to be a bit crazy to work there every day. So the skull and crossbones are almost justified.

And finally the two Groupes Crime, where all the murders committed in 93 end up. Six offices separated by a changing room, where the bloody clothes of the most recent victims are hung up to dry before they are sealed. Since the room is usually full, it's not uncommon for the officers to hang shredded sweaters or torn skirts out of their windows.

To roam the corridors of a police headquarters is to come face to face with all the worst aspects of mankind.

More or less opposite the police headquarters stand the five floors and three basements of the Bobigny criminal court, built in a clashing Lego-brick style.

On one side, the Police; on the other, Justice. Side by side, at the heart of Seine-Saint-Denis, facing wave after wave of tower blocks like two warships.

Behind the door of the office marked GROUPE CRIME I, Coste booted up his computer. The mailbox icon pulsed. The fingerprints had found their owner. He connected to the network, went into the criminal records database, and read the report out loud for Aubin to hear.

"I don't know if you'll appreciate the irony, but our giant is called Bébé. Bébé Coulibaly, born 1985 . . . which makes him twenty-seven now. Last known domicile Paul-Vaillant-Couturier estate in Bobigny."

Sitting at his desk at an angle to Coste's, Aubin was pounding at his keyboard to check this information in police records.

"Got him. Bébé Coulibaly. No current investigation, no vehicle, no driver's licence. On the other hand, he does have a whole list of honours in the S.T.I.C.* I'll pass on his misdemeanours as a juvenile, but there's armed robbery when

* S.T.I.C.: Système de traitement des infractions constatée. Database of all crimes committed in France, including the names of perpetrators and victims.

he was an adult . . . and since 2005 he's specialised in drug trafficking. Sentenced to two years in Fleury prison in 2005, he got out in 2008 and disappeared under the radar until 2010, when he made a spectacular comeback . . . An accusation of rape that ended with the complaint being withdrawn. Classic."

"Nice guy. We'll see what he has to say when he wakes up. Meanwhile, get working on the S.A.L.V.A.C."*

Aubin scowled. Somewhat arbitrarily, he had been appointed the go-to man for the S.A.L.V.A.C. programme by their departmental head, who herself had been given orders by Commissaire Stévenin, who had doubtless in turn been following instructions from one of the high-ups in a tailored suit.

S.A.L.V.A.C. is one of the most powerful crime databases. It compiles, analyses and searches for links to flag up similarities between different police investigations. M.O.s, places, dates, offences, descriptions and psychological profiles of known criminals. If the crimes appear to have been committed by the same person or criminal organisation, the investigations are pooled, and the investigating magistrate authorises their transfer to the most appropriate police force. Invented and used in Canada for more than twenty years, S.A.L.V.A.C. finally arrived in France in 2005. In *Département* 93 Mathias Aubin was the one stuck with it, doing the best he could.

He opened the database. S.A.L.V.A.C. wished him a good day. He put in his user name and password. The screen flickered, then the interface identified him. AUBIN Mathias – MLE 46556X – SPJ 93.

"O.K.! I've put in the M.O. and the preliminary descriptions . . . If there's a match with another case, the analysts will give us their answer tomorrow."

* S.A.L.V.A.C.: Système d'analyse des liens de la violence associée aux crimes.

Sam and Ronan entered the office continuing their heated argument. The gist of it was that riding a motorbike at more than 140 kilometres an hour on the Paris Périphérique was fucking stupid, and that at a speed like that even an android would find it hard to avoid being hit by a car. They both sank onto the old red sofa in Aubin and Capitaine Coste's office.

"Nothing. No C.C.T.V. footage, and no witnesses."

Sam continued:

"Anyway . . . in abandoned factories in the middle of the night, what else can you expect? I'd like to add that Ronan drives like an arsehole and I'm never getting on a bike with him again. At that speed, even an android . . ."

"Shit, what is it with you and androids this morning? Instead of being such a wise guy, tell them about your geeky little discoveries . . ."

Feathers ruffled, Sam explained:

"O.K., you're going to say I'm a teenager in search of thrills, but I've been looking on the net . . . D'you know what a zombie is?"

Coste blew a fuse.

"Are you taking the piss or what?"

"Just wait before you start shouting at me."

He took a touch-screen tablet out of his backpack, and scrolled down the text until he came to the paragraph he was looking for.

"In Haitian voodoo mythology, they're known as the living dead. It's a belief that extends from Africa to South America. I found all this on a site called 'Dark Refuge'. A zombie is some poor peasant who falls victim to a voodoo priest known as a *houngan* who administers tetrodotoxin. It's a drug you find in puffer fish or cane toads. It cuts out all feeling and deliberate movement, but the zombie remains conscious and can still hear what's going on around him. He is buried, then dug up, and thanks to an antidote comes out of his lethargic state, but is forced to become a slave. The site's author goes on to say that in this century there are still testimonies of agricultural establishments that use these zombie slaves."

Unconvinced, Coste replied more calmly:

"If you don't mind, I'm going to look first at the blood results. If that gets us nowhere, I'll personally pay for your ticket to Haiti."

Ronan chimed in:

"I'll contribute to that."

Coste turned to Aubin, who was laughing in spite of himself.

"Aren't you going to miss them when you're transferred to Annecy?"

"You know very well why I'm clearing out of here."

"I know, your family. That's important."

Aubin teased him gently:

"What would you know?"

7

Coste gave himself permission to attend autopsies on his own. Ronan, a past expert in male–female relationships, had quickly picked up on a certain electricity between his capitaine and the pathologist. With a sly smile, he handed Coste the receiver, winking exaggeratedly to convey the fact that Dr Léa Marquant was on the other end of the line.

"Victor?"

Without looking at Ronan, he pointed to the door. His colleague walked out, dragging his feet like a kid being sent to bed before the end of a film.

"Speaking."

"Two things. First, the Institute switchboard is being flooded with calls from journalists who want to know more about our ghosts. Can you imagine what a pain that is?"

"I'm really sorry, but I can assure you the leak hasn't come from my team. I'd never want you to get caught up in this."

"I believe you, and the fact is I'm not sure how discreet my colleagues here are. But most of all . . . it's tomorrow's papers I'm worried about. It'll be dreadful publicity for our service."

"What's the second thing?"

"Oh yes, forgive me. Your guy was crammed full of barbiturates. In some cases that can produce a deep coma in which all neurological signs or even all brain activity cease. The pulse is very feeble and can be missed altogether, which could explain the error made by the first doctor who saw him, especially considering how cold it was and his probable lack of attention owing to the time of day and the circumstances. And the massive dose of barbiturates in his blood could bring on a hypertonic coma; that's what I confused with rigor mortis. That was my first mistake. Those same drugs also lead to hypothermia – which I took to be cadaveric cold. Second error. Coste, your corpse was nothing more than a huge trap, and I walked right into it."

"If it's any consolation, you won't be the only one with some explaining to do. Stop blaming yourself: we brought you a dead body and you followed the standard procedure."

"One should never just follow the standard procedure with an autopsy. Keep me informed. I'd like to understand, for Christ's sake!"

Coste wondered if she swore like that over meals with her family.

In his mind he revisited the invitation to have a quiet coffee together, but could not bring himself to suggest it. Instead, he hid behind "I'll give you a call."

As expected, he was summoned for a meeting with his departmental boss. Clutching the telephone, Commandant M.C. Damiani reeled off "Yes, sir" several times as she gestured to Coste to take a seat. "M.C." Damiani because that was how she always signed her messages. She probably thought Marie-Charlotte wasn't the kind of first name that went down well for someone in charge of the two Groupes Crime in S.D.P.J. 93. She halted in the middle of a "Very well, s—" and hung up, as the person on the far end of the line had just done, without giving her time to finish.

She straightened up, somewhat embarrassed.

"Have you heard about the press?"

"I have."

"You know this case is . . . unusual to say the least. The boss wants the lowdown a.s.a.p. to cover his back with the Préfet. It's a very, very bad affair."

If it had been up to him, Coste would have added one more "very". The commandant went on:

"It reflects badly on *Département* 93 that we've got a madman who has fun torturing his victim, and it makes us look stupid too. This isn't Hollywood, it's Seine-Saint-Denis."

"I know. You're saying it as if I had something to do with it."

"I'm saying it in the hope you'll sort this mess out as quickly as possible so we can get back to normal. I want peace in this region, not the movies."

With her cropped white hair and a face showing fifty well-lived years, all Damiani wanted was for her appointment as commandant to be confirmed in order to augment her pension and allow her to go off and live in the house she had built for her family, at a time when that word still meant something. She was hoping she could hand in her weapon, badge and paid holidays and get on with various outstanding projects.

This meant she found the story of the black giant who had decided not to die only mildly amusing.

"What about the blood on the sweater: is it his, or is that another headache?"

"We're waiting for the D.N.A. results from the lab."

"O.K., I'll chase them up, and you'll get an answer tomorrow. But before that, see what you can get out of this guy as soon as he wakes up! I want a story that makes sense and an arrest, if that's not too much trouble."

"As do we all, madame."

"No, Coste, I assure you, I do far more than you."

Coste took this to mean the meeting was at an end. He had barely stood up to leave when Damiani was already taking another call. She waved him back for a moment.

"You're losing Aubin, but you're gaining a new lieutenant. A woman. I've got her C.V. out for you. She's still too young to take over responsibility for the S.A.L.V.A.C., but the boss is making sure he finds someone."

As though anticipating possible complications, Damiani added:

"Victor, you haven't chosen this new recruit, but don't take against her. Be kind, don't destroy her in three months, she's only just out of the École de Police. Let's just say she's with you on probation. And keep Ronan away from her, I don't want any sex scandals in the force, if you please."

8

The top floor of the glass ocean liner. In his office, Commissaire Stévenin, head of S.D.P.J. 93, was engaged in a similar damage limitation exercise.

"An individual by the name of Bébé Coulibaly, sir. He's being closely guarded at the Jean-Verdier Hospital. My men are waiting for him to wake up so they can grill him."

"Grill him? Tell me, Stévenin, haven't they done that already?"

The commissaire gave a quiet sigh. When the director of the Police Judiciaire is in a bad mood, it's best to keep your trap shut. So he just listened as the other man went on:

"Obviously, we can't keep this under wraps, the press are already on to it. It's far too good a story not to get them going. Which I can understand: if this were happening somewhere else, it would probably intrigue me too. But as it is, it's a nuisance. Do you follow me?"

"I follow you, sir."

"Who's on the case?"

"Coste and his team. With Lieutenant Aubin, though he's leaving tomorrow."

"I know. We've been offering him the same carrot for two years now, he needs to know when to let go."

"Have you already thought of someone to replace him for the S.A.L.V.A.C. programme, sir?"

"Naturally. If I left everything to you . . . I've got someone who will fit the bill. He just needs to be reinstated."

Stévenin almost had to beg to find out more.

"May I be so bold as to ask who . . . so that it at least looks as if it was my idea?"

The director of the Police Judiciaire had a reputation for being a ball-breaker, combining a love of humiliating his colleagues, sometimes in public, with sly perversity.

"Malbert. I'm sending you Lucien Malbert. My assistant has already given him an outline of what's expected of him. I'll leave it to you to settle him in: that'll make you feel you're involved."

9

The rest of Wednesday had gone by without Bébé Coulibaly's condition improving sufficiently for them to be able to interview him. The next day, Coste was the first to arrive at headquarters. Taking advantage of this moment of calm, he was already polishing off his second cup of coffee. He cast a routine glance at the A.P.E.V.* poster taped to the vending machine. The faces of ten or so children smiling at him, all looking perfectly happy. These posters have to be prominently displayed in every French police station, where everybody, police officers and visitors, can see them. Coste imagined distraught parents in a silent, empty room, searching through their family albums to find the best likeness, unable to avoid choosing the most striking one. The result was an unlikely mosaic of portraits of kids smiling broadly beneath the word MISSING in red capital letters. It was enough to undermine anybody's morale. Some of the children had been missing for so long that alongside their original photograph was another PhotoFit picture, created by experts in the evolution of faces to show how they might look now. Coste knew from experience that once you started imagining how a missing child's face could have changed that meant that there wasn't much hope left.

* A.P.E.V. Aide aux parents des enfants victimes. Aid to Parents of Child Victims.

He left the break room – three mismatched chairs next to a coffee machine – and went back to his office. He made space for his cup by pushing some of his files onto Aubin's desk, which a few hours before his departure was already empty.

He dialled the laboratory's direct line. The female head of the Institut national de la police scientifique picked up and greeted him with an accent he placed somewhere near Perpignan.

"The blood samples correspond to a man called Bébé Coulibaly, but I suppose you already know that. The blood on the sweater isn't the same, however. I'm afraid you're looking for somebody else."

Coste closed his eyes. Of course, it would have been too easy.

"Is this somebody else already on file?"

"Yes, Franck Samoy, born 15 March, 1982. I'll ping my report over to you now."

Franck Samoy. Coste studied the police record. Nothing that serious. An addict, known for dealing small quantities. Compared to the usual clients, you might almost say he was a good boy. No current investigation, never been in prison, the owner of a red B.M.W. 633 from 1982, the year he was born.

The possibility that they were dealing with another dead body hovered like a ghost over these statistics. Commandant Damiani took it badly, and Coste was instructed in no uncertain terms to get his finger out. He sent Sam and Ronan to check the sweater owner's address, and asked Aubin to get in touch with the Jean-Verdier hospital to find out how their Sleeping Beauty was getting on.

The guard on duty, sounding somewhat stressed, begged

them to hurry up: the giant had woken up and was starting to kick up a fuss.

As they drove past, the *choufs*, the lookout kids in the tower block foyers, whistled a warning to the dealers, even though their car was unmarked. Kids knee high to a grasshopper shouted, *"Artena! Artena!"**

You need to be sharp-eyed to get a job as a lookout, but in this case two tough-looking guys in the front seats of a grey Peugeot 306 made it dead easy for them. Coste and Aubin crossed Pont de Bondy with its gaggle of beggars clustered at every traffic light. Pont de Bondy, the Court of Miracles.

They parked their car and walked into a building with peeling paintwork and torn lino. Coste came to a halt at the news-stand hidden in a corner of the entrance lobby.

"You going to take him something to read?" Aubin said.

Coste did not react. The headline THE DEAD COME BACK TO LIFE IN THE PARIS MORGUE had pulled him up short. Beneath it was a photograph of the Institut medico-légal under a lowering sky that made it look like a haunted house. He thought of Léa Marquant. He would call her later.

Of course.

He skimmed the article while Aubin was showing his I.D. at the reception desk. A nurse grudgingly led them to Room 21, then turned on her heel without a word.

Stretched out on his stomach, Bébé Coulibaly greeted them with a groan in which Coste could make out the word *"flic"* punctuated by a stream of abuse.

He sat beside a bed that was scarcely big enough to contain the giant.

* Meaning "drop it" or "leave us" in Arabic. The call lookouts make to the dealers whenever a police patrol car is in the area.

"O.K., so your name is Bébé Coulibaly, you're twenty-seven years of age, your home turf is the Paul-Vaillant-Couturier estate in Bobigny, and yesterday evening . . ." – he searched for the right words – ". . . you were, to say the least, attacked and mutilated. That's serious stuff. Are you aware how serious? What was the reason for it?"

"No idea."

"Having no idea isn't much of an answer. Can't you guess who might have done it?"

"If I knew, I promise you I'd sort the fucker out myself."

"Yeah, I get it, you're the masked avenger. Do you know someone called Franck Samoy?"

"I don't know anyone."

"Yet you were wearing his sweater."

Two deep furrows appeared on the giant's brow, giving the impression he was trying to think this through. That could take a while. Coste removed his coat and hung it on the back of his chair, then said:

"Listen, I understand we're not your favourite people, and I can assure you we feel the same way, but we're in a situation where both of us need to make an effort. You need to talk to me, and I need to be sufficiently bothered to investigate when the victim is somebody like you, an armed robber turned dealer. How tall *are* you, anyway? Close to two metres? How could you let yourself be kidnapped?"

Bébé turned a quarter of the way towards the two policemen and looked at them resignedly.

"Look, pig, I remember three things. First, I was trying to repair the electricity in my storage unit. I felt something cold on the back of my neck. Then the sound and lights went out. Second, I came round. I was on my stomach, I couldn't move, and I had a hell of a hangover. At first I thought I was in the dark. I heard footsteps. But when I turned my head to either side I could feel some material on my skin. I had a fucking hood on. Then I felt somebody winding something round my . . ."

Despite his size and looks that would make anyone apologise even if they had done nothing wrong, Bébé Coulibaly didn't seem ready to relive that experience any time soon.

". . . and then I passed out."

"What was the third thing?"

"You pointing your gun at me in the morgue, you cunt."

"Yeah, I have to say you caught me by surprise. Did you have a laptop on you?"

"No chance. When did you ever hear of a dealer handing over his laptop to a police officer?"

"I couldn't give a fuck about what you do, I'm not in the Groupe Stups. But if you had your laptop with you, maybe we could track your journey. And if somebody stole it, we could locate exactly where it is now, right?"

"My laptop never left my place. I didn't take it down into the basement."

Coste turned to Aubin.

"You can start the interview. Get all the details. I want the number of his storage unit as well. In the meantime, I'll call the others."

Aubin opened his computer and began:

"O.K., let's take it from the top. Surname? First name? Date of birth?"

Coste was making notes in the hospital foyer, mobile clenched between ear and shoulder. Ronan and Sam had gone to Franck Samoy's address.

"He's the despair of his poor mother, who he lives with on the Gagarin estate in Romainville. His own room, a few pieces of clothing, and some twists of cannabis. His old lady offered us coffee and the mobile number of the offspring causing her so much grief."

Ronan's capacity for empathy had never risen above zero.

Sam, now in his element, was already trying to use geo-tracking to locate the mobile. A list of all recent calls and a precise itinerary for the previous forty-eight hours. They had the blood; all that was missing was the donor.

Coste was pacing up and down when Aubin rejoined him in the hospital entrance.

"Fancy visiting Bébé's basement?"

Block F, Paul-Vaillant-Couturier estate

To gain entrance to most of the buildings on estates in 93, all you have to do is push the front door open. Bébé's was no different. A digicode torn from the wall, hanging by a wire. Broken windows in the foyer, lock smashed, letter boxes vandalised by opportunists, burned by others. Welcome.

In the second basement, they walked along a corridor as narrow as a tunnel, sporadically lit by naked light bulbs fed by wires running along the ceiling, until they came to storage unit 38. Coste pushed in the pass key he had borrowed from the caretaker, and opened the door. It opened to the left, so the light must be on the right. He ran his hand down the wall to find the switch. A bright glow revealed a pile of boxes full to overflowing with clothes, and two bikes crushed under the weight of a scooter frame.

"Either he had time to repair it before he was abducted, or there was never any need to replace the bulb here."

Coste nodded and left the unit to inspect the nearby ones. At the far end of the corridor, number 55 had a padlock on it to reinforce the lock.

A few minutes later, Aubin reappeared with a jemmy. He made short work of the padlock, and the pass key opened the lock. Nothing happened when he pressed the light switch. Coste

took out his Maglite, and on the floor counted ten or so con-
doms, a few joint stubs, two sixpacks worth of beer in scattered
cans, and a filthy, brown-stained mattress with no blankets.

Aubin switched on his torch.

"The electrics here need work."

The beam from his torch picked out a silver package. He
bent down and picked up three empty blister packs. He un-
folded them to read what they had contained.

"Viagra and Cialis. Good stuff. God forbid you fail to get it
up in front of your mates."

Coste saw things differently.

"No, what I reckon is that a young girl who gets trapped in
here has no chance of getting out."

"Shall we send all the rubbers for D.N.A. testing?"

"At four hundred euros a test, no investigating magistrate is
going to slap ten thousand onto the budget of the justice
department for a cheap love nest. And if we ask the police lab
to do it, we'll have to wait six months for the results. Besides,
there's no evidence linking Bébé Coulibaly to . . ."

Coste took a step back.

". . . storage unit 55. All this does is shed a different light on
matters."

When they re-emerged into the light, Aubin took an age to get
rid of the caretaker and her list of grievances. Kids in the foyers,
scooters racing up and down the car parks, deafening music,
squatters, the police breaking down the doors at six in the
morning and of course no-one came to replace them. She was
still pursuing her endless list when he left her cubbyhole. He
told Coste what he had learned.

"Evidently, unit no. 55 doesn't belong to anyone. Or rather,
it belongs to an apartment the council hasn't yet allocated. So,

as the caretaker, who's something of a philosopher, put it: 'Nature abhors a vacuum' . . ."

"What about the apartment?"

"According to the old witch it's as good as new, waiting to be handed over to a family."

"Maybe we should . . ."

"I have the keys."

They climbed ten floors that smelled of urine and burnt remains, and opened the door to a furnished five-room flat that, in complete contrast to the surrounding filth, looked like a show apartment. Newly fitted carpets, new wallpaper, clean smell.

Coste went and looked out of the living room window at a view of factories and tower blocks. He lit a cigarette.

"You do realise this is going to be one of the most fucked-up cases I've ever had to deal with?"

"To tell you the truth, my mind's already elsewhere. I can't even feel sorry for you."

"Your replacement is a school-leaver. A girl. De Ritter, Johanna. Never set foot in 93. It's going to be just great."

II

Sam and Ronan, meanwhile, were completing their visit to Suzette Samoy, who was sitting in her living room. She was struggling with a plastic frame, trying to pull out a photograph of her son in his Sunday best at a cousin's wedding, while at the same time shoving off her lap an ancient cat that wanted to see what was going on. Annoyed, it jumped clumsily under the table, slipping between the two officers' legs and climbing up onto a T.V. unit that had no set on it. One of the disadvantages of having a drug addict for a son: he was liable to sell everything he could.

As they sat there, a picture of Franck Samoy from police records pinged on to Sam's mobile.

Set alongside each other, the photograph at the wedding and the one taken while Samoy was in custody looked like a before and after advert. Before junk, after junk. Take away fifteen kilos, add grey circles round the eyes, colour the few remaining teeth yellow, add ten years of exhaustion and the look of a hedgehog caught in the headlights of a four-by-four, and you might recognise it as more or less the same person.

"You can keep the photograph, but if you're going to throw him in jail, could you please swing by so I can give him some clean clothes and a hug?"

Ronan sighed. Sam promised they would. The cat took

advantage of the open door to make its escape, and Suzette remained dignified until they were out of sight.

"Did you have to sigh like that?"

"You get the kids you deserve," Ronan said.

"I bet that's what your mother says about you . . ."

Armed with the two pictures, they set off in search of Samoy's buddies and any information they could find. Sam told Ronan to hurry up: he had no wish to spend the afternoon trailing round the Gagarin estate in Romainville.

"Seriously, get a move on . . . We're going to have to ring on hundreds of doorbells if we want to do this properly. We'll start on the northern towers and come back via the south."

"So you're a Cherokee tracker now, are you? Which way is north?"

"Look at the satellite dishes on the windows. They always point south. Now you know where south is, do you think you can find north?"

"I'll follow you anywhere, Pocahontas."

In this unlikely pairing, Ronan was the one who asked questions, while Sam, who had the air of a broadband engineer, took notes. They came up against closed doors, families who preferred silence to problems, old people who never heard a thing, and young people who told them to go fuck themselves. End of story. A typical N.S.W.N.R. in 93: "Neighbourhood search with no results."

Sam had been careful to park as far away as possible from the tower blocks. Despite this, the C3's front tyres had been slashed, and the contents of a fire extinguisher sprayed inside the car through a smashed window. The intrusion of a couple of officers asking questions had not gone unnoticed. Four wasted hours, and a return journey on public transport.

By the time they arrived back at headquarters, Aubin had already organised his farewell drinks. Bottles of champagne had been set up like bowling pins on the big table in the meeting room. Ronan took Coste to one side and reported back.

"The C3 is out of service. The tow truck has left it at the police garage."

"An accident?"

"We were spotted on the Gagarin estate."

"We've still got the 306, but it's on its last legs. I'll borrow a car from another team for tomorrow. You ring your mate at the garage and make sure he puts it first on his list. Otherwise you're going to have to walk everywhere for the next few weeks."

Glass in hand, Commissaire Stévenin praised Lieutenant Mathias Aubin as an outstanding officer and an excellent colleague. Apparently, no matter who the officer was, when he was leaving it seemed he was always outstanding and the best possible colleague.

The bosses made themselves scarce when the champagne ran out and was replaced by less sophisticated drinks. The evening went on and on, and conversations became increasingly slurred. At two in the morning, Sam slung Ronan into his car like a bag of dirty washing. Coste took it upon himself to deliver Mathias to the door of his family home out in the suburbs. On arrival, he parked across the drive and staggered with drunken discretion up the ridiculous garden path, taking great care not to crush any plants as he linked arms with his colleague like a First World War casualty. The porch light came on and Laure Aubin, still half asleep, came out to greet the two men. She winced as she saw the damage to her flowers. She put one of them to bed fully clothed and prevented the other one from leaving before he'd had a good strong cup of coffee.

In the empty house, only the coffee machine and an alarm radio were still plugged in. Everything else was in boxes.

"You wouldn't have any sugar, would you?"

"It's already packed, but if you want to search . . ."

"I'll do without. Did you come back for the move?"

"Seeing how little time off you give Mathias, let's just say I did it all on my own."

She lit a cigarette and passed Coste one. He told himself she looked beautiful, even in a dressing gown and with her hair a mess. He told himself his friend was right to get out, and told himself as well that he was probably a bit tipsy.

"It's a bold step," he said eventually.

"Maybe. We're giving the house keys back tomorrow, so I see it as one last big effort. I'm so fed up with doing everything on my own. Mathias has been depressed for two years, that's two years when we've hardly seen each other, even when we were together."

"Don't worry, I'm handing him back to you."

"Victor, I swear we both love you, but getting Mathias away from you, from 93 and from his job is without a doubt the best thing that could happen to him."

Coste took this on the chin, and with this thought running through his mind went home to try to get some sleep. For some time now, he had sensed that Aubin was distant. Distant from him, from the others, from his work. A family man robbed of his family, in self-imposed isolation. He couldn't have gone on like that much longer.

Coste tossed and turned in his bed until he took the duvet and went and lay down on the sofa, letting himself be hypnotised by the repeats on his T.V., the only piece of furniture in his living room.

12

Coste received the first anonymous letter the day Aubin left. Among the run-of-the-mill mail he picked up from the office he found an envelope with his name handwritten on it. He tore it open, took out a sheet of paper folded in two, and read it.

Code 93.
Overdose – 16 March, 2011.
Squat in the former Les Lilas Town Hall.

His first reaction was to curse: his problems seemed to be piling up. Then he thought for a moment, marshalled the facts, and drew up a list of everything that needed to be done. Picking up the envelope and the sheet of paper by a corner so as to leave as few prints as possible, he took advantage of the fact that the corridors were still quite empty to photocopy them both. Then he slipped the originals into a bigger manila folder that he hid in one of his desk drawers. Brown paper preserves D.N.A. better.

The letter referred to a case from a year ago. And that case must contain a mistake, an omission, a slip-up, a grain of sand which meant that this morning he had been rewarded with this letter.

The envelope made no mention of his rank or unit. That

made it sound very private, and he decided that for the moment that was how it would stay.

Half past seven. He still had a few minutes before the early risers appeared.

He picked up the copies and headed for the unit archives. Closing the door behind him, he scanned the big room filled with seemingly endless rows of files. The S.D.P.J. 93's memory like a ship's log of crime.

Running his finger along the dossiers, spooling back through the months. The names of criminals, victims and crimes passed before his eyes, as he recalled scenes etched on his memory. As the letter suggested, he stopped at March 2011.

He had no problem finding the case file. He took it out of the box, then sat on the threadbare carpet with it on his knees.

The first reports described a young woman found dead in a squat in the former town hall of Les Lilas. His correspondent had good information. Maybe he was another policeman?

The authorities' arrival had made the usual residents of the squat take flight, and questioning the neighbours had thrown up nothing. Since no I.D. had been found on the victim, she became a corpse identified with an "X". He pulled out the forensic pathologist's report and skimmed the paragraphs, concentrating on the most relevant details.

Unidentified body X, a female aged approximately twenty. 160 centimetres, weight 49 kilos. Registered in the Institut medico-légal with the number 11-1237, received on 16 March, 2011 at 17.30 hours. Autopsy carried out by Dr Léa Marquant.

Multiple vaginal tears caused by the insertion of a blunt instrument. Identical anal wounds – massive perineal destruction.

Bruises to left and right upper limbs in areas of injection, indicating a drug habit – skin scraped on left and right knees compatible with the body being dragged along the ground.

Blood analysis – significant quantities of heroin, cocaine, cannabis.

Ulceration of nasal mucus – bruxism with decaying of teeth – compatible with heroin-cocaine addiction.

Infectious necrosis around injection points: inside of elbows, fingers, toes and back of feet – compatible with heroin-cocaine addiction.

Cause of death – overdose of heroin – massive pulmonary oedema.

Attached to the report, a series of photographs of the victim summed up her way of life. Her means of survival? Nights desperately searching for a fix; mornings already needing more. Fingerprint identification: underway. Identification from D.N.A. database: underway. The standard procedure had been followed whereby the photographs of an "X" body were distributed nationally.

Coste had not forgotten that day. Mattresses strewn about the floor of what used to be the town hall. A two-storey building, one floor serving as a vast toilet, the windows covered in newspaper. Sam's first case when he joined the unit. The smell of shit and rotting garbage had been so potent he had refused to take down the details or even set foot in the old building. Ronan had not been able to resist twisting the knife: "Too sensitive, you poor little snowflake?"

Coste read to the end of the dossier. The remaining statements had led to the case being quickly closed. Aubin, the lead investigator, had consulted the S.A.L.V.A.C. programme. The software revealed that the young drug addict's case was similar to numerous other deaths as a result of injecting heroin cut with lethal products such as plaster or strychnine.

Aubin had written to the investigating magistrate suggesting the case be transferred to one of the central agencies in charge of the fight against illegal drugs. This was accepted, and he was no longer responsible for the case.

Fifty-three sheets. A bit skimpy for a criminal investigation. But Aubin appeared to have done his job properly. Perhaps not properly enough for whoever who had taken the trouble to write an anonymous letter. Coste must have missed something. And that annoys a detective.

Ten past eight. The department was starting to wake up. He left the archives, peering all around him as though he had something to feel guilty about, and walked back to his office with the sensation he had committed a crime in a place crawling with policemen.

13

About ten metres above the enclosed garden, in the glassed-in corridor linking the north and south wings of the S.D.P.J. 93, eighty officers were standing to attention, some of them with their eyes closed, others staring into space, all of them perfectly silent. The previous evening, one of their colleagues had been run down by a Porsche Cayenne travelling at 130 k.p.h. belonging to a gang of escaping armed robbers. The officer was killed instantly, and instantly won posthumous promotion and the right to a minute's silence. The year had hardly begun, but this was the second time the S.D.P.J. had assembled here. Given the statistics – ten thousand policemen wounded every year, an average of ten or so killed, plus the suicides – this gathering was definitely not going to be the last. At the end of the sixty seconds that served as a brutal reminder of the reality of their jobs, they all went back to their investigations.

The telephone operator pinged his results to Sam's inbox. Franck Samoy's mobile signal had been traced, and showed a strange pattern. A call lasting a few seconds exactly every three hours. The first at nine in the morning, the last at nine in the evening. All of them went through to voicemail without any message being left. This had been going on for three days: far too regularly to be a coincidence. Sam analysed the networks the calls activated and traced the mobile to within a few streets. He threw some paper clips at Ronan, who was sitting opposite him engrossed in a magazine he had surely read before.

"I'm not going to waste my time trying to explain to you what different networks are in the world of telephony. The only thing you need to know is that Samoy's mobile is somewhere in Pré-Saint-Gervais, an area of villas in the Belvédère neighbourhood, within a four-street radius."

"Who?"

Sam looked at him as if he were subnormal.

"Franck Samoy! The guy we're looking for. The blood on the giant's sweater. Shit, we saw his mother yesterday! Are you really here during the day, or is this a hologram?"

Ronan closed his magazine and swept the paper clips off his jeans.

"I really like that Belvédère area. It's one of the most middle-class parts in all 93. Shall we go door-knocking?"

"I'll tell Coste."

14

Seeing her at first only from behind, Coste just managed to swallow a "Good morning, monsieur" and avoid an awkward moment. She was a head taller than him, with crew-cut light blonde hair and a physique that meant she would have no problem applying for any of the anti-criminal brigades or rapid response units in 93. Green combat trousers and a polo-necked black sweater added to her ambiguous appearance.

Without rising from her desk, Commandant M.C. Damiani did the introductions:

"Lieutenant Johanna De Ritter – Capitaine Victor Coste, of Groupe Crime 1."

Coste could not help thinking of Ronan who, when he'd been told of the arrival of a new female recruit in their team, must have imagined anything but this kind of woman. He was in for a shock.

"Welcome, lieutenant," he said.

Damiani gave De Ritter no time to reply to the greeting.

"O.K., that's done. Now clear out of my office. Coste, you sort out the details for De Ritter, then get back on the ground with your castrated giant and the guy who stained his sweater."

They left the office together and walked down one of the S.D.P.J.'s interminable corridors.

"So your name's De Ritter?"

"Affirmative, capitaine."

Even though Coste was a good metre eighty tall, De Ritter had to lower her eyes to reply.

"O.K., let's get some things straight from the start. I'm called Victor or Coste. I prefer Coste, only my mother ever calls me Victor. There are two Groupes Crime in 93, and almost all murders come to us. I head Groupe Crime 1. For your trial period you can use Lieutenant Aubin's desk. I worked with him for ten years, and his departure is tough on all of us, so don't expect to be received with open arms."

"I'm used to it."

Coste enjoyed her irony.

"Ronan is part of our team. Now that Mathias has left, he automatically steps up to become my deputy. Don't pay too much attention to what he says, just keep in mind that if we have to go to an emergency, it's always good to have Ronan by your side. But be careful how you handle him. Even I see him as an unstable explosive."

"Noted."

"And last but not least, there's Sam. If there's an emergency, Sam will be no use to you, but he's a human tick. He leaps on someone and never lets go. I also leave all the technical stuff to him, because neither Ronan nor I are very good at it. So all you have to do is work out how you fit in. Keep your eyes open and your mouth shut; don't push yourself forward and everything will be fine. Do you remember your management classes?"

"That wasn't my favourite subject at the École de Police, but I remember the three-month rule."

"Well done. For the first ninety days, you just observe. That's the time you'll need to win respect, or at least to be accepted. We'll see how you've got on after three months. Groupe Crime 2 is our back-up team, headed by Capitaine Jevric. You'll get to know her, and when you do, you'll loathe her like everybody else does. Winning respect comes from doing a good job, but she tries to get it by shouting at everyone. As a result, there's a high turnover in her team and no cohesion. She's a petty tyrant I do all I can to avoid working with, but, unlike her, the rest of her team are good officers."

"Noted."

They came to a halt outside the reception office.

"O.K., here you introduce yourself, sort out your working hours, get your codes, your login for the police files and a new e-mail address. Then you go to the armoury to get your gun back, your baton and your police armband. The people in admin are like nurses – you can be the best surgeon in the hospital, but if they're not on your side, things can quickly become difficult. After that, you'll have to go to the shooting range with the firearms instructors before you're allowed to carry your weapon. The team will go with you; that'll help knock off some of our rust and we'll see what you can do."

"Roger."

"Do you ever say more than one word?"

"It's just that . . ."

"I'm teasing you. We all started out like that, not knowing what to say. Don't worry, be straight with people, don't gossip too much, and nobody will know you're there. That's what your aim should be for the first few days. Invisibility."

Sam appeared behind Coste's back. Without bothering to ask if he was interrupting, he cut into their conversation.

"The number Samoy's mother gave us is somewhere in Pré-Saint-Gervais. A call every three hours on the dot."

"Any other calls?"

"Not one. Only that number, every three hours for the past three days, redirected to voicemail but no message left. The first call is at nine in the morning, then one at twelve, one at three, and one at six, and the last one at nine at night."

"So from nine in the morning to nine at night: that's almost the same as our working hours. What do you think it means? An invitation for us to locate him?"

Sam was no longer paying attention but was staring openly at De Ritter.

"Sorry, Sam. This is Lieutenant Johanna De Ritter. Johanna, Sam. Now we leave you to the admin people. We have to go and take a look in Pré-Saint-Gervais. Someone seems to want us to go there."

As they walked to their office, Sam could not contain his smile.

"Is that really De Ritter? Has Ronan seen her?"

"Not yet."

"You know he's been fantasising over her first name for the past two days at least?"

"Yeah, I know. It's going to be a hoot."

15

"On the case as ever, your honour. We're heading for Pré-Saint-Gervais, the Belvédère neighbourhood. The blood on Bébé Coulibaly belongs to someone called Franck Samoy, an addict who's known to us. We went to see his mother. She's had no news of him for several weeks, but she gave us his mobile number. That's the number we've traced to Belvédère."

"Do you think you'll find him there?"

"Well, it's only a G.P.S. tracking: that gives us an approximate area, not a precise address –but it's all detached villas, not twenty-storey towers. Apart from that, seeing that it's his blood on the sweater, I have my doubts about his health. I'll call you if we discover anything."

Coste ended the call and slipped his mobile back into his jacket. Ronan was driving, and from the back of the car Sam was giving him a misleadingly flattering description of Johanna De Ritter.

"It's about time! We could do with a nice arse in the team, I'm fed up with ogling your backside, Sam. I'm no fan of prison romances, and in 93 there's no-one you can pick up."

"That's because you don't know where to look."

"No way, the thing is they hide. They all wear sweatpants and spit on the ground to show how macho they are. When they come back from a night out they have to change in the métro before they reach their estate. Some people round here think a girl wearing a skirt has to be a prostitute."

"You're exaggerating, Ronan."

"What about the young girl who was burned alive down-stairs from where she lived?"

"That was because she was going out with a guy who wasn't from the same neighbourhood. No, you mean the one who had a chequerboard cut on her face."

"Oh yeah, I'm always confusing them."

Their patrol car pulled up on the brow of Pré-Saint-Gervais hill.

"Sam?" Coste enquired.

His colleague laid his touch-screen tablet on the dashboard. After a few swipes, a map of the area appeared on the screen.

"O.K. The neighbourhood is a square of four streets. Inside the square are three avenues all named after trees – personally I prefer when it's poets, but you can't have everything. So we've got Acacias, Maronniers and Saules. I went onto a property site, and we're going to snaffle seventy-four villas. The mobile is inside one of them."

"And with a bit of luck, next to the mobile will be Franck Samoy."

"Ever the optimist, Ronan. How do you want us to do this, Coste?"

Coste thought for a few seconds.

"I know the area well. None of the villas goes for less than four hundred thousand; Samoy couldn't pay that much, even if he was renting. Either he's been taken in, or he's squatting in an empty villa. I go for the squat. We can go from villa to villa, or look for the old biddy who knows the neighbourhood, the kind who spies on her neighbours and hears all the gossip. If we discount gardens with children's equipment in them, the villas with a new car parked outside and those with a satellite dish, we ought to be able to find our old lady. Ronan: you take Acacias, Sam Marronniers, I'll do Saules. The first one to find anything calls the other two."

They split up. About twenty minutes later it was Ronan who called. Sam and Coste joined him outside 15 avenue des Acacias.

"You're going to love this. I've found a good one. Do you know what this is?"

He pointed to a round pink child's walkie-talkie hanging from the iron railing of a villa with an overgrown front garden. A small statue was half-buried in a mass of tangled weeds. A sign warning BEWARE OF THE DOG was stuck to the letter box.

"It's a fucking two-way baby monitor. She's hung them up all over her shack."

Sam whistled in astonishment.

"Bravo, you've landed on the neighbourhood paranoiac."

The baby monitor crackled into life.

"That big gormless one can stay outside. I'm not having him in here! He'll see if I'm paranoid!"

All three of them looked up towards the house and saw they were being spied on by a silhouette obscured by the sun's reflection on the window. Then it disappeared.

Ronan was beside himself. He couldn't have asked for more.

"O.K, you big gormless one, wait here for us like a good boy while we do the police work. If you like, you can replace the guard dog, he's been dead for years."

"May he rest in peace," the monitor said.

Another one of the same make and colour was hanging above the front doorbell. The door was ajar, and a persistent smell of cat's piss filled the air. Ronan invited Coste to follow him.

"Come on, she's at the back, in the living room."

A woman of indeterminate age was ensconced in a thread-bare armchair. The headrest bore a big greasy stain. Squeezed into a flowery blouse, she had short hair dyed an unlikely shade of blue. She barely took her eyes off the T.V. screen. Laid out on the table in front of her were eight baby monitors, each of them crackling with their own tone, and so loud they almost drowned out the sound of the T.V. newsreader.

"Always on the alert, my lads. Seven windows and one door, eight talkie-walkies so I can hear everything. That means I know if anyone is coming towards the house, or prowling out-side. Better than a burglar alarm."

"Yeah, grandmaman, but those alarms are directly linked to the police station, whereas if somebody comes in here, you'll be the only one to know. And probably the last as well."

The old lady strained to hear.

"What was that?"

"I was saying—"

Coste interrupted him.

"You were saying nothing, Ronan. You were going to sit down and let me speak to the lady. That's what you were doing, wasn't it?"

"Oh, so he's the boss. Would he like some coffee and biscuits?"

In addition to the unwelcoming smells, the thin layer of grease apparently covering every surface in the house guided Coste's answer.

"No thanks, but it's very kind of you."

He took a seat next to her and spoke more loudly.

"I'm sure you're the kind of person who knows the people living round here. We're looking for a villa that might be being squatted. Does that ring a bell?"

"Seventy-seven villas. I know every one of them, because my

cats get everywhere. People say they stink, but cats can't stink because they're always cleaning themselves."

She craned her neck as if to see if any of them were around, then remembered the question.

"Two villas for sale. One's clean, and one my cats got stuck in once, but that won't be sold, it's abandoned. It's 23 avenue des Saules, if you want to go take a look."

"Thank you for your time, madame."

Ronan went over to the baby monitors so that Sam wouldn't miss a word.

"Yes, thanks, and I'm sorry about our colleague. He's never been taught how to talk to a lady."

Out in the street, Sam gave him the finger.

They made their way to 23 avenue des Saules, and discovered that their new informer's description was accurate. A small two-storey house, shutters closed, faded paintwork, a few tiles missing, whitewash peeling off the walls and every square centimetre covered in climbing shrubs. "Abandoned" was a pretty good description.

"Sam, take a look in the letter box so we can see the last time the mail was taken in. Ronan, climb over the railing and break the front door down. We can say that's how we found it; we're not going to hang around for a couple of hours waiting for a locksmith."

"The letter box is locked. Can I break into that too?"

Ronan was already astride the railing, but even in that uncomfortable position could not help poking fun at his colleague.

"Go for it, Sam. Your arms are so short, a letter box is a bit like a door for you, but don't hurt yourself."

With that he jumped down into the garden and made for the house. At the same moment, the latch on the letter box gave way. Ronan put his shoulder to the front door, but it didn't yield. Sam plunged his hand into the letter box. Ronan took several steps back to get a better run-up. Sam took out the only thing he found in the box: a laminated card. He handed it to Coste. Ronan took a deep breath and launched himself at the door a second time. It collapsed in a crash of splintered wood. Coste shouted:

"Don't go in!"

He was holding a worn, crumpled national identity card bearing the photograph of Franck Samoy, with Afro hair and smiling eyes.

"We've got mail!"

Sam was triumphant.

"We've found the right spot, haven't we?"

"First his mobile pointing us to here, now his identity card in the letterbox. We didn't find a thing, we were led here by the nose. And I don't like that."

16

He had got into the habit of advancing with his head turned to the left. Only his right eye worked – the other one had been put out in a street fight. In this way, year in, year out, he gradually refocused his field of vision. He climbed onto what was left of the knees of a man seated on a chair. The smell of roasted flesh had brought him here. He had tried to lick the least charred parts round the ankles, but didn't like the taste. Calculating the strength he would need, he jumped gracefully down to the floor. Even though his empty eye socket made him look like a pirate in a child's story, he was still a big cat who always landed on his feet.

He walked down the stairs to the ground floor. If he followed the corridor towards the front door and then turned into the room that had once been the kitchen, he would find the hole in the wall where he could get out into the fresh air. That was how he had got in. Inside the house it was as black as ink, but on the bottom step he sensed danger, and came to a halt, ears pricked. He turned his head a bit further to the left to see what was going on. He dropped one paw to the floor, but couldn't decide whether to leave the staircase.

The combined effect of the door exploding and crashing violently against the wall together with the blinding white light suddenly flooding the house almost gave the cat a heart attack.

He did a sudden sprint on the spot, his paws scrabbling on the floor, then crashed headlong into the wall before hurtling back up the stairs in two bounds.

Framed in the doorway, Ronan took out his service revolver and flicked off the safety catch. The other two quickly joined him. Without speaking, the three men immediately recognised the smell. Going from room to room, they checked the downstairs rooms, calling out to each other:

"Kitchen, clear!"

"Living room, clear!"

"Up to the first floor!"

The light from the ground floor barely pierced the gloom upstairs. Coste took out his Maglite. He swept it round the only room there, in the middle of which was a plastic folding chair. A body charred through and through, mummified by the heat, was waiting for them. Man? Woman? Franck Samoy or somebody else?

"O.K., let's get out of here, we don't want to mess up the crime scene. Ronan, call the forensic crew. It'll soon be six o'clock, by the time they get here the sun will be setting. Tell them to bring spotlights. One for the outside, two for the interior. Sam, find out who owns this place and get in touch with them. I'll call the duty doctor and the public prosecutor to get them to agree to an autopsy. Sam, what time was the last call to his mobile?"

"According to the list of incoming calls, at three this afternoon."

"So if there's a call every three hours, there should be . . ."

The ring tone that sounded at 6 p.m. precisely had a Cuban rhythm somewhat at odds with the situation. Stuck between two of the corpse's ribs, the mobile flashed as it announced an "unknown caller". The mobile had been vibrating every three hours for the past two days, and this last call shook the charred bones between which it was lodged, causing them to finally give way. The ribs crumbled into ashes, sending the mobile spinning down inside the thoracic cavity until it vanished, still playing its rumba, though by now it was more muffled. Even so, Ronan managed to make a joke of it:

"We'll have to warn the pathologist there's a surprise inside, like a Kinder egg."

"I'll consider that. Don't touch anything else, we're out of here."

Sam did not appear to have got the message.

"Sam, what are you doing? Don't go near him."

He ignored Coste's order.

"The chair . . . It's not burnt. Look, it's plastic, but it's not at all melted. Nor is the floor. Shit, nothing's burnt but him."

17

From a distance, with the spotlights throwing a violent light onto the front of 23 avenue de Saules, passers-by might have supposed a film was being shot in the neighbourhood. The C.S.U. team's work did not finish until long after eleven. Once they had completed their survey, the body had to be removed. The undertaker's team hesitated. The first one tried to slip his arms underneath those of the corpse, while the second man tentatively got hold of his ankles. The bones snapped at the left shoulder and the arm fell to the floor. One of the men almost brought up his supper. They laid the arm gently across its owner's knees, and the two men were forced to accept they would have to carry the body out on his chair if they were going to be able to tuck him into the body bag waiting outside. Coste approached the C.S.U. team and handed them Franck Samoy's identity card.

"I need you to look for fingerprints on this. Tell 'Can't Touch This' that two of us have handled it: Lieutenant Dorfrey and Capitaine Coste. Say I'm sorry."

"Don't worry, we can collect your prints back at headquarters to rule them out. We're good here, all done."

Intrigued, he stared at Coste.

"Wasn't it you three days ago with that story of the ghost?"

Coste nodded, eyes tight shut.

"And now you've got spontaneous combustion. You boys have strange tastes these days!"

"We've also got a case of werewolf bites. If you're interested I'll keep some hairs for you."

"Seriously?"

Coste bristled. He knew this was a foretaste of what the press would headline over the next few days.

"Are you stupid, or what? Make sure you look for petrol. It's more likely he was set on fire somewhere else and then dumped here, rather than your theory about spontaneous combustion. How long before we can have the results?"

"Tomorrow morning, if I work on it tonight."

"So get going, Fox Mulder."

Coste left him and lit a cigarette. Leaning against the railing next door, he slid down until he was crouching on the ground. Head in hands, he listened to the reports from his team. Sam first:

"The owners are in Cannes. They handed the sale over to an estate agency that went bust; they haven't had time to deal with it since then. The place has fallen into disrepair and they've been waiting to get back on their feet a bit before putting it on sale again. They haven't been here for the past six months."

"Anything else?"

"Nothing special inside the house. I've inspected both floors. But there's a back door with signs of a forced entry. Almost certainly opened with a crowbar. That's probably how they got in. More discreet than through the front."

Then it was Ronan's turn:

"I contacted the Institut medico-légal. They've got a slot at one o'clock tomorrow afternoon."

"Nothing before then?"

"Yes, an hour earlier, but Dr Marquant comes in at one, so I thought . . ."

"O.K., one o'clock is fine. Let's clear out of here."

"Listen, playing the mysterious, good-looking, steely-eyed detective is fine for a while, but if you want to get anywhere you're going to have to talk to that girl somewhere other than over a corpse. I can coach you if you like, it's becoming more and more popular, I've seen it on T.V."

Sam added his money's worth:

"Especially since you must have shaken her with your zombie three days ago, and now with your . . ."

"If you use the words 'spontaneous combustion', you're fired. No, I'll make you work over Christmas, and fire you after that. You really are the only one who could get excited by that sort of thing."

The three officers walked back up avenue de Saules. Ronan turned when he heard a soft meow. Sam was carrying the pirate cat in his long, skinny arms.

"You *cannot* be serious! What are you doing with that stinking creature?"

"My good deed for the day."

As they passed 15 avenue des Acacias, Sam tossed the cat over the garden railing. The baby monitor thanked him.

18

Shooting range in the basement of S.D.P.J. 93
Saturday, 14 January, 2012, 8.30 a.m.

Sam was like a dog with a bone. He teased Ronan:

"So the fact that you're wearing a new shirt with the top two buttons undone and that you've more or less shaved has nothing to do with it?"

"None. Give me a break."

"I'm sorry, I just think it's very odd you make such an effort for Lieutenant De Ritter's first day. Then again, I can understand it: I reckon she's in a class you've never had much to do with."

Coste came in accompanied by the new recruit. Despite being well built, next to her he looked like an eight-stone weakling. He addressed his team and the instructor.

"Gentlemen, most of you know our new lieutenant. Johanna, this is Benjamin, our firearms instructor, and this is Lieutenant Ronan Scaglia, my second-in-command, the only one you haven't already met."

The two of them said hello, unsure whether to give each other a kiss on the cheek or shake hands, and in the end doing neither.

As they separated, Ronan whispered:

"I'll keep a bullet for you, Sam."

'I told you, she's way out of your league."

The instructor took over.

"Alright ladies, line up on the range. Safety catches on. Insert your fifteen shot clips. Stand five metres from the target for five rounds of rapid fire. Helmet and glasses on. Shooters, are you ready?"

The three replied as one:

"Shooters ready."

"When I give the signal."

His whistle unleashed a salvo of fifteen rapid-fire shots.

"Safety catches on. Shooters, move back to ten metres for another round of five shots. Helmet and glasses on. Shooters, are you ready?"

"Shooters ready."

The three automatic Sig Sauer S.P. 2022 pistols spat their cones of flame.

"Safety catches on. Last round. Stand twenty metres from the target for your final shots. Helmets and glasses on. Shooters, are you ready?"

"Shooters ready."

The targets were shaken by the power of the 9mm parabellum bullets.

"Safety catches on. Holster your weapons. Shooters examine the results."

Ronan, whose target was next to De Ritter's, got his second shock of the morning. His shots were good enough – he'd always been gifted – but compared to hers they looked pathetic. Five shots to the heart, five to the head, five to the abdomen. It got to him.

"Who exactly are you? Calamity Johanna?"

The instructor came up to them.

"Good work, Jo."

Ronan could not hide his surprise.

"You two know each other?"

"A little. I guess I should introduce you. Johanna, national champion at pistol shooting, let me present your team; team, let me present Johanna De Ritter. I can't believe it: you had no idea who you'd recruited?"

De Ritter tapped the instructor's back in acknowledgement.

"Jo, come back whenever you like, make yourself at home."

Coste took her to one side while the other two were putting their things away.

"Didn't I say you were to keep a low profile? That wasn't shooting practice, it was an exhibition. You know how sensitive men are."

"Yeah, when I no longer see 'big lesbian' signs flashing in Lieutenant Scaglia's eyes I'll make the effort to miss occasionally, if that helps add a couple of centimetres you know where."

"Fine, fine, fine. I can see we'll all have a great time. We'll sort out your ego problems straightaway. Ronan, you take Calamity with you and bring her up to speed on the Bébe Coulibaly and Franck Samoy case. Then the two of you go and see the C.S.U. people and find out if the results are ready. You'll see, champ, you're going to love it."

19

She pressed the RECORD button on her dictaphone and leaned over the blackened body.

"Criminal technique commonly known as a 'barbecue'. Murderers change their M.O.s according to advances in police scientific research. A colleague in Marseilles told me about it recently. Six cases in the first five months of the year, essentially settling of accounts. Generally used to delay identification of the victim."

"Not in this specific case. We were led directly to him."

She leaned over again:

"Skeleton of a male. Fourth degree burns. Volume and weight of body reduced, skin with spontaneous tears, fractures produced by heat. Forget any hope of fingerprints, they're burnt to ashes. But we should be able to find some D.N.A. There's just enough flesh round the ankles. They must have been protected by leather ankle boots. If he's on the database you'll get your man."

"What if he'd been totally burnt?"

"Then there's mitochondrial D.N.A. in the medulla, but that's more complicated."

"What about his dental imprints?"

"That's only when there's really nothing else. Medical odontology could possibly help us date things, or where dental surgery took place, depending on the techniques employed. But in this case that wouldn't be of any use. Just take a look."

She waved Coste closer and opened the corpse's jaw with a soft crack.

"Some of the teeth are broken. In front, an incisor and a canine on the bottom jaw; at the back, two molars snapped off. But not pulled out. It looks very much as if he was tortured. Did you say nothing around him was burnt?"

"Oh, you're not going to start on that as well, are you?"

"I'm a rational sort. When I see a non-identified object in the sky, I think first of a weather balloon rather than a U.F.O. I just wanted to point out that if your two cases are linked, then some bastard really is taking the piss out of you."

Some vulgarity at last. Coste was beginning to get worried.

"Yes, they are linked. The charcoal skeleton in front of you may well be the source of the blood on the ghost's sweater."

"Victor, they're playing with you. You're going to have to be very careful if you don't want the press on your back for a second time."

Asking him to wait a moment, she left the room, and came back carrying Bébe Coulibaly's file. She took the photographs of the bloodstained sweater from it and held it next to the body.

"As you can see, the holes match. I can trace two impacts at chest level and here, an abrasion on the spine. Those are your three wounds. Because of their position on the body, any one of them could have been fatal. Death by carbonisation could also be the cause, but I don't really see why someone would shoot three times at an already charred corpse. As for when he died, I'm going to have to consult a paleoanthropologist colleague. Given the state of the corpse, we can use only his bones."

Coste watched her with an amused expression.

"All this seems to really turn you on."

"I'll be honest with you, Victor. It's a great way to attract a woman."

20

In his spotless white coat, "Can't Touch This", the head of the forensics department, was dealing calmly with Capitaine Lara Jevric, the boss of Groupe Crime 2.

"We'll be as quick as we can, Capitaine."

"And that's still too slow. Do like they do in 'C.S.I.', it's not difficult. I'll leave the official request here, O.K.?"

She straightened up when Coste came in.

"Hello there, Victor."

"Morning, Lara."

"How are you getting on with your loopy cases?"

Coste did not rise to the bait.

"We're making progress. What are you up to?"

"Grievous bodily harm and rape. Well, not really rape . . . The kid nicked a kilo of shit from some villains in Saint-Ouen, scooted off to sell it in another region, then tried to disappear in Thailand."

"It didn't work?"

"Not really. Holidays always come to an end. We got a call this morning from the Jean-Verdier hospital. His buddies found him. They chopped off his first finger with a bolt-cutter for revenge. Then, for a bit of fun, they forced him to suck off their dog. We found fragments of hair in his mouth, and I want the 93 experts to get a move on and tell me if they're from the mutt or not."

"As I told you, Capitaine, we'll be as quick as possible," muttered "Can't Touch This".

Capitaine Levric raised her eyes to the heavens and left the room.

The head of forensics picked up the request from his desk and slipped it under the pile of those he had received earlier that day.

"What are you doing?" asked Coste.

"Whenever some arsehole mentions 'C.S.I.', I put their request at the bottom of the pile. Seriously though, do I call you Columbo? No, I don't."

Coste laughed.

"Have you got the results of traces of hydrocarbon on the body from Pré-Saint-Gervais?"

"Yes, I thought I was going to have to push the fire specialists in our main lab, but they were already on it and knew pretty much what was going on, like everyone else, I expect. You should steer clear of all that, the spotlight's on you, Columbo."

"You see how you can be nasty as well."

He put his hand on the man's shoulder. His bushy 1968-style beard went quite well with his role as a white-coated scientific expert. On his desk, the usual framed photographs of kids and family were replaced by snapshots of the most gruesome crime scenes he had been called on to investigate. Coste knew some of them because he too had worked on the investigations. The one involving the woman partly devoured by her former partner who had gone mad. The sex game that had ended badly, with the guy found dead nailed to a St Andrew's cross. There was nothing morbid about the collection, simply habit and a skin thick enough to see nothing but the professional side of these images. The two men were linked by an indestructible bond. One that had arisen in a shared personal experience that neither of them had forgotten but which did not need to be talked about.

Coste left the department with their report, skimming it as he walked along. When he reached his office he saw Sam standing in the centre of the room reading from his laptop to the rest of the team.

"The first recorded case took place in Verona, Italy in 1731. The victim was Countess Cornelia Bandi, aged sixty-two. The magistrate wrote in his report: 'A mysterious fire seems to have been lit in the Countess's chest.' A similar case in Caen in 1782. The examining surgeon: 'The body was consumed in less than seven hours, even though nothing save her clothes were burnt.' In 1977, the expert appointed by the authorities at Nancy raised the possibility of the existence of a case of spontaneous combustion. A woman found carbonised in her apartment whose bones had been reduced to ashes must have been subjected to a heat of more than 2,000 degrees Celsius, without anything else in the apartment showing signs of having been burned. In addition there are occurrences that had witnesses. 1938, Chelmsford, England: a young girl catches fire in a ballroom. And there's another case in 1980, at a disco in Darlington, also in England. No trace of accelerant was found in any of these cases. In 2010, the Irish police themselves concluded that the death of a pensioner in Galway could be attributed to spontaneous combustion, and . . ."

Coste interrupted him, tossing the forensic report onto his desk.

"And in 2012, Franck Samoy fried to a crisp, sprinkled with petrol. End of story. To be exact, with lead-free 98."

Ever the joker, Ronan added:

"The most expensive. A nice touch."

Sam was visibly disappointed. He had already had his theory

about zombies demolished, and now nobody wanted to listen to his stories about spontaneous combustion. Still more seduced by the mysterious version than the scientific explanation, he wanted confirmation.

"Are we sure about the lab results?"

"Does their use of a gas chromatograph with a flame ionisation detector satisfy you? I for one reckon that's incomprehensible enough to be convincing."

Coste sat on the edge of his desk.

"I've just been harpooned by Damiani. She's had a call from Marc Farel, a crime reporter who doesn't usually spare us."

"A shit-stirrer for anything to do with the police," Ronan said. "Farel must have such a hard-on from all this that he could at least offer to collaborate rather than stab us in the back."

"That's true, and we can use that to our advantage. The press is already informed and hasn't needed any proof to link the two cases. I can imagine tomorrow's headlines. It won't take much for the rumour to spread and our bosses to become scared witless. For your information, Damiani is already being courted by the Brigade criminelle in Paris. They're interested in the case."

Although she knew she ought to keep quiet, De Ritter dared to ask:

"My thoughts exactly: they deal with homicides when the perpetrator is unknown. How come these two cases haven't already been handed over to them?"

"The Brigade criminelle is an old lady who has already celebrated her hundredth birthday, whereas the S.D.P.J. 93 is a young stripling, a mere thirty years old. Here we have to deal with an annual average of ninety cases of murder and attempted murder with a team of twenty people. In Paris they receive an average forty-five cases, fewer than half we have. They have fifty-five officers there, that is, three times more detectives, so you can see the imbalance and understand why they have a record clear-up rate. For the moment, we have no leads, so they're biding their time. Conclusion: all this mess is down to us. So let's get to it, and see who does what."

He opened the files and glanced at the different statements.

"We saw from our records that Franck Samoy was the owner of a red B.M.W. 633. Sam, send the traffic people a request to locate that car. I want it and I want forensics to pass the whole thing through the cyanoacrylate fuming chamber to search for fingerprints. I want the names of everyone whose backside has been in it."

Sam looked at the new lieutenant and could guess the question she was dying to ask.

"Cyanoacrylate. It's better than powder to identify fingerprints. It's a kind of superglue that's vapourised: when it dries you're left with a solid cast of the print. No chance of a mistake. Don't hesitate to ask."

Coste went on:

"When you've finished, Sam, get in touch with the press, all of them, and find out how they know as much as we do and almost as quickly. They'll say they want to protect their sources, you'll have to convince them. As a last resort, try Farel."

"I'm on it."

"Ronan and Calamity, go back to Pré-Saint-Gervais."

Ronan looked at Coste as if he had just been punished. Some partnerships don't work straightaway, and he sensed he was going to have trouble with this one, whom he was already thinking of as "Juggernaut". He thought female recruits to S.D.P.J. 93 were too few and far between, but it was just his luck to be paired with someone who in his eyes was the archetypal lesbian. Coste ignored his filthy look and said:

"We found the body but still haven't questioned the neighbours. Find a witness, and while you're at it say hello from me to the old lady with the baby monitors. Ronan, after that, get in touch with your contact at the Jean Verdier hospital. Bébé Coulibaly has been there for two days now, that's time enough, don't you think?"

"Yeah, I think we've waited long enough, he must have had a delivery by now."

De Ritter looked lost again, but chose to let it go.

"I'm going to pay a visit to Suzanne Samoy," Coste said. "We promised her."

21

Yuri Gagarin estate, Romainville

Suzette Samoy broke the silence.

"The television is new."

"So I see."

"It's bigger. The man in the shop said it was a plasma model, but I don't know what that means."

"Isn't it plugged in?"

"Well no, I never watch it, I prefer the radio. I put it in the window just in case my son is in the neighbourhood, notices the T.V. and thinks of coming to see me. The cat's the only one who's upset. The T.V. table is his lookout post."

The cat was purring peacefully on Coste's lap. Franck's mother wasn't used to seeing it so friendly.

"Do you like cats, then?"

"I've been coming into contact with a lot of them recently, but not in the best of circumstances. How many T.V. sets have you bought by now?"

"This is the seventh, but sometimes people give me them."

Coste sat there without moving much or saying a lot. He had to make an effort though. He opened his mouth, took a deep breath to begin, then bit his lip. Suzanne Samoy gave him a weary smile. Coste thought he could glimpse a hint of renewed calm in her eyes. For a mother, an unconfessable sense of relief.

"There's no point my waiting for him, is that it?"

Coste's voice was barely above a whisper:

"Yes, that's it."

He was close enough to take her in his arms. He didn't move. She put her hand on his cheek and tapped it gently, like grandparents do their grandchildren.

"For a policeman you don't like death much, do you?"

"To be honest, I couldn't care less about it. It's the poor people left behind I worry about."

"You must stay and eat. I made a roast with potatoes, there's too much for me on my own."

He glanced at his watch. 4.20 p.m. Precisely the time not to refuse Suzanne Samoy anything.

Without waiting for his reply, she shuffled off into the kitchen. She was not going to cry as long as he was there. Heartbreak is personal, not to be shared.

22

Unité médico-judiciaire at the Jean-Verdier hospital

The cold had decided to take a grip on this late afternoon. February was just around the corner. Ronan parked the unmarked Peugeot 306 in one of the spaces reserved for the police, and told De Ritter:

"Five minutes from now, a nurse is going to appear. She's a friend who lends us a hand from time to time. If you don't mind, you're to stay in the car. I'll open a window and put the radio on. If there's a problem, give me a shout."

He walked the few metres to the entrance for emergencies and people being held in custody. He leaned against the outside wall, took out his mobile and sent a message. A couple of uniforms went past, escorting a prisoner in handcuffs. The men recognised each other: Ronan had arrested him for rape the previous year. He was not astonished to see him getting out so soon. He was surprised to find himself wishing that one of these bastards would one day pick on the daughter of the public prosecutor or a judge, just to see if he was given a sentence of less than a year.

"Greetings, pig."

Ronan did not look up from his mobile.

"Greetings, arsehole."

A female voice said:

"Classy as ever, I hear."

"Sorry, Latifa, I didn't see you. It's just that . . . oh, forget it. Do you have anything for me?"

"Yes, you were right, he took delivery of a mobile the second day. He's having his bandages changed in the treatment room at the moment, I have to put it back in his room in less than ten minutes."

"Go on, call me."

She looked all around before taking out the mobile. Bébé's number appeared on Ronan's mobile.

"Great, got it. Go into recent calls and erase the last one."

"I've done that already, James Bond. Do you need anything else, or was this merely professional?"

"Could there be anything else? You're the one who dumped me, remember."

"No, I made a choice. You gave me hell for six months. I like you a lot, but not your job or your womanising."

"But when you asked me to, I deleted all my girlfriends' numbers."

"Yeah, but you still kept the one of your most clingy mistress: Victor Coste."

"Very funny. Can I call you later?"

"Don't go to the trouble, Mister playboy. Go break some other hearts."

When Latifa turned on her heel, Ronan put on a big smile to hide his dismay: he had noticed that De Ritter had not taken her eyes off them throughout their conversation. He settled back in the driver's seat. She could not resist saying: "I see you're getting personally involved in this case."

"It's the cross I have to bear every day. I look good, and make the best of it. Why, does she attract you? Would you like me to introduce you?"

"Thanks, I have all I need at home."

Ronan pulled out, glancing in his rear-view mirror at Latifa. He would never admit he had been so keen on her. He handed De Ritter his mobile.

"The top number is Bébé Coulibaly's. Call Sam and pass it on to him so that he can ask the prosecutor to authorise a tap. With a bit of luck, Bébé will have something interesting to tell us."

23

It is common knowledge that the only star that seems to shine at 36 Quai des Orfèvres is that of the Brigade criminelle. Yet it is here that all the big central units are to be found, from the anti-gang team with their rapid response vehicle permanently stationed in the courtyard, to the Brigade des Stups.

On the second floor, once you've climbed the polished wooden staircase, shown your credentials at the bulletproof security check and crossed the spacious lobby of the waiting room, you come to the offices of the director of the Police Judiciaire. From here, he controls his army of chief inspectors in every département of outer Paris: Hauts-de-Seine, Val-de-Marne and Seine-Saint-Denis, as well as all the arrondissements in the city of Paris itself.

Having adopted an authoritarian style of command bordering on the unacceptable, a style he applied to all his subordinates without distinction, he had chosen for his deputy a pen-pusher who would have been happy to be his master's shadow, and was reported to wag his tail and fetch the ball whenever he was ordered to. Jacques Galienne, the deputy director, could put up with this unpleasant gossip as long as the director continued to further his career. During ministerial reshuffles, he had already seen one head of the national police force suddenly become a road safety spokesperson. As humiliating as putting a chief inspector at a crossing to help children cross when they came out of school.

In the waiting room a man in his fifties wearing a tight suit was sitting patiently. From behind his round glasses he was spying on everybody who went by. A smartly dressed woman came up, and he immediately pigeonholed her. A secretary, no use to him, no point smiling or being friendly.

"Commandant Malbert, the deputy director will see you now."

Without a word, he stood up and followed her. At the end of a thickly carpeted corridor, she opened double doors lined with padded brown leather. He also knew where to pigeonhole the man behind the doors, and adopted his most ingratiating attitude.

"Deputy director, sir."

Behind a huge lacquered desk, a balding man screwed the top back on his fountain pen and closed the file in front of him.

"Commandant, please take a seat. Coffee?"

Without waiting for an answer, he despatched the secretary from the office.

"I hope you won't mind that the director himself cannot join us. I speak for him, and it's on his behalf that I wish you a successful return to the forces of law and order."

In view of the way in which he had quit the profession ten years earlier, Malbert was even more appreciative of the polite tone the man adopted. He knew that the reasons given to justify his early departure were exactly why he was now being recruited as a reservist. Irony creeping into his voice, Deputy Director Galienne said:

"What a splendid concept being a reservist is, Commandant! To be able to call on our most qualified pensioners so that they can pass on their knowledge to younger people. As in every profession, the transfer of expertise is . . ."

Lucien Malbert was perfectly aware when someone was mocking him, and preferred to cut out the polite formulas.

"That's what's written officially, but you and I know very well that my expertise is from another time and I doubt very much if anyone wants me to pass it on."

The other man sought to mollify him:

"Those are old stories from your time in Paris, long since forgotten . . . Now you're part of S.D.P.J. 93. You'll be the link between the Groupe Crime officers and the criminal analysts of the S.A.L.V.A.C. system. You are to report to Commandant Damiani, the head of the Groupe Crime units there. Your predecessor Lieutenant Aubin did a fine job, and is now enjoying a comfortable position in Annecy, close to his family."

"You know my conditions: they're purely financial. I couldn't give a damn about Annecy. I'm laying aside other commitments, and you're going to line my pockets. That's all there is to it, no need to dress things up."

"There's no need to be rude either, Commandant."

Accustomed to swimming in the muddy waters of hints and half-truths, Malbert knew when he had won. He had the match ball in his hand, and simply wanted to confirm he was in a position of strength.

"What you're asking from me, which I've agreed to, means we depend on one another. A bit like my relationship with my informants in the past. The only difference between you and me is what we stand to lose. Personally, my track record will always be against me, but you have your career to consider. I could take a piss on your carpet and neither you nor I could back out from our agreement, so you can keep your rudeness. Tell the director that our interview was a huge success and that

I'll be in touch with Damiani tomorrow morning at nine. And on that note . . ."

He stood up and strode out of the office. The deputy director smiled, convinced he had recruited absolute scum. They could not have made a better choice: Lucien Malbert would be perfect.

24

Coste had heard the news that same day. Malbert was to take the place vacated by Lieutenant Aubin as head of the S.A.L.V.A.C. programme. Damiani had asked him to have to hand all the details of the latest two murders so that Malbert could inspect the database to see if anyone else in France had been enjoying themselves castrating or setting fire to their victims. The name Malbert rang a distant bell in Coste's mind, although he was unable to trace it back to any particular period or unit. When that happened, he was in the habit of calling Noviello, his encyclopedia.

Now well into her seventies, Noviello had spent her entire career in the Brigade de protection des mineurs* at the Quai de Gesvres. In addition to having to her credit the fact that she had put a fair number of paedophiles behind bars, she had another passion: the history of the Police judiciaire. She knew all there was to know in all its different periods: the brigades set up by "Tiger" Clemenceau and the Bonnot gang at the beginning of the twentieth century. Commissaire Massu, known in novels as Maigret. Pierrot Le Fou and his Tractions Avant gang, and how chief inspectors Truchi and Mattéi had failed to capture them. The indelible links between Commissaire Broussard

* Child Protection Department

and Jacques Mesrine. The cock-up by the head of the Brigade de répression du banditisme* when trying to arrest the Postiches gang. The mishaps of Commissaire Inspector Neyret, whose working methods were tolerated for twenty years in Lyons but then became unacceptable, despite the Légion d'Honneur pinned to his lapel.

The moment Coste cast the Malbert bait, the cork float bobbed underwater. Noviello knew all about him.

"Lucien Malbert? My God, you're scraping the barrel there."

"Tell me more."

"He's a former Brigade des moeurs† officer who didn't manage to get to the end of his career despite a bright start in the Eighties. He worked in gambling dens and strip clubs in the XVIIIth. He began building up a list of contacts where influential people featured alongside girls of easy virtue, shall we say? From there it was a small step to organising some private soirées, a step he took all the more easily because of what he got out of it. For a few years, the name of Malbert opened all the doors in sleazy Paris, but he got more and more careless. As you know, in that line of business the hardest ones to keep quiet are the girls. One of them tried to blackmail a minister. She ended up dead, and the Inspection générale des services‡ latched on to Malbert and wouldn't let go. That was young Abassian's first investigation."

"Dariush Abassian? The guy who now heads up the I.G.S.?"

"Yes, but back then he was just a young whippersnapper with jet-black hair and the looks of an Iranian immigrant. He never managed clearly to implicate Malbert, or he wasn't allowed to: no doubt the guy was protected by the politicians

* Organised Crime Squad
† Vice Squad
‡ Police Inspectorate

he allowed to fuck for free. However, Malbert was advised to retire, for the good of the police force, if I may say so. And now they've had the brilliant idea of bringing him back into the fold. That's interesting. If you want my advice, Victor, there must be some reason behind it. Keep your distance, he's the kind of guy who splashes everyone around him with the brown stuff."

"I'll make sure I don't get splashed. Thank you."

But Noviello was not going to let him go that easily.

"Victor, don't be rude. You can't abandon an old woman just like that. Tell me a bit about yourself. Unless I'm mistaken, two dead bodies means two trips to the I.M.L. Tell me, that pathologist, Léa Marquant, isn't it? Does she at least know you exist?"

"I think she does now. But what with all the work . . ."

She had known Coste for too long not to realise he was going to evade the question, so she finished his sentence for him:

"And above all because you're so scared of letting anyone near you again."

The silence on the line became awkward.

"I know all your excuses, Coste, you've been making them for years. Except that some day or other you have to give yourself permission to turn the page. She's gone, and it's not your fault."

"I could have been there an hour earlier," Coste muttered, before he hung up.

And yet getting there an hour earlier wouldn't have changed anything. Coste knew she would simply have done something different, somewhere else, at another moment.

But even though he had come to accept that, the day it happened still stuck to him like tar.

* * *

That day, Coste had got home after nightfall. Despite the silence, the sight of the white coat draped over the chair back told him he was not alone. Glancing down at his watch, he sighed, prepared an apology. Because he was late. Because he had not called. Because she never felt too good without him and needed him to be there.

For a long time he had managed to dodge any commitment, to stay a bachelor, even if that worried his entourage. He mistrusted love: couples who held each other's hand, gazed into one another's eyes and finished each other's sentences. Love spreads as untidily as a child's drawing. Then love crossed his path. In such a fragile fashion. Coste had thrown the guy who had destroyed her into prison, but that hadn't been enough. She was still haunted, wounded, empty. And since the police are there to protect, he fell in love with her. In love with this girl who had sought refuge in his flat for almost two years now and who no longer loved anything about life but him.

On the dining room table he noticed an extinguished cigarette in the ashtray, and the blue cup. She had given it to him, pleading with him to take the time to have a coffee before he went to work. Just one. With her. He had tried hard, but his old habits had resurfaced. After that, she had borrowed the cup from time to time before making it hers. For good.

He called out to her increasingly loudly, then looked in every room. Finally he came to a halt outside the closed bathroom door. He laid his hand on it, not daring to push. Refusing to admit what he already knew, he whispered her name several times before making up his mind.

On the other side of the door, in red-tinged, already cold water, floated her body. Her long black hair was spread round her face like a crown. Pointing to the ceiling, her slashed wrists. He was sure he shouted something. He plunged both hands into the tub, under her legs and back. Staggering, he collided with the toilet.

The note fell.

He lifted her as if she were asleep, water streaming from her hair, the tips of her toes and fingers. Engulfed by sadness, drained of all strength, he slid down against the wall, still clutching her to him. He had wept, he was sure of that. He hugged her – too tightly, she would have said – and kissed her full on the mouth, as if there were still time to love her.

He struggled to his feet and laid her on the bed. As gently as he could. He stretched out beside her, talking to her, pulling up the blanket, asking her forgiveness as well as why. Why?

He ran back into the bathroom, searching everywhere: on the toilet seat, the shelf where she kept her perfumes, even the floor. Then he knelt by the bathtub. In front of him floated two sodden sheets of paper, stained all over with a blue ink that had traced the excuses or reproaches he would never read.

The rest of his memories were one big blur. He was filled with rage and pain, and the combination of these two feelings gave him simultaneously a desire to cry out and to collapse, to be comforted or to gun down the first person he encountered.

He went back to her and thought he would say nothing, ever, to anyone, just lie there. Then in the middle of the night he had called Mathias Aubin. Although all he asked was for him to come, his tone of voice had said the rest. His friend had driven through all the red lights, probably smashed several wing mirrors, and in less than fifteen minutes was banging on the door with his fists. Refusing to wait, he had used the spare keys Coste had given him, just in case. He had run down the corridor, put his head into the bedroom and seen the two entwined bodies. With the incredible gentleness he could display despite his massive build, he had tried to separate them.

Coste had objected, defended himself, struck out, and Aubin had accepted the blows for as long as it had taken.

Only Mathias and the head of forensics had entered the flat. His friend had refused to let him stay on his own that night, and had called his wife, who came to pick him up. Coste had spent two days being watched over by the Aubin family until finally he decided to return home. There he conscientiously smashed everything to pieces. Then threw it all out.

That evening, in his devastated flat, he ran a bath and for a moment thought he would never again have the strength to climb out of the water.

From that day on, apart from a bed, a low table and a sofa, the flat was empty.

For many months he continued to receive letters addressed to her, but he did nothing to stop them. A few authorities and some mail order cosmetic or clothes companies thought she was still alive, and that suited him. However pathetic.

He still refused to sleep on her side of the bed.

25

By the end of the day, no new element likely to advance inquiries had been discovered, as the police would say. Ronan and De Ritter had not found any witnesses in Belvédère. The wire tap on Bébé Coulibaly was turning round and round, still waiting to pick up any calls. As for the press, only the journalist Marc Farel had agreed to say a little more about the source informing the media in real time. The letter-writer had apparently contacted him from a number that Sam had traced, which led them to a phone box. Block no. 14583, Zone 75056, Exchange 10681, a booth at 95 rue Chevaleret, Paris XIII. Farel had added that the informer was a man. Impasse. Sam had ended his report with the journalist's final words:

"He insisted I stress his 'prompt collaboration with the police, who owe him one in return'."

A classic stock phrase for this sort of freelancer, for whom a contacts book and business cards were the main tools of their trade. Farel saw himself as much as a policeman as a journalist, and, like the police, he was so fascinated by the profession that he devoted his life to it. Like the police, he had his snitches, the ones he paid and the ones he didn't, the basics for any crime reporter. Like the police, he spent nights staked out in his car. Like the police, he investigated. He respected the profession so much he gave himself the right to cause trouble, to question it, force it to improve. He ate with them, occasionally got drunk with them, partly because that was what the job demanded, but above all because he could not see himself leading any other life. On the cusp between the good and the bad, even the very bad, the "public enemies", the leading criminals who held the same fascination for him as the police did. Like the police. That did not make him exceptional. There were at least a hundred similar journalists in the Ile-de-France region who knew both wolves and hunters. Each had their own way of working, but one thing in common: their contacts. Without them, the best crime reporter wrote mere literature. Without them, there was no investigative reporting, and to judge Farel by his contacts among the police and justice communities, he was worthy of the reputation he had among his colleagues.

He had quickly grasped that information was more reliable the closer you got to the bottom. Although his contacts covered every social class, he had to admit there were more secretaries than commissaires, more non-ranking officers than capitaines with lots of stripes, more people who wrote memos than read them. Across more than two decades as a journalist, he had built up a network fine enough to trap all kinds of information and rumours. And yet there were only a few from 93, and Coste wasn't one of them. Lieutenant Aubin was.

Their meeting concluded, Coste sent his team home to get some sleep, telling them to be back on the bridge at 0700.

Twenty minutes later, he was at his apartment. His key turned only once in the lock. Coste was in the habit of always double locking his front door: one turn was missing. Ever since "*her*", he never returned home without a voice inside telling him that behind every door a life could be slipping away. The corridor light was on, and so was the one in the living room.

He took off his coat and threw it on the sofa, but kept his gun in his waistband, half-hidden by a sweater. The sound of a tune being hummed came from the kitchen.

"Good evening, Alice."

"Hi there, Victor. You could at least come in like a real *flic*, with your gun at the ready. I might have been a burglar."

He pretended to be annoyed.

"A burglar who has keys and closes the door behind him? By the way, we exchanged keys 'just in case' either of us needed a spare set. It wasn't so I could find you here at any time of the day or night. What are you doing?"

At first glance it looked as if she must be cooking an elaborate meal, but when Coste peered at the contents of the saucepan he was astonished to see that all the mess she had made in his kitchen was apparently for little more than pasta in tomato sauce.

Nineteen, bare-foot, standing there in a pair of cut-off jeans too short to be worn decently outdoors and a thin, baggy black jumper bare over one of her shoulders: Alice had been his neighbour for less than a year and was already starting to acquire bad habits.

"What if I'd been with someone?"

"You? You're a lone wolf, Victor, you never let anybody in. Besides, just between us, who do you reckon would come? Have you seen your apartment? There's no woman who would put up with it for more than a quarter of an hour."

She surveyed the living room.

"There's no furniture. It looks as if you moved in yesterday. No, I've no reason to be afraid, there's no room for anybody else in your cave."

"But you're fine here, aren't you?"

A few months earlier, in haste and without thinking too

much about it, he had grudgingly promised her parents he would keep an eye on Alice. She had managed to convince them that they ought to let her live on her own in Paris for her studies, even though all she could afford was a studio on the outskirts. That was how Coste had acquired an intrusive young girl as his next-door neighbour. She was studying at the Florent Acting School, and he could believe she was good-looking and charming enough to succeed.

"Whatever you're experimenting with in that pan, you can count me out. I ate earlier."

"With a woman?"

"Yes."

"A pretty one?"

"An unhappy one."

She did not give up.

"But pretty?"

"Very."

Playacting, she gave a childish pout and turned the cooker off. That was it for tonight. The mess she had prepared was going to go to waste.

He stretched out on the sofa and turned on the T.V. news channel, with the sound off. A rapid sequence of images of the Institut medico-légal, abandoned factories in Pantin, villas in Pré-Saint-Gervais. It had begun. A red carpet for collective paranoia, and more headaches for him. He closed his eyes and concentrated on his breathing. He sensed Alice's body next to his.

"What are you doing?"

"Making sure I'm safe. You promised to protect me, didn't you?"

"Never. I simply said I'd keep an eye on you from time to time."

She lifted his arm, slid underneath, and placed it back round her, making herself his prisoner. Turning on his side, he removed the gun that was digging into his back, ejected the clip and the round in the chamber with a whirring sound, and laid everything on the table.

When he reopened his eyes, he had no idea how much time had elapsed. Long enough for the newsreader to have disappeared and no doubt gone home, to be replaced by a programme about the police. That was all there was on T.V. these days. Police series, police films, police reports. Coste had never understood why people hated them so much in real life and yet adored them in fiction.

Alice was breathing softly, her breath feathering his neck. He got up without making a noise and took her keys to open the studio door. He left the door to her bedroom ajar, then went back into his own apartment, picked her up, carried her across the corridor and laid her down on her own bed. He pulled a blanket up over her.

"I know you're not asleep."

"No, but I love it when you carry me like a princess. All girls want a Prince Charming. I make my girlfriends at the theatre school fantasise. I tell them that during the day you pursue murderers . . ." She turned so that she could plunge her eyes into his and said more softly: ". . . and that at night you're mine, Coste."

"You've got the wrong prince."

"Will you kiss me?"

"Not this time, Alice, not this time."

Closing the studio door behind him, he went back to make coffee. It was ten to twelve, but his night wasn't over yet. In his kitchen he smiled at the brand new packet of sugar. On the faded Post-it that for weeks had been begging him to buy some, she had written "Done", and added: "Pay a bit more attention to your pretty neighbour."

Carrying the blue cup by its rim so as not to burn himself, he sat on the sofa again and took an envelope out of his pocket. He had received it that morning. It was handwritten, with his name and first name on it. Inside, a sheet of paper folded in two said accusingly:

Code 93
Death by suffocation – 23 June, 2011.
Roma camp in La Courneuve.

He took out his car keys, and when he opened the letter once more, he was in the archive room of the S.D.P.J. 93, deserted at that time of night. Even the office of the poor bastards on duty was empty. Coste knew they must have responded to some call or other, so he would not be bothered for a while.

Thanks to the date in the letter, he had no problem locating the dossier. This time the victim had a name: Violetta Djuric. Once again, the information was correct. Found dead in the Roma camp at La Courneuve on 23 June, 2011, with a rag forced deep down her throat. All the murderer had to do was to pinch her nostrils, the way you do to annoy a child. She must have died in less than two minutes, but even so, in certain situations two minutes are 120 eternal seconds.

Yet again, the investigation report seemed to him rather brief, maybe too brief for a murder inquiry. The case had been handled by Groupe Crime 2 under Capitaine Lara Jevric, but Coste's former deputy, Mathias Aubin, had quickly taken the lead after a comparison of cases on the S.A.L.V.A.C. programme. The official report mentioned a series of murders of prostitutes among the traveller community. The crime analysis software linked them to that of the deceased Violetta Djuric. On paper, the case had been transferred to the Brigade de répression du proxénétisme de Paris,* which was already looking into similar murders.

Coste closed the dossier, his stomach churning. He saw that what he had been fearing ever since receiving this second anonymous letter was coming true. It was enough to list the facts out loud to himself to understand that unfortunately it all fitted far too well.

In the same week, Coste had come up against two bizarre murders, very visibly and deliberately staged. A castrated man and another one burned alive – or, depending on your point of view, a zombie and a case of spontaneous combustion. In tandem with those cases, his attention had been drawn to the deaths of two unknown women, one a girl raped and drugged in a squat, the other a prostitute killed in a Roma camp. Two invisible victims, with no family or friends. The investigations into their deaths, handled by Mathias Aubin, had been rapidly dropped thanks to the S.A.L.V.A.C. programme. This same S.A.L.V.A.C. that was now going to be put in the hands of a shadowy figure from the past, Lucien Malbert.

In the silence of the archives, Coste muttered to himself:

"Mathias, Mathias, what have you got yourself into?"

Then he told himself that he had never visited Annecy.

* Paris Anti-Prostitution Squad

26

Ronan parked outside the address De Ritter had given him the previous evening.

"Are you sure it doesn't bother you?" she had said.

"It's on my way. Almost. Coste wants to meet at seven, and if you take public transport you're almost bound to have to catch a night bus, so just say yes."

At a quarter past six she was out on her porch, wrapped up like an Inuit. She gestured to him to join her.

"Coffee?"

Stepping out of his car he clapped his hands together, as if that was enough to ward off the cold.

"A quick one then."

He sat at the kitchen table while she refilled the machine. The decor inside the house confused him. It didn't fit somehow, it was far too "Happy Families" for his liking. Then there was the sound of an earthquake on the floor above. The sound rumbled down the staircase and slammed into the kitchen: two young kids who wrapped themselves round De Ritter's legs, sleepy-eyed with dishevelled hair. The decor suddenly made more sense.

"You were going to leave without giving us a kiss," the one in blue pyjamas complained.

"Yeah, you didn't have kissed us," the girl in green blurted out.

"I'd never have done that, my little angels."

Their eyes turned to the intruder.

"Who's this?" Green Pyjamas wanted to know.

"This is Ronan, I work with him now."

"Is he nice?"

"He'd better be," said a gruff voice.

The man standing in the doorway in T-shirt and boxers introduced himself.

"Karl. The husband. Jo has told me all about you."

Ronan could imagine what that meant.

"Ronan. Pleased to meet you. Everything she's said about me is doubtless true."

"I sincerely hope not," replied Karl with a smile.

Johanna was obviously enjoying this moment of gentle revenge. Karl De Ritter separated the two coloured balls of fire from their mother.

"Come on, you two, back upstairs. You've won the right to finish the night in our bed."

Green and Blue allowed him to carry them off, saying brief goodbyes to their mother. Green stuck her tongue out at Ronan.

Embarrassed, he polished off the coffee as quickly as he could. Johanna could not resist a final jibe.

"Maybe you'll stop calling me Juggernaut now?'

Ronan wished the ground would swallow him up.

Before opening the door to the cold outside, De Ritter disguised herself as an Inuit once more. Normally her outfit, and in particular the Nordic jumper with its snowflake pattern, à la Sarah Lund in "The Killing", would have given Ronan a field day for sarcastic comments. But that would have to wait.

Making plain that she did not bear him any real grudge, Johanna made conversation as they drove.

"Tell me about you and your group. How long have you worked with Coste?"

"Almost seven years now. Sam's been with us for two."

"Were you recruited, or did you join him by chance?"

"As far as I know, you're the only one who hasn't been hand-picked. Coste recruits his team himself."

"So why you, and why Sam?"

"Those are long stories. I'd need more than a coffee to tell you all that. Ask me again some evening when I'm good and drunk."

When they arrived at the S.D.P.J. 93 building, he drove the unmarked car down the lane to the underground car park. There they met up with men from the Rapid Response Unit. Five big guys rummaging in the boot of their squad vehicle, already strapped into their bulletproof vests. Ronan called to the first of them, busy checking his pump-action shotgun:

"You heading out?"

"Yeah, there's something kicking off, we don't want to be late."

"Why so early in the day?"

The man stuck the rifle between the two front seats, then added, speaking like a character in a western:

"The gang from the Basse estate at Noisy-le-Sec carried out an armed raid on the one in Cité Haute. There's 105 cartridge cases on the ground, but only one wounded, and in the knee at that. They can't even shoot each other properly. Fuckin' amateurs. We're joining two rapid response units to deep-clean the estate."

27

Sam came in with the croissants and woke up Coste, who was stretched out on the office sofa.

"Did you spend the night here?"

"No. I couldn't get to sleep at home, so I came to listen to the tap on Bébé Coulibaly's phone. I must have dropped off."

"Anything interesting?"

"Not a thing. He mostly called his mother. Just shows there's no place like home."

"The poor guy. Don't forget he's lost his balls. That's a high price to pay."

"Yes. For what, I wonder."

"Has Jevric told you her story? The guy who had his finger chopped off for a kilo of cannabis? So if a finger is worth a kilo of shit, what's a pair of testicles worth?"

"You seem to have a knack for maths. You should have kids. You could really help them with their homework."

De Ritter and Ronan entered the room.

"Did you two little lambs sleep together?"

A few breakfast crumbs later, and Coste gave instructions. He asked Ronan to use his contacts on the street to find a link between Coulibaly and Samoy. Sam was given the task of checking the C.C.T.V. footage around the telephone booth that the journalist Marc Farel had received the anonymous call from. With a bit of luck they might see the silhouette of the mystery man. De Ritter was to call Léa Marquant to find out if fishing the mobile out of Franck Samoy's ribcage had been successful, and whether it could be used again.

"As for me, I need you all to cover for me. I'm taking the day off, and I don't want that to get around. So if Damiani asks after me . . ."

Sam cut in:

"Don't worry, there's no way she would come in on a Sunday."

Coste was embarrassed.

"Is it Sunday today?"

What with this work at weekends and the nights spent at headquarters, he was beginning to feel like the caricature of a TV officer. He knew that this was not a good thing.

"When you've checked all that, buy yourselves a meal on the squad's account and then go home. I'll see you all on Monday."

Once De Ritter had carried out her task, she went over to Sam and allowed her curiosity to get the better of her.

"Does he often go off like that, without saying where?"

"He goes off when and where he likes. He's the boss, you see."

"And you don't ask any questions?"

Ronan butted in:

"Because we don't want any answers. You need to know this is a two-way street, and that a police officer's career is a long one, and far riskier than a baker's. You're bound to need him some day or other. Now put your coat on, we'll take you for lunch on the boss's orders. If you're good, we'll tell you a story over dessert."

28

Rue de l'Egalité runs between Bobigny criminal court and the 93 police headquarters. What better name for the territory between Police and Justice? In a one-storey building on the street, Luigi Maldonado, his family recently arrived from Italy, had decided to open the restaurant La Molisana. The main area for meals is in the living room, and the terrace is built out into the garden, so that the customer has the impression that they are a guest in somebody's home. Parked as an advertising hoarding in the middle of the lawn is an old Fiat 500, painted green and red in honour of the country it was made in, as if a drunken pizza delivery man had ended up on the grass and decided it would be best to leave the car there. It's been stationary ever since. In spite of this, the restaurant serves the best pizzas in the area, good police food, and it was here that Coste's team had decided to have lunch.

Not entirely steady on her feet, De Ritter got up from the table.

"I'll just give my husband a call to tell him I'm staying a bit longer."

She righted the empty glass she had just knocked over.

"And that he'll have to come and fetch me."

As she left, she bumped into one chair, and then another, without even realising it. Ronan winked at the waiter to reassure

114

him everything was under control. Stunned, Sam had stopped chewing.

"Her what?"

"Her husband . . ."

"But isn't she . . . ?"

"Not at all. Married with two kids, and I made a real fool of myself there this morning."

"I can imagine who opens the jam jars when they're stuck."

"No way. He's the big, strong Danish type. Not such a bad guy, either."

De Ritter knocked clumsily against the same chairs on her way back, but this time they didn't fall over.

"What were you saying?"

Ronan repeated what he had said without softening it. The second bottle of Lombardy *vino amabile* had liberated him from any need to be polite.

"I was saying your arsehole husband is rather better than I would have imagined."

"I'm not sure if I should take that kindly where I'm concerned, but it's nice for him. I see you're in the mood for gossip, so speak, man."

Ronan waved his fists in the air for an imaginary fight.

"O.K. sock it to me. You're allowed two questions, no more, so make sure you get your priorities straight."

Given the state he was in, the last words of this sentence ended up like so much chewing gum. His colleagues burst out laughing; they were the only customers still in the dining room. De Ritter thought for a moment.

"My first question is about you. How come Coste, who seems to be pretty clued up, came to recruit you, Lieutenant Ronan Scaglia? And besides, Scaglia's a Corsican name, isn't it? So what on earth are you doing in 93?"

"My mother's Corsican, but I've never set foot there. I don't like the sea, I don't like mountains, I don't like bombs. And your second question?"

Sam insisted he hadn't properly answered the first one.

"Oh yes, I promised to tell you over dessert how I, Ronan Scaglia, came to be part of the Corsican team."

"The Coste team."

"Yeah, the Coste team."

As if on stage, Ronan began his story with extravagant gestures and with little in the way of volume control.

"A few years ago, I was in charge of a team of detectives in Aubervilliers. One summer morning I was called out to a suicide in the Canal de l'Ourcq. We managed to haul the guy out of the water and I called the Fluviale* to come with their sonar launch, but apart from attracting the attention of some rubberneckers, there were no more surprises in the water."

"Rubberneckers?"

"It's a term the traffic police use when there's a road accident. Rubberneckers are the idiots who turn their heads to ogle as they drive by. Shall I go on?"

De Ritter gave a lopsided smile.

"Please, you do it so well."

"The problem with the suicide was that he had his hands tied behind his back. That's pretty unusual as a method, but it does happen, and I knew why. But the duty magistrate didn't want to listen to my explanation, and called in the Groupes Crime, convinced it was a murder. My first contact with the S.D.P.J. 93 was with Capitaine Lara Jevric, the boss of Groupe Crime 2. You can imagine how that went. She waddled over wearing too much make-up and began shouting orders at us in

* River police

116

that nasal twang of hers that makes me want to punch her. I tried to give her some advice, but I'd have done better to keep my trap shut. She barked at me that it was none of my business and that she'd never seen a suicide with his hands tied behind his back. So I stepped away. That was when I met Coste."

"Hang on: Coste and Jevric were working on the same case?"

"No. Coste was there as chaperone, keeping an eye on things. Jevric is as delicate as a broken-down bulldozer and has put up the backs of most of our local colleagues, which isn't very good P.R. You'll soon learn that three-quarters of the key investigations that the Groupes Crime get come from local police stations. So it's best to stay friends with them."

De Ritter admitted to having doubts.

"For the moment, I tend to agree with Capitaine Jevric. It looks like a homicide to me."

"Trust me. I started out at in a town at the far end of Finistère, where they have one of the highest suicide rates in France. So I've got a lot of experience regarding the thousand and one ways to put an end to life. When Coste took me aside and asked me to tell him what was bothering me, I explained to him about the slipknot trick. There's no such thing as a suicide simply by drowning. The survival instinct means you won't stay underwater."

Intrigued by his story, De Ritter remained silent. This encouraged Ronan to continue.

"O.K., I'll explain. First you tie the rope round your feet and then you use the end to make a slipknot round your wrists. You take a few seconds to remind yourself what a heap of shit life is, and you jump. Obviously, as soon as you hit the water, the survival instinct kicks in. You try to regain the surface, you struggle, but the slipknot only tightens, making it impossible to come up or swim. Conclusion: maybe a crime, but also possibly a suicide."

"Clever. Macabre, but clever. And then?"

"And then? Still convinced she was investigating a murder, Jevric was absolutely determined to examine the body to see if there were any signs of a struggle or attempts at self-defence. So the body had to be turned over. But with the scorching heat we'd had since the beginning of July and the length of time he'd spent in the water, the guy's stomach was swollen and the skin was all soft. In short, it was a really bad idea, but since Jevric doesn't often have any ideas as such, she insisted and got the uniforms to push the body onto its back. I suggested she wait for the undertakers, who are used to that kind of thing, but yet again she blew me out, so I let her get on with it."

De Ritter began to suspect the worst.

"Don't tell me that . . ."

"You've got it . . . As the body was turned over, the skin on his stomach split, and everything in it poured onto the tarmac. Ten litres of frothing intestines liquefied by putrefying gases spattered all over the shoes of the nearest rubberneckers."

"The idiots who come to ogle?"

"That's right. Some of them fainted, others groaned, but most of them simply threw up. We left Capitaine Jevric to tidy up the mess, and I suggested to Coste we went to inform the family of the death."

Informing about a death. A test that every policeman has had to face some day or other. One of the eventualities De Ritter was most afraid of.

"Isn't that very tough?"

"You'll get used to it. You don't know them, you don't know their loved ones. It's not your loss. You're simply the messenger."

Sam put in his pennyworth:

"The thing is, Ronan's world revolves around Ronan, and he couldn't give a damn about anyone else."

But De Ritter wanted to know the end of the story.

"So? Was it homicide or suicide?"

"If I remember correctly, that was the first autopsy carried out by Dr Marquant, who had just joined the I.M.L. She confirmed the suicide theory, and that was the end of the matter. A week after that I got a call from Coste, and two months later I joined his team."

De Ritter emptied their second bottle of wine, pouring it into the three glasses. She turned to Sam:

"What about you? How did you join the team? Another incredible story?"

Ronan cut in:

"Sorry, you're out of ammo. You had the right to two questions, and I've answered them both."

29

Coste took his ticket for Annecy out of the machine at Gare de Lyon. He had not bothered to go home first: he was planning on staying only long enough to have a proper conversation with his friend.

As the train pulled out of the station, he grew annoyed with the window blind, trying and failing to adjust it to prevent the dazzling winter sun shining in his eyes. In the end he gave up wearily, and a few minutes later felt ridiculous when he began to actually enjoy the gentle warmth on his cheek. He sat back and allowed himself to be hypnotised by the speeding landscape.

He had sent a laconic text to Mathias announcing his arrival. In return he had received a "Looking forward to it", and then a few minutes later "Everything alright?" He had not replied to that one because no, everything wasn't alright.

When he got out at Annecy station, everything struck him as fake compared to 93. It was a sort of Disneyland, the impression reinforced by the snowy Alps in the distance and his fellow passengers carrying skis or snowboards depending on their age. Fresh air and a clear view. His mind went back to the groups of tramps and kids from the estates who clustered around the métro in Seine-Saint-Denis. Different scenario, different way of working. To be a policeman here must be a bit like being on holiday.

"Like what you see?"

Coste turned round, and for a moment it was just two friends hugging one another.

"Taken in by it, you mean."

The chat continued in the car, the reason for Coste being there tacitly set aside as they made small talk. Mathias gave him a guided tour.

"Do you remember that case with the Yugoslavians in the XVIth?"

"Of course. Theft of all the cheques from that company in Montreuil, then they bought champagne at upmarket wine merchants in the smartest area of Paris. Almost a million euros lost."

"We surrounded them as they were loading cases of Cristal Roederer at nine hundred euros a pop into their truck. Do you remember when we got our guns out and shouted 'Police!'? The whole street froze."

"Yes! In the XVIth, when they hear 'Police!' everyone freezes, even if it's nothing to do with them. When you shout 'Police!' in 93, the criminals hear 'Pull!', and pull their own guns out."

"Well, just imagine that here you're in the XVIth. I went to say hello to my new colleagues yesterday. It appears that down here nobody insults them or tries to punch their faces in. Great, isn't it?"

"Not bad, I have to admit. It looks as if you'll fit in. And if you happen to know of a good restaurant round here, I'm in."

"Forget it. Laure's expecting us. She's been at the stove ever since I got your message, so if you want me to live a while longer, we're heading straight home. And I expect you to say 'mmm . . . delicious' to everything she puts in front of us."

*

Laure Aubin greeted them on the threshold. The house had Mont Blanc in the background, as picturesque as a screen-saver, and was lost at the end of a winding track only wide enough for a single vehicle. Coste gave her a big hug.

"So you came just like that on a whim, with no luggage? Are you missing us already?"

Mathias had been asking himself the same question. A surprise visit that clearly was not by chance. Not least since, for Coste, Annecy was a long way. He was expecting trouble. He whispered to the capitaine:

"We'll have lunch and talk afterwards, O.K.?"

Coste agreed with a friendly squeeze of his shoulder.

Coste could have wished the meal would never end. As he had been warned, Laure had massacred everything, from main course to dessert. He sensed that Mathias and she had changed in some way. Their gestures were slower, the way they spoke calmer, and their usual backbiting had vanished from the conversation. Happiness in a house of cards that he was about to bring crashing down.

"What does Gabriel make of his new life in the mountains?"

"There are ten or so kids his age in the village of Bluffy. By yesterday afternoon he already had a bunch of new friends. We're pretty relieved."

Laure took Coste's plate and piled it with the others.

"Why don't you come and live down here? We ought to be able to find you two or three murders, if that's all that's keeping you in 93."

"I'll think about it. For now I just came for half a day to see how Mat is getting on without my help."

Neither of them was buying that, so Laure made two cups of coffee, put them on the living room table, made the excuse that she had some shopping to do in town, and left the men on their own. As she was going out, she met Coste's gaze and without a word gave him a look that promised she would kill him with her bare hands if when she returned he had in any way upset the delicate balance of their new life.

Coste checked that the two anonymous letters were still in his inside jacket pocket. He knew he was going to lay them on the table and wait for his colleague to explain. He was hoping that the years they had worked together, protecting each other's backs, meant he didn't have to face the pantomime of suspects who pretend to fall off their chairs when presented with devastating proof. Mathias was not as rotten as that.

30

Aubin remained silent. He had no idea where to begin. Without even touching the two sheets of paper in front of him, he had read the contents.

Code 93
Overdose – 16 March, 2011.
Squat in the former Les Lilas Town Hall.

Code 93
Death by suffocation – 23 June, 2011.
Roma camp in La Courneuve.

"I was going to call you."

"No need. Here I am."

Mathias stood up and went over to an old wooden sideboard where the alcohol was kept. He filled two glasses that were as small as the spirits he was pouring were strong.

"Laure wanted a divorce . . ."

He gulped down his drink.

"I'm not trying to excuse what I did, but she was going to leave, Victor, and take Gabriel with her, obviously."

"I'm not here to arrest you, I simply want to understand. I can imagine why you got into this mess, it's the mess itself I don't follow."

"Two years ago I was called in by Galienne, the deputy director of the Police Judiciaire. He was the one who pressured Commissaire Stévenin to have me put in charge of the S.A.L.V.A.C. in S.D.P.J. 93. He promised me a transfer to Annecy within a year if I did a few things for them."

"What kind of things?"

"To sideline some very special cases. Only homicides and only invisible victims."

"What do you mean by 'invisible'?"

"Addicts, whores, the *sans-papiers*, people with no family or friends close enough to claim the body."

After receiving the two anonymous letters, Coste had prepared himself for an ugly, twisted story, but hearing it was another matter.

"And how did you do it?"

"Thanks to the S.A.L.V.A.C. I say that the programme has found a link to other investigations, I take it over, call the duty magistrate and tell him that another police force in another region is investigating similar cases. He authorises me to transfer everything to them. I close the investigation, and it no longer shows up in our statistics."

"Just a moment: what happens to the case file?"

"I put one copy in our paper archives just in case the investigation bounces back to us, and destroy the other three copies. The officer I took the case from in the first place doesn't ask any questions – for him, it's one less thing to worry about."

"What about the examining magistrate?"

"He never bothers to contact his colleague in the department where the file is supposed to have been sent. Have you ever seen a magistrate's office? They're surrounded by piles of legal files almost two metres high: do you really think they're going to worry about cases they've managed to get rid of?"

"What about the S.A.L.V.A.C. crime analysts?"

"I never get in touch with them. I simply say I've found similarities in the M.O.s but don't pass the details on. Everything is done and stays in my office."

"Our office."

"Yes. Obviously I waited until you were out on the street or on leave."

"You say the case no longer appears in our statistics, but everything is registered in the national S.T.I.C. database, and there's no way you can alter that."

"The national S.T.I.C. sounds very grand, but in fact it boils down to a single person who checks and registers the info. I leave the rest to your imagination. The lever in my case was a family that was going to explode if I didn't get a transfer soon. At the S.T.I.C., they must have come across some poor administrative assistant with a handicapped child, drink problems, or whatever other pressure point they found to get him to press the delete button and expunge the cases I had managed to bury. To conceal murders requires meticulous organisation, but they only need to put pressure on two individuals: the one dealing with the dossier and the one registering it."

Coste shook his head as if trying to rid himself of the whole affair.

"But shit, it can't be that easy."

"The simplest things, Victor . . . the simplest things."

"But why do it? O.K., so the murder rate in 93 may be higher than anywhere else, but from there to making dead bodies vanish into thin air is going some."

"It's not so strange as all that. There are precedents. You know the rumour about some regional police chiefs who asked their local forces to stop compiling figures before the end of the month so that they looked better, and swept the remaining

126

crimes under the carpet? At one stage, twenty-five per cent of misdemeanours weren't being registered. Result: the crime rate stays the same, the minister can remain in office without encountering any turbulence. He thanks his Préfet, who has earned his place in the sun. In turn, the Préfet compliments the regional chief, who is sitting comfortably and gives a very welcome bonus to his commissaire, who doesn't share it with the rank and file. They simply have to keep their traps shut and get on with it. These offences were hidden under an accountancy entry disguised under the name 'Code S'. Spiriting away shoplifting or small consumers of shit isn't very complicated, nobody really cares – but to get rid of cadavers, they needed another organisation. So they had to find a new title. That's 'Code 93'."

"Well, at least that's clear enough," Coste said sarcastically.

"I imagine that when it comes to deliberately erasing murders, they don't really care. And if it works, the good thing is that it can be put into practice elsewhere. Marseilles will probably soon have its 'Code 13' if it goes on sticking out like a sore thumb."

Coste raised his glass to his lips for the first time. His friend's explanation had been as smooth and clear as a recitation. He concluded that Mathias had been preparing his defence for a long while. Not to face justice, but someone far sterner: him.

"So how many 'invisibles' have you made disappear?"

Mathias was about to pour himself another glass when Coste put his hand on his arm.

"Don't pull a face like that, Laure will be back any moment. How many, Mathias?"

Aubin hesitated, even though he knew the figure by heart. Whenever his step counter showed a figure ending in 23, it leaped out at him. When his watch showed – on either hand

– the number 23, it leapt out at him. When it was 23 degrees outside, it leaped out at him.

"Twenty-three."

His eyes closed, Coste pinched his nose, just like the gangster about to dish out punishment in Georges Lautner's films.

"I can't conceive of an organisation like that and such a huge number of victims wiped out simply to massage the figures. It's too serious. Where's the money in all this?"

"How do you come to that conclusion?"

"Money and sex make the world go round; the rest is the exception to the rule. And in this particular case, I don't think there's any room for tits and bums."

"You're right. I asked myself the same questions, and it was at that point I was led to understand it was in my interest to know as little as possible."

"Twenty-three! Give me a break!"

"Shit, Victor, I haven't killed anyone. I've simply—"

"Shut it! The best thing you can do now is to keep your trap shut. Does anybody know about this?"

"Yes."

"Tell me you're joking! Who?"

"Marc Farel."

"That's all we needed! My God, you know how to choose. The worst journalist imaginable."

"I don't think he'll give us any more trouble."

"This is beginning to sound like a Mafia discussion, but go on, tell me how you reckon you've shut up a nosy hack like him?"

Mathias had no choice but to tell him everything, from the very beginning. And the beginning went back to the end of 2011, two years earlier.

31

Farel had been lucky enough to catch him on a good day. Aubin was expecting at any moment to be fired, and was trying desperately not to go to pieces.

He was leaning over the parapet of the S.D.P.J. 93 head-quarters' roof staring out over the city as he finished a cigarette. His left ear was still burning from a fresh argument with Laure on the telephone that had again ended in drama and threats. The words "separation" and "child custody" were still pounding in his brain. He threw away the butt and watched it fall. That could be me, he said to himself. He calculated how high he was above the ground. Not high enough. At best he would break a leg and simply end up looking ridiculous.

He felt his chest tighten. The police shrink had given him a simple exercise to do when the choking feeling became too much. She advised him to search in his memory for a calm spot far away from anxiety or pressure, an idyllic place. A sanctuary where he could shelter and take stock. He had never found one.

He took a step back, his mind in turmoil. He decided to go and tire his body out in a gym. Not the one in the building, of course. Strategically placed between the cloakrooms and the car park, all it contained were three adjacent tatami mats that a leak from the toilets above had soaked with a mixture of water and piss. And yet they were encouraged to stay fit.

Gym bag on his shoulder, he was about to get into his car when a man's voice brought him up short.

"Lieutenant Aubin?"

It was a rhetorical question, so he didn't reply. He simply glared at the man.

"Good morning. Marc Farel. I'd like to take a few minutes of your time, if possible."

Three sorts of people set off an internal alarm in policemen. Lawyers, criminals and journalists. In ascending order of irritation. This Farel was definitely in the uppermost category.

A tailored brown suit, unruly dark hair: the casual look, with a scooter helmet under one arm. Lieutenant Aubin had thought naively he could brush him off.

"Sorry, I don't have the time. Leave your details at reception, I'll get back to you."

Then Mathias realised the man had addressed him by his name and rank and waited for him outside instead of coming in to the front desk. Maybe he had better take a moment to hear what he had to say. Throwing his bag onto the back seat of the car, he turned towards the journalist.

"O.K., five minutes."

In the back room of one of the few cafés in the area, they had sat down facing one another. The journalist did not mince his words.

"You don't look well, lieutenant."

"I don't have a relaxing job."

Marc Farel had long since developed the ability to quickly capture his listener's attention. As a crime reporter, he had chosen a specialisation in which, bizarrely, everyone he tried to approach was trying to get as far away as possible from him. The legal profession, the police, criminals. He pressed home his attack.

"Remorse, perhaps. It can be very exhausting."

In questioning, this technique is known as casting the bait. Throw out the vaguest accusation possible and wait for the reaction. He didn't have to wait long.

"Listen . . . Farel, isn't it? Either spit it out, or I'm off, but above all, don't play cops and robbers with me."

Aubin was as abrupt as his physique suggested. Caught off guard, the journalist pulled out a notebook and riffled through it, looking for a specific page.

"I'll be as brief as possible. A fortnight ago, a private detective came to see me. A Monsieur Simon. I never knew if that was his first or last name. Our paths have crossed a few times: I'm a writer who's been around a while, and as far back as I can remember he's always been in the same line of work. Private eyes, journalists, police, it's a small world where the main players know one another because we're all doing more or less the same job. We investigate, try to understand. But you lot do it on the cheap."

When this brought no reaction, Farel returned to the point.

"Alright. Simon is old school, he likes personal contact. He had some specific questions, so naturally he thought of me. I know, my reputation goes before me, I'm a shit-stirrer."

"Funny, that's exactly the word I would have used."

"Thanks, that's touching. Monsieur Simon had been hired to find a young woman. Photograph in hand, he had stubbornly retraced her steps and gone through all the places she might have dossed down until finally he tracked her to a squat. In exchange for a few notes, one of the human wrecks haunting the place told him about an addict who looked quite similar to the person in the photograph. She had died of an overdose. His contact apparently also told him that the police had come that day and forced them to run away. She remembered this all the more clearly because after that the old building was boarded up, with the trolley containing all her possessions inside it. So the private detective thought he had found the lost sheep, even if the wolf had got there before him, and duly informed her family. Can you recall the case now? You ought to: you were the one in charge of identifying the body almost ten months ago."

"O.K., a junkie who snuffs it from an overdose isn't exactly glamorous, but it's common enough. What do you want me to do about it?"

"Of course, lieutenant, of course. But give me a few more seconds to explain where you come in, because from the start, as I'm sure you realise, you are my target. What followed is rather embarrassing for your unit. When he tried to get in touch with his contacts to gain access to part of the case dossier, Monsieur Simon discovered there was no record of it in your files."

Aubin showed no surprise. Obviously. The journalist was at pains to tell him a story he knew all about, because he was at the centre of it. He merely lowered his hand to show what cards he still had.

"I'm sorry to disappoint you, Farel, but the case was transferred to another police force. I work for the Groupes Crime, and the little addict you're so worried about overdosed on adulterated drugs. The central Brigade des Stups was interested in the affair, so they took it on. A lost file or computer glitch isn't that uncommon. I can check, if you like."

The journalist looked disappointed. Not by the explanation, but by this policeman still desperately trying to keep his head above water. He said:

"Don't go to all that trouble, I've already looked into it. Even if the case had been transferred, there would be some trace of it in your computer records. But it wasn't sent anywhere else. It never left your office."

He allowed himself a theatrical pause.

"It's said that after years of experience, police officers learn to tell the truth from lies."

"No. It's from hearing so many lies that the truth has a different ring to it, that's all. Am I to gather you don't believe me?"

"I'm trying hard, but somehow I'm not convinced."

Aubin made to bring their conversation to an end.

"If that's the case I'm sorry, but I've got a long day ahead of me, so if that's all you have to say—"

"That's all about the girl in the squat perhaps, but what am I to do about the sixteen other similar cases?"

At that point, Aubin should have checked Farel did not have a microphone. Better still, he ought to have got up and left, but that day he didn't have the strength either to fight or to run. Maybe he had even been waiting a long time for this moment. He listened for more.

"In total, seventeen people found dead. The majority of them murders or suspicious deaths. Seventeen cases, and all trace of them disappears when they arrive in your unit."

Aubin downed his coffee mechanically. In his hands, the cup and spoon looked like something from a child's toy tea set. He reflected that if the hack had dug a little deeper, they could have agreed on the exact figure. Twenty-three. Not seventeen. He remembered every single one of them. Caught up in his own thoughts, he missed part of what the other man was saying.

". . . anonymous individuals, ones with no family, cases that would have no repercussions. Of course, those are the most common ones, so they quickly add up. You look for the stone that won't create ripples when it hits the water, pick those who die silently. And with that little addict, you thought you'd hit on a sure thing. But you slipped up, Aubin. She should never have been part of your scheme."

"The family assured me they didn't recognise the body. Did you find some other friends of hers?"

"No. The family were just taking you for a ride."

"How can you be so sure?"

"Well, because in spite of everything, Simon is still being paid to search for the girl, when there's no reason to. So, be honest with me, did you really decide to do it?"

"What are you talking about?"

Farel's eyes betrayed his excitement, the excitement of a kid on Christmas Eve, a junkie presented with a new, full syringe, a hack sniffing a scoop. He could hardly contain himself.

"The big clear-out. Are you really doing it?"

"Steady on, Farel. You find there's one case missing and immediately think there's a conspiracy. Haven't you learnt to keep a cool head in your job?"

"Not one missing file, lieutenant. I've already told you, I counted seventeen altogether."

"So why wait until the seventeenth before coming to see me?"

"I was waiting for a mistake, lieutenant. There always is one. I just had to be patient. There was bound to be a day when one of your ghosts woke up and tapped you on the shoulder one night."

There was no more room to sidestep, so Aubin went straight to the point.

"What do you want?"

"It's one thing to know, but without concrete proof I'm nowhere. Tell me, where are those case files?"

"Destroyed."

"That's a shame. I was willing to do a deal. You're taking ridiculous risks for something that goes way beyond you. I'm even convinced you've no idea why the gravediggers are doing this. You must have been promised a lot. What price did you put on your conscience?"

With that Farel stood up, ready to leave without paying. He knew he had the upper hand. Slipping on his coat, he added:

"I'll leave you my card, Mathias, with my home address. Just in case you feel like paying me a visit this evening."

"Don't call me Mathias."

By ten-thirty that evening, Aubin had finished his second packet of cigarettes. His throat was sore, and he was coughing painfully. He opened a fresh pack. Gave himself another two minutes to decide. A copy of each of the twenty-three case files he had removed was in a box in the tool shed at the bottom of his garden. Clashing emotions had led him to keep them but make sure he would never see them. Aubin was a good policeman, he even considered himself honest. Until now. But circumstances, love and fear had led him to make the wrong choice. He was angry he had accepted the deal his bosses had offered, but it was impossible to back out now. He picked up his service weapon and his car keys, and checked that the business card was still in the pocket of his jeans.

At eleven that night he parked in upper Belleville, in the heart of the XXth, opposite Farel's apartment. Still behind the wheel, he checked his handgun, slipped a round into the chamber. He breathed softly, eyes closed, then got out of the car and walked over to the building. In the ill-lit entrance, one of the mailboxes had the name Farel on it, with the floor and apartment number. He climbed the stairs to the second floor and found himself outside No. 26. He stood there for a moment in silence, gun in hand. He thought of his son. He thought of prison. He told himself that Farel was a scorpion willing to die for a scoop, even if he stung himself getting it. He told himself that, above all, he could shut him up. He felt for the butt of his gun. Closed his eyes. Took a deep breath.

No. He wouldn't have the courage. And shit . . . killing someone?

He turned on his heel, raced down the stairs and ran back to his car. In the quiet street where all the lamps had been smashed to make things easier for the local dealer, he began to cry. His life was escaping him. He was making mistake after stupid mistake. It was getting out of control.

Leaning back against the head rest, he poked the cold metal of the gun barrel into his mouth, and gently squeezed the trigger. The hammer was cocked, ready to strike the cartridge that would blow off the back of his head. Then the pressure of his finger on the trigger eased, and the hammer slid back into the frame.

He did not have the courage for that either.

At ten minutes past midnight, Marc Farel's doorbell rang. He left his computer and opened the door to Aubin, who was standing outside, a heavy box in his hands.

"I'd given up on you."

"It took me a while to decide."

"You could say I was lucky."

"You could say."

Far luckier than he imagined.

32

Mathias Aubin was carrying his son on his shoulders so that he'd be tall enough to untangle the basketball net set up in the garden. He was swaying from left to right to make it impossible for the boy, who laughed out loud at each failed attempt.

Coste was watching this happy family scene through the kitchen window. He was mulling over his choices, between what reason dictated and what in fact he was going to do. Naturally, these two points of view were diametrically opposed.

He felt Laure's arms encircle his waist, and her face press into his shoulder.

"I live with him, Victor, so don't imagine I don't know when my guy has been really stupid. I know you as well, and I know that if you came here today, it was to decide whether to take responsibility for that stupidity yourself."

"Near enough."

"A policeman's wife is almost in the force herself, isn't she? So, have you decided?"

"I'd like to be able to answer you, but I've got no idea where this business is going to lead me. I'll do my best to ensure you enjoy the Alps as long as possible, but I'm making no promises."

"Is it that serious?"

"Try not to blame him."

"Blame him? Mathias wouldn't do anything illegal for his

own benefit. I know that, whatever the problem is, he did it for us. I threatened him until he became crazed with fear. I even brought Gabriel into it; I was at my wits' end. I feel responsible in some way, even though I haven't the slightest idea what we're talking about."

She clasped Coste a little tighter.

"How could I have hated you so much when I realise now that if Mathias was able to survive up there, in your crappy squad, with me harassing him the whole time, it was entirely thanks to your friendship."

Coste did not trust women in love. They had led him up the garden path in far too many investigations. He could not say for sure that she was trying to manipulate him, but it did not matter: he had already made up his mind, and he knew that meant he was encasing both feet in cement. What he had most of all to avoid was falling into water.

PART TWO

"Do you think he's playing with us?"
"No, I think he wants us to join in; that's different."
Capitaine Victor Coste

33

Lucas Soultier was in the habit of lunching with his mother. He would leave the Ministère des Finances shortly before noon and be driven to the family manor house nestling in the heights of Saint-Cloud. Even though it looked nothing like a small chateau or an aristocratic stately home, the Soultier family insisted on calling it that rather than the more appropriate "town house". The imposing, luxurious two-storey mansion opened onto a wide entrance hall leading to a central staircase. Halfway up, this staircase split into two, one side leading to the east wing, the other to the west. These contained the bedrooms, most of which had been shuttered for years. The ground floor was taken up with the reception room, the big salon, and the kitchen areas. Lighter patches on the walls indicated where paintings long since sold had once hung. Over the years, the staff had become reduced to one faithful retainer whose first name, Brice, was all one needed to know about him.

It was said that Lucas's great-grandfather had built the house with his own hands immediately after the Second World War. But another part of the family history suggested the Soultiers had acquired an important part of its wealth in shady deals done between 1941 and 1943.

It was with Lucas's father Jacques Soultier, a brilliant entrepreneur, that the manor house had enjoyed its glory years.

Sumptuous receptions were given, attended by Parisian high society. Financial investments in a right-wing party had allowed Jacques to put one foot into politics, but at sixty cancer of the liver meant he ended up with both feet in the grave. From then on, it had been unusual for the walls of the big salon to echo to the sounds of lively conversation.

Passing through the wrought-iron gates, the official limousine advanced at walking pace, crunching the gravel in the courtyard lined with yew trees that the winter had blighted. The driver braked gently: he had been advised to leave no tyre marks in the gravel. Lucas Soultier hung his overcoat in the hall and headed for the dining room, where his mother was waiting for him, imprisoned in her wheelchair. Dispensing with any polite greeting, she spoke as if she were continuing a discussion left in abeyance.

"Did you meet the minister, as I asked you to?"

Lucas took a seat and dropped that day's newspaper on the edge of the dining table.

"Good morning, maman. No, I haven't had time."

The old lady glanced at the newspaper, whose headline was the same as in all that day's media: SECOND STRANGE DEATH IN SEINE-SAINT-DENIS. The article must have mentioned 'spontaneous combustion' ten times, and made a direct link to Bébé Coulibaly's surprising return to life. The photograph of a charred body took up almost half of the front page.

"Brice, my son has no manners. Would you be so kind as to remove that horror from the table?"

Lucas said sarcastically:

"Is it the photograph that upsets you?"

"No, my dear. Life is full of dramas; I'm used to it. But newspapers that could have been handled by anybody have no place on a luncheon table."

"I thought it would take something more shocking to affect you."

Not allowing herself to be distracted by this veiled criticism, Margaux Soultier again turned the conversation to her son's career.

"You know I'm only trying to get you to meet the right people. You're not intending to spend your whole life in that research department and actually enjoy it, are you?"

He knew his mother was deliberately pretending not to remember his exact position, but he corrected her.

"That research department, as you call it, is the Bureau of Economic Forecasting and Evaluation in the Ministère des Finances."

His mother shrugged.

"In other words, an unknown bureau of a sub-directorate. Your offices aren't even at the Bercy headquarters."

"But if I was at Bercy you wouldn't be satisfied. You would only throw the Elysée in my face. I know you, mother, your ambition for others knows no bounds."

Only Margaux Soultier's fatigued body was seventy-eight years old. The rest of her could have continued for several generations more. She had played her role of mother like a tragic actress, seeing herself more as the wife of a man of power, one of those women who push their husbands on and isn't troubled by the thought of the collateral damage that a high-flying political career invariably causes.

"So you still find it amusing to call me maman?"

"That's what you are, aren't you?"

"Don't be ridiculous. That's obvious, but at your age you don't need a mother anymore."

The word *maman* had scalded her tongue as she pronounced it. She saw her son's lack of ambition as a distressing blemish. Yet she had pulled strings with all her acquaintances to secure him this ministerial post as well as entry into the masonic lodge to which her deceased husband had belonged. None of her efforts had succeeded in prodding her son out of his lethargy. She hated to see him waste everything his social position offered him. She hated to see him come back with his tail between his legs to have lunch with her, like a fledgling that refuses to leave the nest. Above all, she hated his excessive displays of affection. She did not give him time to pick up his fork.

"We've received more invoices from Monsieur Simon. Do you still have dealings with him?"

Lucas Soultier's reply was vague.

"Just some information I needed. Nothing that wasn't professional."

"Let's say I believe you."

Her habitual reproaches had ruined his appetite. Without looking at her, he pushed away his plate.

"I'm going up to my room for a bit of a rest."

He stood up, meticulously rolled down his shirtsleeves, and picked up his jacket from the back of the chair. As he passed behind her, he laid his hand on her shoulder. She shuddered. She hated unnecessary contact.

In the silence of his room he stretched out in the middle of his bed, eyes fixed on the ceiling. Dropping his arm over the side, he touched the jacket he had left untidily on the floor. He pulled out an invitation.

In the dining room, Brice helped Margaux Soultier leave the table. He pushed her wheelchair out to the terrace where her glasses and a thick leather-bound book were waiting on an iron table. As he was preparing to leave her to her reading, she quizzed him:

"Brice?"

"Madame?"

"Did you find it?"

"I searched in every corner, but it's not there."

She looked perturbed. She realised that a German Luger P08 was not a large handgun, but all the same, for it to have gone missing . . .

"Would you like me to ring the police?"

"Don't be so vulgar, Brice."

They smiled at one another. Her factotum certainly deserved the best that an embittered old lady like Margaux Soultier had to offer.

Lucas had got up from the bed and gone over to his desk. He hesitated a while, the invitation between his fingers. The instructions were almost obsessively clear. Embossed lettering, expensive card, glossy finish. No address, no name, merely a date to remember. On the back, he was offered a simple choice:

HOME

OFFICE

OTHER

(Please tick one)

The unpleasant memory of his first time resurfaced in a wave of nausea.

34

A year earlier, he had ticked OTHER and indicated the address where he wanted to be picked up. Then he had slipped the invitation into another envelope and sent it back to the post box whose details he had been given when he agreed to join the club.

A few days later, a black limousine with tinted windows drew up three minutes early less than a kilometre from the Ministère des Finances. Discretion in the already dark street.

Sex and power have always been linked. Every politician has a desire for power. And sex is never anything but an exercise of power over the other. In addition, politicians have known years of frustration, from lycée to elite university, without ever being popular. They have rarely seduced anyone, preferring to study than to waste time on romance. And once they reach the summit and are straitjacketed in the routines of a marriage of convenience, all that lost time comes back to haunt them, and it is not their wives they are going to whip or call a whore. That is where the club comes in.

Unable to avoid looking guiltily around him, Lucas dived into the car. Yet everything had been devised so that no-one would know who the members were, and the 'goods' could never blackmail them. Two canvas bags were on the back seat for his use. The contents of the first guaranteed absolute

discretion. A black mask to ensure anonymity, a box of con-
doms and a tube of lubricating jelly to avoid having to visit the
pharmacy.

The same care had been paid to the girls. They too would
wear a mask, not to protect their identity or their reputation
(those were not things that mattered), but simply so that they
would not recognise one another. Perfume and lipstick were
prohibited, so that no indiscreet souvenir would be taken back
to the conjugal abode. A guilty excitement led Lucas Soultier to
lose all sense of time, and he was unaware of how far he had
been driven when the limousine pulled up outside a detached
villa. He looked into the second bag: it was empty. The driver
didn't even bother to turn round.

"Empty your pockets. Mobile, wallet, I.D., credit cards."

Several seconds hung in the air, betraying his hesitation.

"I'm sure that sir wouldn't like to lose any of them. They'll
all be returned to you first thing tomorrow."

"And my briefcase?"

"I'll look after it, sir. All these preparations can be unsettling
the first time, but you'll soon get used to coming without any
personal belongings."

"O.K. Shall I get out?"

"Are you wearing your mask?"

"No. Don't you ever turn round?"

"Never, sir."

Lucas saw that in fact there was no rear-view mirror. He
rummaged in the first bag and put on the mask. It covered
two thirds of his face, leaving only his mouth visible. He felt
ridiculous.

He got out of the car, climbed the three steps up to the
house, and rang the bell.

A giant of a man opened the door. Lucas could get some

idea of how he himself looked when he saw his own reflection in the masked man facing him.

"Welcome, sir."

He turned to look for the limousine, but it was disappearing into the distance. With empty pockets and no means of turning back, he stepped inside the house. The door closed behind him.

He found himself in a dark hallway that the man almost completely filled.

"Arms out, please, sir."

He did as he was told, and the man slipped behind him like a nightclub bouncer. He felt something sweeping along his legs, his back, his arms. A strident beep went off at the level of his metal belt buckle, and then again as the apparatus reached his left jacket pocket. The man held out a bowl.

"Please empty your pockets, sir."

Again, he did as he was told and dropped some change into the bowl. Then he was led into a small, windowless room containing a low coffee table and three sturdy, bright red armchairs.

Left to his own devices, Lucas found it impossible to stay still. He began pacing slowly up and down the room. Put his hands in his pockets, then took them out again. He resigned himself to sitting down, then got up and began pacing once more. He jumped at the "Good evening" from someone he had not heard come in. He was startled a second time when he saw the man. This mask thing really disturbed him. At first he thought it was the athletic doorman, but soon realised that his size, his shape and the colour of his mask were not the same. This new arrival did, however, seem more welcoming than the giant at the front door. Lucas tried to reply to his greeting, but his voice failed him, so that only the end of his "good evening" was audible.

"Please, make yourself at home," the stranger said. "Would you like something to drink?"

"I'm not sure. In fact, I'm not sure if . . ."

The man interrupted him. Lucas's hesitation came as no surprise.

"Do you remember the top diving board?"

Beneath his mask, Lucas frowned.

"I don't follow."

"The highest diving board in the swimming pool, do you remember it? All the time you took staring at it, challenging it, climbing up towards it, only to stop at the one beneath. Then the day you finally made your mind up to dive off it, and found it was impossible to change your mind because of the braver boys pushing behind you. The leap into the void, like a small suicide. The second in the air, hitting the water, the feeling of being still alive, then the underwater guffaw before you resurfaced in a state of grace. The indescribable sensation of wanting to do it again without waiting, as if to regain all the time you had wasted making excuses."

He paused, settled in one of the armchairs, crossed his legs.

"Now you're on the highest board."

"And you are?"

"I'm as anonymous as you. If you like, you can call me Monsieur Loyal. I don't really take part: I supervise, keep an eye on things, take care of any problems. I have the only mobile allowed in here; slip-ups are part and parcel of this kind of evening, and I deal with any surprises."

"So you're the organiser?"

"I'm going to answer that question, and then we're going to agree you've asked enough for this evening. No, I'm not the organiser: no-one knows who that is, nobody knows the identity of the club members or of the goods supplied. You're not here to make new friends. Agreed?"

Lucas was uneasy, and shifted in his chair without feeling any better.

"Yes, sorry, that's fine."

"Now, since this is your first time, I'll explain the rules of the game. Don't try to find out who is in your arms, who is in the adjoining room, or, depending on your wishes, who is looking at you or joining in. The pillow is a sly truth drug. To make love is to offer up your body and soul. But don't ever forget that you're here only to take. Don't talk about yourself or your work, don't try to find out anything about the girl who gives you whatever you ask for. Don't try to continue the night somewhere else: everything takes place here, and nobody leaves with company. We change locations twice a year. You can ask for whatever you wish, no-one will judge you. Special requests are considered, though anything more elaborate can take some time. The first visit is free. After that you pay. The cost of becoming a member of this club is offset by the quality of the goods on offer and the discretion we guarantee. Membership is annual. Every room is equipped with an intercom so that if need be you can contact me. The sheets are used only once, and thrown away afterwards. Glasses and any other objects are also disposed of. I'm sure that will compensate for the lack of decoration in the rooms. I am here until the last member has departed. If there is any problem, I am easy to identify – I'm the only one with a white mask. I think that's all."

"What happens now?"

"If you wish, we can go into the main room."

They plunged into a long, dark hallway lit only by a sliver of light from the bottom of the door in front of them. Lucas was relieved to hear laughter, soft background music and the tinkle of glasses. The door was pulled back like a theatre curtain to reveal a scene of debauchery. Monsieur Loyal announced:

"Gentlemen, please welcome a new member."

Lucas's arrival was followed by silence, and he stood there feeling ridiculous in front of all these naked masks. Then the conversation started up again, and nobody paid him further attention. All the men there remembered having been in the same situation. He was led to a leather armchair and, at the sight of the goings-on around him, he gradually relaxed.

Monsieur Loyal went over to the only girl without a partner and whispered something in her ear. She stood up, put on a smile, and crossed the room towards Lucas. She passed a man whose lower belly was hidden by a mass of red hair that he was clutching in his left hand. Another man was cutting two lines of coke on a mirror on the tabletop, with a plump woman astride his lap. One last couple was leaving through a door at the far end of the room. The man had a firm grasp on the girl's wrist, and with a mindless giggle she grabbed a bottle of champagne as they walked out. When the young woman reached Lucas, she said:

"My name is Star."

She knelt down.

"I'm going to take off your shirt and trousers. If I'm not what you want, two other girls are getting ready."

She pronounced the words slowly, and despite the hoarseness of her voice there was still something feminine about it. She untucked his shirt and began to undo the buttons, which gave way easily. He said nothing, slightly ashamed of wanting this. But he did want it.

Inside his pants, she took his sex in her hand and stroked it. No reaction. She lowered her head and rubbed her lips against the fabric. Feeling uncomfortable, he stopped her. She offered him a little purple pill, which he refused. She tried with cocaine, and then champagne, but received the same response.

He told himself that his unease would dissolve more easily in the vodka she brought him. Unable to see her face because of the mask, he surveyed her body. She was very attractive, a cut above anything he had seen before. Her long black hair hung halfway down her back, and when she turned to rejoin him, he could see a red star-shaped tattoo in her groin, to the left of a perfectly shaven pubis. So that was why she was called Star.

She poured him another drink, and without trying to hide it added a large sprinkle of cocaine. He gulped it down. Less than an hour after his arrival, things had started to become clearer. Everything that might have been a problem at the outset had become self-evident and normal. He felt his mind was sharp, his gestures precise. And his thoughts . . . shit, how clear things were! He was a politician, he had power. He was made of the kind of steel that can cut through the most complex decisions, and she was made of the kind of flesh that satisfies the desire of men of his standing. He accepted another glass that she also dosed. As she bent over his crotch to arouse him, he asked if they could go somewhere more discreet.

He followed her across the room, and let her lead him down the corridor towards one of the bedrooms. He smiled when he saw the intercom next to the door, and sat down on the bed. She began a lascivious dance, smiling, sensual, almost happy, though he knew it was only for show. He stared at her red star changing shape as the muscles moved beneath her white skin: it made it seem as if the tattoo had a life of its own. Thanks to the drugs' filter, everything around him took on a beautiful sheen. If he had witnessed her movements two hours earlier, he would have seen that the lascivious dance was nothing more than a succession of stumbling steps, her sensual caresses nothing but vulgar pornography, and that her smile could barely disguise her weary resignation. And yet at that moment she was beautiful and available. So he took her.

Turning her round, he pushed her face down on the bed. She stretched out her arms in front of her, laying them flat on the duvet. His swollen sex started to ache like an accidentally cut finger; he could feel his heart racing. His breathing accelerated, scorching his face beneath the mask. He tried to penetrate her, had to push a little, then harder still. She was not getting moist, and he resented it. His fingers clawed at the flesh of her thighs to get a better grip and thrust deeper inside her. Excitement mingled with pain. He grabbed her hair and pulled her head back. He saw the side of her face: she was crying. This made him even more resentful. He was engulfed by a mixture of emotions: self-loathing, the pressure of the imminent orgasm, frustration. He came in a silent grimace, then everything subsided. Sex vanished from his mind like a passing storm, and everything became clear once more. Too clear. A feeling of nausea swept over him; he raised his hand to his mouth.

"Are you alright, monsieur?"

Her cheeks were still damp from her tears. The fact that she was worried about him made him feel even more wretched. Guilty. Despicable. He looked down, and his sex was shrivelled and tiny, as if it too were ashamed. The effects of the alcohol and drugs evaporated on the spot, leaving him to face up to what he had done.

"I'm sorry. Star, isn't it? I'm sorry, I'm not that sort of . . ."

She seemed more terrified than hurt.

"You won't say anything to Monsieur Loyal, will you? If you like, we can start again, we can . . ."

He laid his hand on her thigh to reassure her, then immediately pulled it away. He no longer felt he had any right to touch her. A furious desire to chop off his prick, to tear it off with his hands, to bang his head against the walls, to call the police, turn himself in. The nausea returned. He left the room without looking back.

At the end of the corridor, Monsieur Loyal was brushing every inch of another participant's suit that might contain a telltale strand of hair. He paused when he saw the new recruit come stumbling towards him.

"Is everything alright, sir?"

"No, everything isn't alright. I want to go home at once."

"Is there a problem with Star?"

"No, no problem, she's fine. I simply want to go home."

A not uncommon reaction: flight and shame after the act. Monsieur Loyal took it in his stride.

"I'll call your driver and fetch your things."

Lucas Soultier realised he was standing there in a mask wearing only his stained, crumpled underpants. He dressed as quickly as possible. Refusing to allow himself to be brushed, he clambered into the limousine already waiting for him. The driver handed him a bag and his briefcase. He recovered all his belongings.

Somewhere between Paris and the outskirts, the limousine came to a halt. The left-hand rear door opened, and the passenger stuck his head out to throw up. At his request, the driver dropped him a little further on at a taxi rank.

That had been more than a year earlier, but the memory of it still pained Lucas Soultier so much that each time he experienced the same nausea, the same disgust. The kind of disgust that is rare enough you remember it all your life.

Now he was holding a fresh invitation; on the back he had finally chosen to tick the box OFFICE. There were only a few days till the next event.

35

On the journey back to Paris from Annecy, Coste had received two messages on his mobile. In the second, Ronan told him there was a bit of an uproar at headquarters over the disappearance of three hundred grams of cocaine and five thousand euros from the Groupe Stups evidence lockers. Which only went to show that police officers are human like everyone else.

The first message, from Alice, had annoyed him. By the time countryside gave way to city, his annoyance had given way to anger. If he had taken the time to step back a little and analyse the situation, he would no doubt have realised that a good deal of his anger was due to the bind he had got himself into, which he already found suffocating.

Retrieving the service car left at the station, he drove fast to 37 avenue Jean-Jaurès in the XIXth.

It was past nine o'clock, and the neon sign above the Florent Theatre School shone on several groups of would-be actors no doubt dreaming of a future of opening nights in Paris and red carpets at Cannes. Seated on a low wall, Alice was waiting for him. When she saw Coste she made to stand up, but with a commanding shake of the head he indicated she stay where she was. She glanced across at an athletic-looking young man who must have been at least a head taller than Coste's six feet. A big red scarf, very self-assured, at the centre of an attentive group, talking far too loudly not to be boasting.

Coste strode towards him so purposefully that the young man was taken aback. The policeman's intrusion into the group brought an end to his boasting. He stared at the intruder.

"What are—?"

A vicious punch to his liver put an end to his query. He doubled up, gasping for breath, gazing at Coste in bewilderment. Coste should have made do with that; what came next was an exaggeration. He straightened up the youngster, who decided it would be better to be polite.

"Monsieur . . ."

Coste punched him again in the same spot, with the same force. This time the young actor sank to his knees in agony. None of his friends dared intervene. Coste bent down and whispered in his ear:

"Don't even think of laying a hand on her again."

The situation and the reason for his getting beaten up became clearer in the budding actor's mind. He looked across at the girl whom an hour earlier he had cornered in the changing rooms. Unfortunately, the word "no" is an abstract concept to someone who can think only of their own impulses. He had pressed Alice up against a locker. Taking advantage of there being nobody else around, he had grabbed hold of her, fondled her with clumsy violence and finally gripped her jaw and forced her to kiss him. So that the kiss almost seemed like a kiss. Then he had slipped his hand into her knickers, pushed his middle finger inside her, scratching her as he did so, sniffed his fingers right in front of her, and walked away, leaving her sobbing.

Alice had resignedly gone to the class anyway, creeping in as discreetly as she could to sit at the back of the room while the idiot strutted about on stage in the role of D'Artagnan.

The contents of the message Coste had received on the train

came back to him, enraging him further. He looked down at the boy kneeling in front of him.

He knew that if Alice brought a charge it would be her word against that of the cretin moaning on the ground. She would have to undergo medical examinations, be brought face to face with her attacker, who would doubtless deny it and say she had led him on. And then the trial, with a defence lawyer who would leave her in tatters.

All because of a finger. It was highly likely the guy would get away with it. That was something Coste could not stomach. Not tonight.

He brought his knee up with such force that the face exploded in blood like an over-ripe tomato. With a dull crack, the nasal bone shifted a centimetre to the left, painfully spoiling the symmetry of a perfect profile. One of the musketeer's canines punctured Coste's leg.

It looked as if D'Artagnan was going to miss his starring role in the end of year play.

The journey to their block on the outskirts of Paris was a silent one. Alice kept her hand on the back of Coste's neck, but nothing had changed: he was still choking with anger. At himself this time. He had always hated violence.

36

Dariush Abassian, head of the I.G.S., the police inspectorate, had very few illusions about the human race. Still fewer about policemen. Power is a source of temptation that is hard to resist. A police I.D. card and a firearm can give the impression of superiority in many ways, sometimes to the law itself. That was when he was called on to intervene, when an officer was toying with the red line in the sand.

And that weekend, in the S.D.P.J. 93, one of these officers had more than crossed it, running off with a large sum of money and enough coke to supply a nightclub for several weeks. Five thousand euros and three hundred grams.

Organising a urine test first thing on Monday morning of everyone at headquarters had been intended to show he meant business. Abassian limited himself, however, to installing a team of two detectives from the I.G.S. and a doctor, and kept out of the process the whole day. Having briefed Commissaire Stévenin, the head of S.D.P.J. 93, who must have been sitting in his office praying that none of his own officers tested positive, he said goodbye and pressed the ground floor button in the lift. When the doors opened, he almost bumped into a little man, and apologised. The doors had closed behind him again by the time his memory came up with who it was. He halted in the middle of the foyer and looked round, as if the man might still be behind him. Malbert.

Both of them were twenty years older, but the man's shifty, unpleasant eyes had remained etched on Abassian's mind like a living insult to the police force.

For his part, Lucien Malbert had recognised Abassian in a quarter of a second, and was smiling broadly as the lift took him up. With exquisite objectivity, he was asking himself how someone as dishonest as himself could be offered such wonderful gifts. How many questions must be whirling round your honest little head, he thought.

Arriving at the Groupe Crime 1 office, Coste found Sam in a state of high tension.

"Where's Ronan?"

"In the toilets."

"It's great to have friends."

Sam did not smile at the joke. De Ritter did not get it. The men continued with their mysterious conversation.

"Did you check? Is it the usual?" Coste said.

"The doc stays outside the door, so we're alone in the cubicle," Sam said.

"Then you can relax, everything will be O.K."

De Ritter caught on.

"You lot are kidding me, right? Ronan is pissing in a bottle on Sam's behalf, is he?"

She could not get over it, and returned to the attack.

"So the medical ethics code is just a game for you?"

Coste opened the office door wide.

"The I.G.S. are in the meeting room. If you want to talk to them, I'll go with you."

She left the room, but Coste chose to stay where he was

rather than face up to her. Sam's stress levels had hit the danger zone.

"What do you think she's going to do?"

"I think she'll get used to the idea. I also think it would be good if you stopped smoking joints – you're not a kid anymore."

"I feel like shit."

Ronan bounded in, tossing a dark bottle to Sam.

"Vintage 2012, drink responsibly."

The smile on his face vanished.

"Where's the funeral? And where's Jo?"

Once he had complied with the demands of Abassian's internal investigation, Coste went back to take stock with his team. On his way he met someone.

"Capitaine Coste?"

Turning round, he didn't recognise the man as someone from S.D.P.J. 93. He deduced that he was meeting for the first time the famous . . .

"Allow me to introduce myself: Lucien Malbert."

"Commandant Malbert, I was planning to talk to you at some point today."

"Retired commandant, actually. I'm here to lend a hand with a bit of administration. Can I get you a coffee?"

In front of the machine, Malbert began jigging about as though searching for coins in his pockets. Coste inserted the money, and with a weary gesture invited the other man to choose the number he wanted. Tomato soup. No doubt about it, Malbert had no redeeming features. What followed confirmed Coste's impression.

When two police officers first meet, it's normal for them to outline their careers, like two dogs sniffing each other's backsides.

"I spent some time with the Paris Brigade des moeurs. By 'some time' I mean twenty years. Then my mother became very ill with cancer, so I chose to take early retirement to look after her. After her death, I thought I might as well recharge my batteries with you, so as not to die of boredom."

Coste could understand perfectly well that Malbert would not have enjoyed having only himself for company.

And yet Noviello, the police history encyclopaedia, had given a very different version of the bogus perfect son's career. With rather less about a sick mother, and rather more about dirty money and prostitutes. Coste allowed Malbert to continue.

"At the start of this year you had a case of an undocumented Pakistani found frozen near a Sikh temple with a bullet in his throat. I've seen several identical cases of executions by the Pakistani mafia, and I was wondering if I could find a match on the S.A.L.V.A.C. database."

Coste proposed they continue their conversation in the office set aside for Malbert. They could talk more easily, get to the bottom of things. As soon as the door was shut behind them, he grabbed Malbert and shoved him up against the wall. He growled at him though gritted teeth:

"That's enough! No more pissing about! Call whoever you like. And tell them it's over. We're police officers, for fuck's sake: that still means something, doesn't it?"

To his surprise, Malbert gave him a broad smile. Coste let go of him. The little man straightened his jacket and clashing tie. Nobody smiles like that unless they have an ace up their sleeve.

"And you'll do what, Coste? Go and see the I.G.S.? You're in luck, they're in the meeting room. If you want to talk to them about your friend Mathias Aubin, I'll go with you."

The son of a bitch . . . Coste let him continue.

"What? So you've stumbled across Code 93 and it's got to

you, has it? You feel a bit inadequate trying to tackle all that. And who exactly are you defending, whores and stinking gypsies?"

"And what is it that you want, Malbert? I imagine that you are not that keen on moving to Annecy?"

"I couldn't give a shit about mountains and mulled wine. My objective is the same as the people who dreamed up Code 93. It's as simple and vulgar as that. And let me stop you right there, before you go on about integrity and honour. I left all that behind me long ago. O.K., so I won't go to paradise, if that is what you want to hear. In fact, I've absolutely no idea what reasons lie behind them wanting so desperately to massage the murder statistics. And, between us, I couldn't give a flying fuck."

Coste tried to respond, but was aware he had lost this round.

"I'll find a way to have you thrown out of here."

Malbert settled down behind his desk before landing a final blow.

"I know your friend Aubin is in this up to his neck, and yet you dare preach to me. So I'll let you into a secret, Coste: either you accept me, or you report your buddy. Because the longer you keep your mouth shut, the more you become an accomplice, and from where I sit, it seems to me you're already in far too deep."

He adopted a business-like tone:

"I expect your report on my desk today, if you don't mind. And you can easily imagine the fate awaiting your frozen Pakistani."

Realising he might be moments away from receiving a punch in the face, he was quick to set the cup of tomato soup down in front of him.

"You wouldn't hit a coward, would you, Coste?"

No. Malbert disgusted him far too much for that. Mean, fearful, manipulating and a liar – the words were so obvious they came into his mind unbidden. What disgusted him most was that from now on it seemed they were on the same team. He stormed out of the office, bemused but feeling slightly better.

If Aubin's initial lie was the flutter of a butterfly's wing, the threatened earthquake was soon going to shake the whole of S.D.P.J. 93, and the aftershock would affect the entire national police force.

Left to his own devices, Malbert picked up the telephone and informed his interlocutor of his worries. His call was taken very seriously. The decisions arising from it would be drastic.

37

When he got back to the office, the expression on Coste's face warned them he was in no mood for jokes. He began the meeting.

"O.K., how did your Sunday go?"

This wasn't addressed to anyone in particular, so Sam decided to go first.

"The press was informed in real time about the body that went up in flames, and about Bébé Coulibaly. You asked me to check if there was any C.C.T.V. round the booth used to call Farel, the journalist."

"And?"

"The booth is on rue Chevaleret, in the XIIIth, and there are no C.C.T.V. cameras there."

De Ritter spoke up, keen to show the other three she was now part of the team.

"Maybe our informer has access to the police record of C.C.T.V. cameras operational in the Ile-de-France. Or maybe he's just struck lucky."

"Not really; it's easy enough to avoid them."

Sam turned his computer screen so that they could all see a detailed map of the XIIIth. It was covered in myriad red dots, like measles. Each red dot represented a C.C.T.V. camera. He explained:

"The site is called paris-sans-videosurveillance.fr. It's updated by the C.D.L., the Collectif démocratie et libertés. It gives you the complete list and position of the cameras in every arrondissement. So all you have to do is pick a street where Big Brother's back is turned. No need to be a policeman: a decent internet connection is enough. Anyway, we haven't had much more luck with the different mobiles. The tap on Bébé Coulibaly's line has come up only with calls of no interest to us, mostly to his mother or friends. He never mentions any names that could provide us with a lead."

De Ritter spoke again.

"The forensic pathologist managed to get the mobile out of Franck Samoy's body. It didn't make his nose light up red."

She burst out laughing, then stopped abruptly when she realised she was the only one who had kids and doubtless the only one who remembered Rudolf the Red-Nosed Reindeer. She went on more soberly:

"I got through to the pathologist. Not very welcoming, by the way. She made me repeat my name twice and seemed very surprised I was on your team, Coste."

He pursed his lips. Had he put his foot in it? Ronan seized the opportunity:

"Victor, didn't you tell Léa about your newest recruit? How tactless of you. She may be getting ideas."

"Don't listen to him. Go on, Johanna, please."

"O.K., so the mobile was fished out and handed over to forensics with a request for the Computer and Technological Evidence Service to take a look at it. I've got their interim report; the definitive one will be ready in a week. But I can assure you they've been through it with a fine-toothed comb – the internal memory and the S.I.M. card. It looks as though everything's been deleted. The only thing remaining is that

166

same call, every three hours, sent to voicemail – which is empty too, of course. And I'm sure your trained police nose can tell me where these repeated calls come from?"

Coste announced the obvious:

"From a booth on rue Chevaleret, I imagine. So there's a direct link between the person who's tipping off the press about the murders and the one who directed us to Franck Samoy's warm welcome. It's either a very privileged witness, or the murderer himself."

De Ritter was uneasy.

"Do you think he's playing with us?"

"No, I think he wants us to join in; that's different."

Coste turned to Ronan, to hear what he had to say.

"Late yesterday afternoon I went to take a look round the Paul-Vaillant-Couturier estate in Bobigny, where Bébé crashed. It's a pretty active place for drug dealing. Samoy was a user, our giant was a dealer, so I went to find out if they knew one another."

De Ritter butted in:

"Late yesterday afternoon? You mean after everything you knocked back at that pizzeria?"

Even though it wasn't aimed at him, Sam replied to the question.

"Yeah, but I was there as back-up, keeping an eye on him."

"Of course, no Tom without Jerry."

"So I checked with the drugs people and the detectives in the local station. The guy pushing the drugs calls himself Brahim. I've already put him away once for a settling of scores when I worked in Aubervilliers. His real name is Jordan Paulin, he was born where no doubt he'll croak, in Bobigny. He's never been anywhere near North Africa, or converted to Islam:

Brahim's just a bit of make-up. I went there to collect info: he turns up every morning between ten and twelve to supply his guys."

De Ritter was imagining the worst.

"And how do you seduce your police lovers? I guess you must have been very persuasive for them to tell you his time-table? Do you slip them drugs, or money? Shit, don't tell me you had something to do with the theft from the drugs people's evidence locker?"

"Whoa, Johanna, you're barking up the wrong tree. We may take a few liberties with the rules, but you'll see soon enough that if you want info – good info, I mean, not the kind where you go breaking down doors at six in the morning to find ten grams of weed – you're obliged to get your hands dirty. Listen, big girl, you can try to get a snitch legally, according to the police code of conduct. You can register with the B.C.S.* and with a bit of luck you'll be able to give him a hundred euros. You can bet that, for that amount of money, your information's going to be really first-class."

"You're a real tough guy from the eighties, aren't you?" she scoffed.

That struck home. Ronan counter-attacked:

"And you don't even have a clue yet, if you don't mind me saying so. I'll explain a bit more. For international drug smuggling or terrorism, the amount the B.C.S. pays informers can be substantial, but for small-time stuff in the Paris outskirts, you'll never get more than a few banknotes. They're not really adapted to that. So it's us who have to adapt. Which doesn't make us bad officers. But if you really think I went into the Groupe Stups to steal so I could get such basic information,

* B.C.S.: The Bureau Central des Sources: the central office registering and paying informers, of both police and State

168

you've still got a lot to learn. I pulled the oldest trick in the book, and that was more than enough."

De Ritter still had no idea what he was talking about, so he went on:

"You show up somewhere where there's a pusher, wait for the visit of a real human wreck, preferably a heroin addict – they talk more readily. You let him buy his shit and tail him for a few metres. When you reach a quiet spot, you intercept him, take his dose from him – and then you can ask whatever you like, he'll be only too keen to talk to you. The shit's usually in his hand, so that he can dump it more easily, but he may have hidden it in his pants or in his hair if he's a Rasta. If he's got two doses, you can tip one away: that encourages him, softens him up. After that, he'd go down on you to get the other half-gram back, so collecting his pusher's timetable is not a problem."

"And do you give him back the remaining dose?"

"Of course! There's no need to be vindictive. And who knows? Maybe you'll need him some other time."

Coste glanced at his watch. They were within the hours that Jordan "Brahim" Paulin operated.

"O.K., let's go and see if your pusher knows our two stiffs. We'll take two cars. Ronan, you come with me; Sam and Jo, you stay within sight at the entrance to the estate. We'll take walkie-talkies, on the restricted channel D.I.R.2."

At the Paul-Vaillant-Couturier estate, Groupe Crime 1's second car – the metallic blue C3, at last repaired – pulled up close to the first tower blocks, the edge of the estate, where nothing ever goes on. The 306 Ronan was driving entered the estate a bit further on, and disappeared from view.

Slightly uneasy, De Ritter turned to Sam for reassurance.

"Weren't we supposed to stay within sight?"

"Try the walkie-talkie, see if they can hear us."

She picked up the apparatus discreetly jammed between her thighs.

"Car 2 to Car 1. Testing, testing . . ."

The reply came: "A.O.K. for Car 1." Sam undid his seat belt and settled down more comfortably.

"Now we wait."

"How long?"

"That's not a question we ever ask."

38

Ronan was driving slowly between the tower blocks. They had forgotten to check the volume on the police radio, and De Ritter's voice deafened them.

"Car 2 to Car 1. Testing, testing . . ."

Swearing, Ronan took one hand off the wheel and replied:

"A.O.K. in Car 1."

He put the walkie-talkie in the side pocket.

"What do you make of De Ritter?"

"Once she's got over some of her misconceptions, she'll be alright. Give her time. Did you print off a photograph of Jordan Paulin?"

"Sam sent it to my mobile."

Ronan held the mobile out as he went into reverse to park discreetly a few metres from an entrance hall. Clustered around it was a group of local kids of different ages, who despite everything had spotted them from the start and had begun to whistle the alert. Coste undid his seat belt and took one last look at the rather dark photograph.

"Wait for me here. Shall I leave the window open so you can get some air?"

"And I'll bark if I see anyone coming."

Ronan let Coste get out alone. He strolled over to the group. Some of them were already sidling off in different directions, taking their panoply of drugs with them. Seated on the wall by the steps leading to the building entrance, a battered black-painted wooden baseball bat across his lap like a royal sceptre, Jordan Paulin was waiting calmly for the policeman to reach him. Surrounded by five guys in sports gear, each one of whom could have had Coste for breakfast, it was obvious that Paulin had nothing on him and no guilty conscience either.

"Brahim? I'd like to talk to you. Preferably somewhere quiet, and without your girlfriends."

"I got nuthin' to say to you."

It's always hard to break the ice.

"Perhaps I should be speaking to Jordan Paulin; you know where I can find him, don't you?"

The pusher took this in, but replied:

"No idea who you're talkin' about."

Coste sighed. He was going to have to do it the hard way.

"Listen. Three days ago, Bébé Coulibaly, who used to sell drugs for you, had his balls cut off. The next day, one of the junkies who probably uses you was burned to death: a guy called Franck. Does that mean anything to you? Even if it doesn't, it would be reason enough to station a riot police van at the entrance to this estate and have uniforms patrolling here 24/7. That wouldn't be very good for business, would it? So I'll try again. Do you think you and I could go and talk things over in my office, or shall I put a bomb under your neighbourhood?"

This hit home.

"Take it easy, man, no sweat. Bébé don't sell for me any-more, he's moved on. As for your other guy, I swear on my mother I dunno him. You think I know the name of all the arseholes who come beggin' round here?"

Coste turned back towards Ronan. He knew he was on his

starting-blocks in case he signalled to him to join them. When he saw who it was, Brahim stiffened.

"You work with that cunt?"

"I know who to choose to have with me. And I could say the same of you: your buddies don't look bad either."

Coste asked Ronan to show the picture of Franck Samoy his mother had given them a few days earlier. When he saw it, Brahim clicked his tongue.

"Yeah, I know him, but he don't come round here no more neither."

"Obviously. I've just told you, he's dead. Concentrate, sweetheart, please."

Paulin's bodyguards burst out laughing. Coste asked him again:

"I thought the arseholes who came round here didn't stick in your memory, Brahim?"

"Stay cool, man, it's not him I remember, it's his bitch."

"His girlfriend, you mean?"

"He used to send her to suck me off for heroin. You might call that a princess, I call it a bitch."

"That makes sense. Do you know where I can find her?"

"It's been a while since I seen her round here. At first I didn't mind being paid in kind, because she was real good at it. But I didn't get much out of it. Some guy came to see me, said he was interested, had plans for her, like ones off limits to under-eighteens, know what I mean? That was the last I see of her."

"And do I have to take you in to get the name of that guy, or do you prefer to tell me here and now?"

"You know it already, Sherlock. It's Bébé."

A whole series of connections clicked in Coste's brain.

"You mean Coulibaly organised orgies?"

"He's too dumb to organise anythin'. No, he just recruited the bitches, that's all."

"And did you go to any of them?"

"I asked several times, but Bébé told me it was a high-class thing, like only for guys who have enough dough to join in. Too much for me. And for you too, I reckon."

"O.K., now you're going to come with us willingly so we can get all that written down."

Paulin turned to his bodyguards then said to Coste:

"Give me two minutes?"

"By all means, get yourself sorted."

39

Nothing particularly interesting had come out of the questioning. Jordan Paulin did not know much more, and behind her
computer, De Ritter was reaching the end of her queries. The
story about adult sex parties had established a probable link
between Coulibaly and Samoy. That might have got them
somewhere, but the link was nothing more than a female user
made none too choosy by the lack of a regular supply: and
besides, she had not yet been identified.

Sam switched on his computer and launched the inter-
departmental Canonge program.*

"Give me a description of our princess. If she's a user, she's
bound to have been arrested for possession, theft or prostitu-
tion, and if that's the case, we'll have a photograph of her on
our files. I'm listening."

"Users like her are like Chinese girls, you never know how
old they are. I'd say somewhere between eighteen and thirty
depending on what she'd been shooting up. She's white, small,
around one metre fifty-five, skinny, hair colour . . . dirty?"

"And eye colour?"

"What would I know? Red most of the time."

The program was buffered for a while, then came up with a

* Nationwide database of offenders, with photographs, fingerprints,
D.N.A.

selection of seventy-eight images corresponding to the details entered. Seventy-eight hapless girls who at some moment in their lives had made a bad choice. Jordan Paulin went through them one after the other, keen to get out of S.D.P.J. 93 head-quarters, which he did not usually visit as a witness. He was insistent.

"Soz like, but she ain't any of those you showed me."

Pushing back his chair, he addressed the team.

"O.K., it's cool, I've been good, so can I go now?"

Coste stood up and motioned for him to follow him along the lengthy corridor leading from his office to the lift. This investigation seemed to be one step forward and two steps back, and he had never been a skilled dancer. In the open area shared by the lifts and the victims' waiting room, Paulin spoke to Coste in a voice he had not heard him use before. Relaxed and almost reassured.

"If I'm honest, I was expecting you to keep me overnight."

"We had a bargain; it's important to keep your word. Besides, I didn't really have any reason to arrest you."

"You mean you need reasons these days?"

"Increasingly, yes."

The lift doors opened, and for a moment Paulin's eyes flitted somewhere over Coste's shoulder.

"That princess bitch of yours . . ."

"What about her?"

"She's right behind you."

Coste turned round in the empty room and stared at the only decoration: the A.P.E.V. posters – aid for the parents of children who had been kidnapped or gone missing. In big red letters above the photos of the kids were the words DISPARU in French and MISSING in English.

"First photograph top left, girl in the green sweater, smiling.

Well, she looked like that the first time I saw her, afterwards she went downhill a bit."

Paulin took advantage of Coste freezing in front of the photograph like a hunting dog on the alert to step into the lift and disappear, the doors closing behind him. If he stayed put, he was likely to be there for another round of questioning. The officer knew where to find him.

Coste read the name written under the face of the vanished angel.

Camille Soultier.

It meant nothing to him. He strode back along the corridor and burst into the office. He shouted to Sam:

"Camille Soultier."

He spelled out the name.

"I want everything we have on her. Right now."

Before De Ritter had even asked Coste what hat he had pulled the name out of, Sam had already plunged into his computer without wanting to know anything more. Explanations would come later. He knew how Coste worked.

"Soultier, Camille. Got it."

40

The telephone remained silent, but a red button flashed, indicating an internal call from his secretary. Galienne, the deputy to the head of the Police judiciaire, pushed the button and his secretary informed him of the caller's identity. The conversation was brief. Galienne hung up and rose to his feet.

He crossed the twenty metres between his office and the director's as rapidly as he could, almost breaking into a trot. Out of breath, he pushed open the padded double doors. The Cerberean secretary peered at him over her glasses.

"You know the mantra?" she said.

"Do not disturb until further notice?"

Thanking her, he went in.

"Sir, we've just had a call from Commissaire Stévenin of the S.D.P.J. 93. You need to talk to him."

A few minutes later, the director's telephone flashed red and his secretary informed him that the call he had requested was waiting. He turned on the speaker for the deputy's benefit.

"Christophe, I understand you were trying to reach me."

"Sorry to disturb you, sir. We received a call from Commandant Malbert."

"Is there a problem?"

"Possibly, sir. A conversation with Capitaine Coste in which Code 93 came up."

"You're right, that's worrying. Tell me about this . . . Capitaine who did you say?"

"Capitaine Victor Coste, sir. Head of Groupe Crime 1 at S.D.P.J. 93. Gets very good results. A few slip-ups in his career, but nothing we could really use as leverage. He's been with the S.D.P.J. 93 almost all of his time in the force, with his partner Lieutenant Mathias Aubin, the man Malbert is replacing."

"And is this Lieutenant Aubin the one who leaked the information about Code 93? Why would he do that? He's putting the noose round his own neck."

"Possibly he had no choice. Coste is an inquisitive and intelligent officer, and his friend."

"Those are worrying traits. What can we use to put pressure on him? A weak point, something in his past, an addiction, a mistress?"

"Nothing like that. He's thrown himself into his work after the suicide of a girlfriend a few years ago."

"It's people who have nothing to lose who are the most dangerous. How do you plan to deal with the situation?"

"That depends, sir. What scope do I have?"

"Allow me to remind you of our mutual interest in this operation. Don't tell me what you're going to do about it, just tell me what you've done when it's done. You're aware that your career is in my hands."

"Was there any need to remind me?"

"Absolutely. Because somebody somewhere in the Ministère de l'Intérieur has got mine in his."

Stévenin sought to reassure the director and himself at the same time.

"Everything is fine for now. Coste went to see Malbert, but he hasn't said anything yet to Commandant Damiani, his section head. What's most likely is that he's trying to protect

Lieutenant Aubin, so for the moment the situation is under control."

"We can't rely on their friendship: we have to watch our backs."

The director wondered whether to be more explicit. On the other end of the line, Commissaire Stévenin knew the step they were about to take was a last resort. The director made up his mind.

"You'll have to scare him off."

That was easier said than done. How did you scare an officer from 93?

41

Ronan was one of those men who do not recognise a girl they have slept with even if they bump into her less than a week later, and even if she's wearing the same clothes. So Sam was not surprised that the photograph of Camille Soultier which had just appeared on his computer produced no reaction. What worried him more was Coste's silence, because he was sure the girl was someone they all knew.

The MISSING poster had been torn off the waiting room wall and was now the centre of attention on Sam's desk. Yet again, there was no resemblance between the photograph taken by the police the one and only time she had been arrested for possessing drugs and the one the Soultier family had provided. Her smile had disappeared, and all sense of a future had drained from her eyes. The contrast astonished De Ritter.

"With the way she looks, how come she was only picked up once?" she said to Sam.

"You'll have to excuse our colleagues if they're not that keen on trying to control users out on the streets. You've only got to walk round the métro exit at Château-Rouge in the XVIIIth to see what looks like a scene from the end of the world. There's a C.R.S. van parked there full of warriors in their rubber armour. All of them are busy looking elsewhere while a few paces away there are small groups of haggard addicts, blinded by the daylight, shoulder to shoulder with the police while they smoke their rock of crack or exchange their drug substitutes."

"Lexomil?"

"Yeah, but that's just the start. If you want something stronger you've got Subutex, Neo-Codion or Skenan, if you're not scared of injections, but they all seem to prefer La Roche. Before you ask, that's the name of the lab that produces Rohypnol, which is like sweets for addicts missing their heroin fix. And when you know they'd sell their little brother's virginity for a dose, you also know there's nothing you can do for them. I mean, as a policeman. So, no, it doesn't strike me as unlikely that she was only brought in once."

Coste printed out the young girl's police record and announced:

"Calamity and me are going to pay the Soultier family a visit. Sam, go over to the station that picked up little Camille and get hold of a copy of their report. I want to read what she had to say and know if anyone was with her that day. I also want you to call the A.P.E.V. and find out if they are aware she is going round 93 with the drug users' crowd. Ronan, get over to the Jean-Verdier hospital and show the photographs of Camille, Paulin and Samoy to Bébé Coulibaly. You risk being told to go fuck yourself, but we have to try. We'll meet back here in two hours."

Coste picked up his coat. He could sense Sam looking at him, but he did not want to meet his eyes. He was just hoping he would trust him.

Before Ronan left headquarters for a highly intellectual discussion with the eunuch, he sat on the edge of Sam's desk. First because he knew Sam hated that, but also because he was wondering how much longer the three of them were going to keep up this pretence.

"I imagine I'm not the only one."

"Be specific, as Coste would say."

"Not the only one to have recognised the girl from the squat at Les Lilas. The girl Brahim identified as Camille Soultier."

"Ronan, you surprise me. I really thought you wiped your hard drive clean every twenty-four hours."

"Not when my buddy Sam almost throws up on his first case. I remember the squat in the old Les Lilas town hall very well, and I'm sure Coste does too. Do you think he's keeping something from us?"

"No, and neither do you. I think he's trying to protect us from something."

"Could be. So do we just wait until he decides to let us in on the secret?"

42

Coste had never seen his inability as a failing, but it was true: he could never remember street names. He had managed to put a name to all the boroughs in 93, but the streets were beyond him. He had a police officer's knowledge of them, from the offences committed there.

Bobigny, Chemin-Vert, meant nothing to him. But there was no way he could forget the case of a kid found crushed under a fridge thrown from the twenty-fourth floor of one of the tower blocks onto a police patrol. He could remember the colour of the boy's satchel when they lifted the heavy missile off him, but there was no way that the name of the street had remained with him.

De Ritter had switched on the G.P.S. when she realised Coste was going to be no help, and that the Soultier place on the heights of Saint-Cloud could just as well have been in India as far as he was concerned. As soon as they entered Paris from the Périphérique, he seemed to lose all interest. They left Bobigny and took avenue Jean-Jaurès along the Pantin cemetery. To Coste, this was nothing more than a long line of clandestine African nightclubs that were the scene of stabbings and drunken brawls almost every Saturday night.

De Ritter left Pantin behind, and the sign telling them they were entering the city of Paris warned Coste that from now on he wouldn't recognise a thing apart from the main historic monuments. He was as in the dark about the French capital as a Japanese tourist.

Since he did not seem in the mood for conversation, De Ritter turned up the volume on the car radio. The phantom of the I.M.L. and the case of spontaneous combustion in Pré-Saint Gervais were still headlines. Irritated, Coste turned the volume down again. De Ritter cut off the tinny voice regularly telling her to prepare to turn right or left.

"You know, Coste, I realise I'm lucky to be involved in such an . . . absorbing affair for my first case."

"That's one way of putting it. If you'll allow me to correct you, I'd say it was a once in a career case. It's a shame it's happened to you so soon. You risk finding all the remaining years before you retire a bit of a let-down."

The front gates that gave on to a tree-lined driveway completed their sense of disorientation. The mansion only revealed its respectable decrepitude to those who really knew it, and they noticed little of it from the outside.

Alerted by the sound of the car engine, Brice appeared on the front steps. De Ritter pulled up abruptly, and Brice told himself he would have to rake the gravel before Madame took him to task.

"Capitaine Coste . . . Police judiciaire. We would like to talk to Monsieur and Madame Soultier."

Brice stiffened.

"Madame Soultier is inside. As for Monsieur, that depends. Neither of them is available. Madame's husband, Monsieur Jacques Soultier, is no longer with us; and her son is in his office at the Ministère des Finances. If you would like to follow me, I'll announce you."

By the time they had gone down a string of corridors and through several small rooms, Coste had given up trying to establish a mental picture of the layout of the house, and simply followed. Vestibule, reception room and morning room were descriptions he had never had to write in any statement for the S.D.P.J. 93.

On the clothing front, De Ritter felt seriously out of step. For the first time her thick woollen navy blue jumper felt uncomfortable. She slipped behind Coste in the vain hope of going unnoticed.

When Brice reappeared, he was pushing a wheelchair occupied by an elderly lady. With her level, staccato delivery, she seemed twenty years younger as soon as she started to speak.

"Coste, Coste, that means nothing to me. Are you a friend of Commissaire Dalerieux? He and the attorney general were taking tea here only a few days ago."

The confident smile the policeman bestowed on her clearly indicated her attempt to impress him had flown wide of the mark.

"No, madame, we're from the S.D.P.J. in Seine-Saint-Denis."

"Then you must definitely be lost," she said with a dry laugh.

"That's true; we would probably never have had occasion to visit this area had we not come to talk about your daughter, Camille."

"My daughter? That's very gracious of you, capitaine, but since I'm approaching my eightieth birthday, I think it would be rather remarkable if I had a 22-year-old daughter."

43

Brice had prepared coffee and biscuits on a plate decorated with a gilded capital "S". De Ritter had no idea if she was looking out onto an English or a French garden; she could not even have said if she were on a terrace or a veranda. When she dipped a biscuit in the scalding hot coffee, the end fell off with an embarrassing plop. She put everything back on the side table and decided to make herself as small and as silent as possible.

Although she was not quite sure how, Coste had softened up the old battleaxe. Possibly it was his calm demeanour. The fact that he did not look stupid, definitely. He had asked her to tell him about Camille. Right from the beginning. De Ritter couldn't always follow Coste's chain of thought, but decided to trust him. So Margaux Soultier began her story in a solemn tone that warned them not to interrupt her until she had finished.

"Camille was not wanted, still less acknowledged, by her father. Isabelle, my younger sister, became a single mother. The void left by the man she was madly in love with was never filled, and her mind began to waver when she saw his gaze in her daughter's eyes. She ought to have died of sorrow the way a fire peters out, but, fortunately for her, her fate was less protracted. She left us in a stupid car accident, if there is any other kind, even though the police never really understood why there were no brake marks on that straight country road. The tree she careered into was almost uprooted. A few months later, before her first birthday, I was awarded custody of Camille. My fortune and my social position allowed me to offer her a good education. I myself had lost my husband two years earlier to cancer, and my elder son Gaël had left home to pursue his studies, so I was on my own here with Lucas. I thought the responsibilities that came with Camille's arrival might help alleviate my boredom. You'll no doubt think me cynical, but some families only seem to write their story in misfortune."

Margaux Soultier thanked Brice with her eyes as he placed a box of pills next to her cup.

"For Lucas, who had just turned sixteen, Camille's arrival was a breath of spring in a house that had not known that season for years. He used to grow furious if I ever dared use the word 'niece', because from the very first day he considered her his sister. I remember the meeting we had with the educational psychologist. Lucas sat there on his chair without moving, staring at the floor. The psychologist used the image of a dammed-up river and the weight of love Lucas could not direct towards either his deceased father, his absent brother, or me – and I am not, I confess, given to demonstrations of affection. Yet I have loved my children. In a certain way. In my way. Does one really have to be kissing all the time, touching each other, talking to one another? Can one not take maternal love for granted?"

The old lady had become rather carried away. She quickly adopted a more neutral tone.

"However that may be, I refuse to see myself as the one to take the blame. You don't mess up your life simply because of a lack of tenderness. At the time we had an African nanny, they're very good, very tactile and maternal. And yet Lucas would dismiss her every afternoon when he got back from school in order to be on his own with Camille. The next morning, I would find him in her room stretched out alongside her like a guard dog. She reached adolescence under his protective wing, and even at that age he forbade me to make her face up to the truth. I had to wait until I was alone with her to explain about her real parents, how her father had abandoned her, and about her mother's death. Lucas never forgave me that betrayal, as he called it, even though it was clearly necessary. I consider that certain secrets become poisonous over time, and that a four-teen-year-old girl is capable of confronting her own reality. That is how I was educated. Against all expectation, it was towards Lucas that Camille turned her bitterness and sorrow. Was she aware that neither emotion would touch me? She chose a more vulnerable target. As she gradually slipped away, he became more and more clingy, trying to spend all his time with her, even though in the end all he received were insults from behind a door now closed to him.

"After that, little by little she went from bitterness to out-right rejection. She no longer dined with us, and when she did us the honour of a quick visit, it was generally to have a shower and ask for money. I don't think I ever saw her again without headphones on, so I'm convinced that towards the end she only saw our lips moving and couldn't be bothered to understand what we were trying to say. She disappeared for days on end and her sadness, which I understood, gave way to an unaccept-able insolence. Even so, Lucas continued to love her and to try to understand her until the very last days she spent here. Where she was concerned, nothing was important or serious. He forgave her everything: the many thefts, although he himself was often the victim, the surprise guests whom Brice sometimes had to escort back to the front gates. The chain of our relationship became too stretched and eventually snapped. She became nothing more than aggression and reproaches. The manor house was split in two: on one side her bedroom, on the other, the rest of the world. Unfortunately, among the rest of the world was Lucas, and in Lucas's desert existence, there was only Camille. I was fortunate enough to have had only boys, and my authority was always sufficient to organise the life of this house smoothly. Conversely, I had no control over that young girl. So little in fact that she left for good before she came of age, after four long years of conflicts that were sometimes veiled and at others the exact opposite. And Lucas never got over that new abandonment."

Since she paused at this point, Coste took advantage of the silence.

"Did you report her running away to the police?"

"You may be surprised to hear it, but our family has only rarely had recourse to your services. For far too long now, my son has been painfully launching his political career, and I did not want in any way to hinder what he might become. We turned to Monsieur Simon, a private investigator whose services my husband had used. Thanks to him, until her final disappearance, we more or less knew what she was doing and with whom she spent her time. On my instructions, Brice searched her room several times, and what Camille's constantly exhausted face suggested was confirmed by the syringes and blackened spoons he found among her things. On the eve of her eighteenth birthday, it was Lucas himself who went to report her disappearance, to avoid what you call an 'investigation on behalf of families'."

"That's understandable. Adults have a right to disappear, whereas minors have to be brought back home. And since then, you've had no news?"

"You would have to ask Lucas. For my part, I've stowed away that episode with the rest of my memories. Camille is twenty-two now, and I imagine we'll find her on the front doorstep again when she's hit rock bottom. I offered her my home and my . . . affection, what more could I do?"

Coste turned towards De Ritter, who took a folder out of her backpack. He searched among the papers and then placed three photographs side by side on the table. Franck Samoy, Bébé Coulibaly and Jordan Paulin. The old lady extracted from a thick tome the pair of glasses she had been using as a bookmark.

"If you would care for my opinion, capitaine, these youngsters don't look very respectable."

"I agree with you. Might any of them mean anything to you?"

She hesitated, then her gnarled finger touched Franck Samoy's photograph, and stayed there all the time she spoke.

"This one. At first he waited politely for her at the front gate, but soon began to drive right in and park as if he owned the place. The last time I saw him, his feet were barely touching the ground when Brice took him by the collar and ejected him from the property."

"You say he used to park outside the house. Do you recall the vehicle?"

"Of course, it was a red car."

"A B.M.W.," specified Brice, who had never really left the room. "An older model."

Margaux Soultier considered she had co-operated quite enough and reversed the roles.

"Perhaps it's time you told me the reason for your visit, capitaine. Have you had news of Camille?"

"No, unfortunately we have not. I'd like to know more about

the man with the B.M.W. because he's involved, to put it mildly, in what appears to be a settling of scores between drug traffickers. He's the one who brought us to your door. As for knowing whether Camille is safe or in good health, I have no information, but, if you wish, I can keep you informed."

Even though she nodded, Coste could detect no sign of urgency about her response.

Margaux Soultier's heavily ringed fingers closed over his hand. A mixture of wrinkled flesh and polished gold.

"Frightful. Is that the word I can glimpse in your eyes, capitaine? You find me frightful, don't you? Don't worry, Lucas looks at me the same way, and I don't tremble at his view of me any more than I do at yours. Camille is not my daughter, and I am trying to protect what remains of a family in decline."

Just like the setting afternoon sun, thought Coste, who decided that this was sufficient for the time being. As he was getting up to leave, something the old lady had mentioned came back to him.

"You spoke of your two sons. You've told me about Lucas. What has become of the other one?"

"Lucas is the younger brother. My elder son didn't want to follow in his father's shoes. He is now a pharmacist in a humanitarian programme. It seems my family wants to get away from me in any way they can."

"Could I meet him?"

"Of course. When you arrive in Mauritania, ask for Gaël Soultier of Pharmaciens sans frontières. According to his last letter, the road to the village of Diaguily has been repaired."

"I doubt if our budget will stretch that far. I'll make do with contacting your younger son, Lucas. Could you please leave him my card?"

The old lady accepted – with pleasure, according to her, but without so much as holding out her hand. It was Brice who took the card from the capitaine's fingers and with a polite aside indicated it was now time to let Margaux Soultier rest.

On their way back to headquarters in the car, De Ritter was the first to comment on the interview that had just taken place.

"My mother has just gone up in my esteem. I wouldn't have liked to be under that woman's thumb."

"You obviously don't know mine."

"It never occurred to me you might have one."

Despite the mess they were in, De Ritter managed to raise a faint smile on Coste's face. He took out his mobile and let Sam fill him in on their expedition. As he could have wagered, Coulibaly had denied recognising the photographs of Camille, Paulin or Franck Samoy. Ronan had tried to apply pressure by threatening him, but he was dealing with someone who had already had his balls cut off, so was rather hard to intimidate. In Sam's inbox was the police report from the station that had arrested Camille Soultier for possession in 2010 when she had been stupidly trying to climb over the turnstiles at a métro station. She fell flat on her face in front of a row of patrolling inspectors. As she had no I.D., the métro inspectors had called in the police, and a search revealed she had half a gram of heroin on her. Nothing very interesting. Even so, Coste wanted more info.

"Did they take a D.N.A. sample? Fingerprints?"

"No, there's nothing. As it was only half a gram of heroin, she wasn't even taken in and was simply let off with a caution. Forensics probably didn't have the time to take any samples. It happens. Often."

"Was she on her own that day?"

Sam scrolled through the report once more.

"The report mentions a guy who was with her, but when they found nothing on him they let him go. No surname or first name mentioned here. If you want my opinion, I'd say it was Franck Samoy."

What Sam had to say next was more revealing, and left them feeling uncomfortable.

"I called the A.P.E.V. They have no info on Camille Soultier's whereabouts, but when I told them she might be in 93 they seemed already aware of that. They explained that after a certain length of time families usually hire a private detective. What with their anguish and police who never live up to the expectations of a family that has lost a child, it's understandable."

"That's what the Soultier family has done."

"Yes, I know. Apparently one of the best."

He kept Coste waiting while he searched through his notes.

"Here it is: Monsieur Simon Beckriche. He even thought he had a lead. In 2011. In a squat. At Les Lilas."

Sam left a tiny pause between each of these sentences, long enough for Coste to respond if he wanted to. Nothing doing. Shit, what was he supposed to tell them? Confess to Sam they were investigating an addict that Mathias Aubin had simply deleted more than a year earlier, but who now turned out to be the daughter of a prominent family? Admit she was a mistake, and that twenty-two other people had followed her path to oblivion over a matter of statistics and results? Coste had no idea how to put any of that into words without sounding absurd. No, he was not prepared to talk, so Sam went on resignedly:

"The detective contacted the A.P.E.V., who advised him to get in touch with the officer in charge of the case to arrange a formal identification of the corpse. All for nothing: the family didn't recognise Camille."

"O.K., thanks for that, Sam."

"Yeah. You know you're not on your own in this, don't you?"

"Give me a little more time."

"You're still the boss."

"One last thing, Sam. Find out all you can about the Soultier family. Concentrate on Lucas Soultier, a budding politician at the Ministère des Finances. And check out his brother Gaël. His mother tells me he's a pharmacist in a humanitarian organisation in Africa. Last but not least, the family butler's first name is Brice: he interests me as well. I've just been talking to the mother, Margaux Soultier, and I think she's been leading me up the garden path."

"O.K. I'm on it."

Coste ended the call. It had taken all this time for the car to emerge from the grounds of the Soultier mansion.

"Have you ever visited the I.M.L.?"

"Once, on my course."

"Put the address into your G.P.S. You're going back a second time. There's something I need to check before you're free to go."

44

From reception he informed Doctor Marquant they had arrived. As usual, she appeared with her hair pulled back, and as usual Coste found her incredibly attractive in her white coat. His heart skipped a beat when she smiled at him through the glass door she opened to join them. He did the introductions.

"Lea, this is Lieutenant De Ritter."

The two women shook hands. The ensuing silence made De Ritter feel she was in the way.

"O.K . . . Coste, I'll make a call outside. I'll check the kids have sat down to eat and done their homework."

The new lieutenant was no threat to a woman like Léa Marquant. Even so, she wanted to make her marital situation clear so as not to have to face such a frosty reception on the telephone a second time.

"I have to admit, Victor, I thought she would be . . . well, more Johanna . . ."

He let her trail off and smiled.

"Anyway, what have you brought me today? A mummy? An extra-terrestrial?"

"I know I've placed the bar a bit high for your next autopsies, but this time I simply want to consult a file. A case from ten months ago. The body of a young woman, never identified, brought in on 16 March, 2011."

*

A few moments later, and Léa was rapidly going through the archives. When she came to the right year and then the month, she slowed down until she found the file he wanted to see. She asked what exactly he was looking for.

"The photographs from the autopsy, and to see if the family came to identify the body."

She took out a series of snapshots of the girl's lifeless corpse and handed them to Coste. She leafed through the other sheets of paper.

"A family did come for the formal identification at the mortuary. Lucas Soultier, the supposed brother, and Margaux Soultier, ditto mother. Negative identification."

"Who was the officer in charge?"

"Lieutenant Mathias Aubin, from your unit."

Coste chose one of the photographs and laid it on the pathologist's desk.

"That's the poor kid from the squat."

He pulled a piece of paper folded in four out of his jacket pocket, and smoothed it with the flat of his hand. The MISSING poster from headquarters.

"And allow me to present Camille Soultier."

Marquant was astonished.

"My God, it's the same girl. Badly messed up, but the same."

Coste let her follow the same deductive process as he had. Her astonishment gave way to fury.

"And that old cow of a mother assured me she didn't recognise her!"

"Her adopted mother, to be more precise."

"And the runt pulled the same trick! What a sick family!"

"I've just come from there and Mother Soultier led me the same dance."

"But how can you deny your daughter – even if she's adopted – on her deathbed? And for what reasons?"

"Exactly, that's what I'm looking into. For now, I'd like to know how I can find an unidentified corpse from more than a year ago. Even if, like me, you think the two photographs show the same person, that's only visual evidence. What I need is scientific proof the Soultier family is trying to pull the wool over our eyes. I want to exhume the body, wherever it is, take a D.N.A. sample, and make a comparison."

Léa Marquant was still so furious she did not appear to take in what he was saying.

"Léa, I need your help with this!"

"You really want to get me into trouble, don't you, Victor? You've already made me do an autopsy on a living man, and now you tell me I've sent some poor girl to a pauper's grave? Well, I guess until I get the sack you've made my job more interesting."

"A pauper's grave?"

"We keep unidentified bodies for a month. After that, the body is buried in the 'paupers' graves' at the Thiais cemetery. She must still be there as we speak. I'll write down her registration number for you. In less than three years she will be incinerated to make room for the next batch of unknown corpses."

"You don't waste time."

"That's right, we're heartless bastards. More seriously though, there are said to be something like fifteen hundred unidentified corpses in France each year, so we don't have the time, space or money to keep them longer than that. What with the autopsy, the undertaker, burial and incineration, each unidentified corpse costs three thousand euros. You would have to add another thousand to analyse the D.N.A. and map it to establish any connection with the cases of missing people. Our administration doesn't appear willing to spend that much. So, for the sake of a miserable thousand euros, some families search for the body of their lost child for years when in fact it's buried only a few kilometres away. These invisible people are no-one's priority. Nothing more than bodies to be stuck in the ground without even a prayer said over them."

"Yes, I know."

Ironically, she too had used the word "invisible". Coste's mobile buzzed: incoming message. De Ritter was growing impatient.

"I can understand the detour to the Institut – she's well worth it, with that Audrey Hepburn look – be careful, she could hurt you – but can we go?"

"An important message?"

He snapped the mobile cover shut.

"Not really, just a recall to duty."

PART THREE

*"93 has always been a den of cut-throats,
so why try to pretend it's a holiday village?"*
Lucas Soultier

45

It was in March 2011 that Monsieur Simon had begun to have doubts. This was when, taking every precaution not to raise false hopes, he had announced:

"I may have a lead."

"Camille?"

"I can't be sure, madame."

This led to a difficult and eventually fruitless visit by the Soultier family to the Institut medico-légal. After that, it would have been logical for them to continue to employ the detective on the trail of Camille, the family's rogue electron. Without being aware of the change in the wind, Simon had found himself on the dark side of the intrigue, unable to understand what was going on, trying to explain to himself why Lucas had instructed him to continue his investigation into the unidentified young woman in the morgue. The one he had not recognised as being his sister.

Like all good detectives, he had become used to keeping his curiosity in check, and this prevented him from asking anything of his employer. But rules like that change over time.

Nowadays, the Soultier family amounted only to the son with an uncertain political future and an embittered old woman. And yet, when her husband had been alive, the family had enjoyed considerable notoriety.

Jacques Soultier had easily made the transition from businessman to man of power without having to change the rules of the game, because to him they seemed identical. He had built his second career in the same way he had previously taken over a firm or closed one down: by digging out the secrets his adversaries were trying to hide. To do so, he had for many years been able to count on Monsieur Simon. It was said that if a politician wanted to give his mistress a gift, he should first consult the person who knew her best, in other words Monsieur Simon.

After Jacques' death, Margaux Soultier had renewed his contract and, out of respect for the deceased, he had agreed to become the family babysitter. For both Lucas and Camille. The first did not seem likely to burnish the family crest; the second threatened to tarnish it once and for all. Even though the work was monotonous, he was well paid, and up until that moment that had satisfied him.

But following the family visit to the Institut medico-légal, the venerable detective began to have his doubts. He knew all about depravity, string-pulling and low blows, and from having to juggle with them every day of his working life had even come to believe he had invented the rules. Finding himself caught up in the midst of such venality was a different matter. He thought he had hit the mark with the girl in the squat, and the more Lucas denied it, the more his doubts grew.

He tried to test his client.

"Would you like me to continue investigating your sister?"

"That's exactly what you're doing," the younger Soultier said calmly. "Concentrate on that unidentified girl, she'll lead us to her. She could be one of her friends. If they have the same bad habits and hang around the same spots, perhaps they know the same people. Do you remember the young man she often went round with and used to bring to the house in secret? The one with the red car?"

"A red B.M.W. 633. I've already identified him as a regular companion of hers. He's called Franck Samoy. I can dig a little deeper if you so wish, Lucas."

Lucas concealed his irritation. Why did the man persist in calling him Lucas, when his mother had won the right to be "Madame Soultier"? Perhaps "Monsieur Soultier" would always and only be his father. He brushed aside his reaction.

"Find him. I want to know all the places he frequents. I'd also like to know the exact circumstances surrounding that girl's death."

"Turning up a page of a log book in a police station is something I know how to do; consulting a criminal case file is more complicated, and I don't think I'm up to burgling the S.D.P.J. 93."

"Couldn't you approach the lieutenant in charge of the case? You are, after all, colleagues . . ."

"In fact we're not, but that doesn't mean I couldn't try. You give the orders, Lucas."

"Monsieur Soultier, dammit."

Finding Franck Samoy in his big red B.M.W. had been easy. Simon made a list of where he hung out and where he crashed and squatted, as well as noting his irregular visits to his mother in Romainville. The detective's investigation took him from hostels to reception centres; he even knew the locations of the pharmacies and neighbourhood Aids centres where you could often find him when he was stuck for a steribox.* All this took him less than a fortnight.

* A kit costing about one euro containing sterile equipment for drug users: two syringes, two teaspoons, two sterile filters, two treated tampons and a condom

Gaining access to the case files had given rise to problems, but not those that Monsieur Simon had been expecting. He already knew who was in charge of the case because he had contacted him about the family's identification of the body. The young girl had been dead for several months now, so he decided to call the S.D.P.J. 93 directly to arrange a meeting with Lieutenant Aubin.

"He's not here."

"Could you tell me who else is working on the case of the young girl found dead in the squat at Les Lilas on 16 March this year?"

"Hold the line, I'll look for you."

Simon loved secretaries. All you had to do was sound like someone in authority and they gave you whatever info you needed over the telephone. He would have bet his shirt on her having a photograph of a kitten in a basket somewhere on her desk.

"We have no record of any body being discovered on that date, sir."

"Are you sure? Could you please check again?"

She became suspicious.

"Could you please remind me of your name and unit?"

Simon hung up.

If his view of the facts was correct, he was investigating a young woman who was not Camille – according to the family, at least – and whose file had vanished in the most unfortunate manner. It did not take him long to contact Marc Farel, who he knew pored over the most sordid cases. The two men knew one other, and the private detective would need to tread carefully.

Without giving away Camille's identity – one of his aims was to keep the hack as far away from the Soultier family as possible – he managed to arouse his interest in the death of the young addict.

"Good morning, Marc."

"Shalom, Monsieur Simon."

"I'd like you to reassure me about something."

"Let's see what I can do."

"I'm looking for a case file. A young girl who died of an overdose in a squat at Les Lilas. I know the S.D.P.J. 93 Groupes Crime were called in because I've already been in touch with an officer there, but when I try to find out more about the case, I'm told there's no such file. Do you think it's possible for there to be no file on a suspicious death?"

"A file could go missing by mistake, but it should turn up some day or other. If it was deliberately lost, that's a different matter . . ."

"Does that happen often?"

"Absolutely not, it's simply a hack's fantasy. Why are you calling me? Have you got wind of something?"

"You're known as a real shit-stirrer among crime reporters, and I said to myself that if I had to ask difficult questions of the police, you'd have been annoyed if I didn't put them to you."

"You're too kind. But tell me, are you still working for the Soultier family?"

This was where he would need to tread carefully.

"Not since the father passed away."

"Right. That must have left a big hole in your business."

"You always vilified him, Marc. Jacques Soultier was a politician, with all the compromises that implies."

"A person who compromises, compromises himself, doesn't he?"

"If you like to play with words."

"So this story about a young girl found dead in a squat has

nothing to do with the disappearance of the Soultier daughter, the one they adopted."

So much for treading carefully. Farel had outsmarted him; he knew the score as well as the main players. Simon had just thrown him a bone and the journalist would not be back until he had sunk his teeth into it and sucked out all the marrow.

46

Farel had a journalist's instinct, and never felt closer to the truth than when confronted by the lie trying to hide it. He knew how to recognise the false note in a voice, the exaggerated sigh, the telltale hesitation, and ever since his conversation with Monsieur Simon he had been infected with the germ of doubt. The old detective had clearly been trying to deceive him with his story about an unknown young woman who had died of an overdose. A story very similar to what might have happened to the young Camille Soultier, even though her profile was different from the others.

He knew deep down that all these disappearances must have taken place, but he had to gather enough proof before dropping his bombshell. Despite all his patient efforts, he was still a long way from publishing his exposé.

In a little less than a year of digging, he had covered the north wall of his living room with press cuttings in his search for potential victims, those whose anonymous status meant they could be silently expunged. Every morning he had set himself the task of reading all the brief items of news, as well as Agence France Presse cables, determined not to miss any. He worked conscientiously, like one of those old people who spend their days cutting out bargain coupons from newspapers.

Parallel to this, he worked on other stories that were

occasionally interesting, and always profitable, but these missing cases were his hobby, his in-depth research, his obsession. On some of the cuttings pinned to the wall he had written the comment "Possible", followed by a question mark. On seventeen others, in red this time, the word "Definite" had been written in capital letters, sometimes so vigorously the ink had run onto the wallpaper.

Without realising it, and above all without meaning to, Monsieur Simon had rearranged the pieces of the puzzle, and the journalist's reading of them was clearer now. Camille Soultier had become his starting point. The majority of homicides committed in Seine-Saint-Denis were automatically referred to the S.D.P.J. 93. This made it the link between them and, thanks to what Monsieur Simon had let slip, Lieutenant Mathias Aubin had become the way in. Confident he had enough information to rattle him, he had contacted the officer and quite simply bamboozled him. Their conversation had told him a lot, and that same evening he had come into possession of a box full of files and a careful explanation of what the police called Code 93.

On his wall, the comment "Definite" had been crossed out and replaced by "Code 93", and the number had risen from seventeen to twenty-three. He was definitely going to need new wallpaper.

If Monsieur Simon's unidentified young woman really had been Camille, her death should have made more waves, and the silence surrounding the affair led Farel to contact Lucas Soultier. Among the chosen cases, only Camille appeared to have a family, or at least a family prepared to come forward. Their conversation very nearly ended after just a few seconds, and yet again Farel had to be convincing to avoid having the telephone slammed down on him.

"My sister's disappearance is not going to be your next scoop, Monsieur Farel."

"I understand, but I'm not bothered about the society pages. I think it's linked to other cases."

Lucas knew that by now there was not much point looking for Camille anywhere other than in a cemetery, but he was still keen to know why and how she had died. He decided not to hang up.

"I have in my possession a copy of twenty-three judicial files related to suspect deaths."

"There's no accounting for taste."

"That's not the point. Whenever I ask my contacts in the Groupes Crime about them, I get the same response. There was no investigation. The deaths don't appear anywhere on their computer system."

Farel chose an example he knew would hit home.

"For example, a young girl around twenty years old found dead of an overdose in a squat at Les Lilas in early 2011. The local police investigated, then the case was handed over to the S.D.P.J. 93. But it appears never to have been received, because they have no trace of it. And yet I have the details here in front of me."

If Lucas had been holding a piece of toast in his hand at that moment, it would have exploded. His fountain pen was more solid. He tried to control his voice.

"And what do you conclude from that? Is it deliberate? They bury some cases?"

"It would take rather too long to explain, but yes, that's what I believe. I think they try to conceal some homicides in 93, the ones the police call 'invisibles', in order to massage the crime figures."

"But 93 has always been a den of cut-throats, so why try to pretend it's a holiday village?"

"I'd like to talk to you directly about this, but I'm convinced that, by mistake, Camille could have become one of these invisible cases."

"This is a lot of information to take in all at once, Monsieur Farel. You say you have proof in the legal reports in your possession?"

"Twenty-three times over, yes."

"And together with those files, you have the autopsy reports?"

Farel thought this an odd question, but he had at all costs to keep Soultier happy.

"Yes, the full summary and conclusions."

Soultier agreed to meet him the next evening. Then he immediately called Monsieur Simon. The detective had one last task to perform for the family.

47

Farel had chosen somewhere he knew well. The Café de la Musique in the XIXth. It offered two different kinds of atmosphere. A public one, on the terrace facing La Villette market, which was open air and generally crowded at all hours and in all weathers. And a private one, with cosy armchairs at the back of the main bar, half-hidden behind a grand piano that was for decorative purposes only and had been out of tune since forever. They had agreed to meet at nine-thirty. Farel left the métro twenty minutes early to take a good look around, a trick he had learned from the police. On his way to the café, he crossed the paved square, in the middle of which stood a fountain with eight seated lions spurting jets of water.

What he had at first taken for a group of students, given the proximity of the music conservatoire, became clearer as he approached. Three not exactly welcoming faces with a strong Eastern European accent that was obvious even if they did not say a word. Farel clutched to his chest the briefcase containing his laptop, and grasped it even tighter when he realised the three men were heading straight for him. When they reached him, the first two blocked his path, while the third looked all round him, unable to prevent himself hopping on the spot. Farel guessed he must be a newcomer to the gang, the loose cannon, the one who did the kneecapping while the other two, slightly older, did the talking. It didn't take him long to realise that he was not the victim of a random attack: they had been waiting for him.

The calm he saw in the eyes of the one closest to him literally disarmed him. The man's hands were covered in smudged tattoos, the sort done at home or in prison, with unsteady lines and blotchy colours, and from his eyes came a pale grey stare as piercing as it was confident. Farel understood that whatever he tried to do would be a mistake. The man tilted his chin towards the briefcase. Farel handed over his computer with a resigned smile. All he could do was obey, unless he wanted to lose some teeth and end up with the same result.

The two men turned on their heels, leaving the young apprentice still hungry. He continued hopping about to contain his excitement, surprised to see them go. Turning to Farel as if he were to blame for his not getting his ice cream, he punched him in the face between the base of his nose and mouth, muttering a "idi u picku materinu",* the way one spits on a prostrate body. A white mist descended on the journalist, then colour gradually returned and sound readjusted itself. Farel wiped away a few pain-filled tears. Ten seconds later he was able to take in the world around him once more.

In the Café de la Musique, he could not help laughing at himself. In one hand he held a whisky with no ice; in the other a paper tissue with which he was trying to stem the flow of blood from his nose. He had just realised how hilarious it would be if he went to the neighbourhood police station to report the theft of his computer containing the scans of the cases their colleagues in S.D.P.J. 93 were trying to erase. How could

* A common Serbian insult

214

Soultier have known he would have his laptop with him? The possibility of error made it a very risky gamble.

He did however have a hard copy of all these cases in the box Aubin had given him, stowed rather than hidden under his desk at home. Downing the last of his drink, Farel suddenly realised that there had been no gamble, and that doubtless his apartment had also just been burgled. He ordered another drink and took out a fresh tissue.

48

Old Simon had carried out his final mission efficiently, and even though Lucas suspected Farel must have been roughed up, he did not allow himself to feel any sympathy. What came next would be far more brutal. He loaded a laptop, a heavy box of recently stolen documents, and a few spare clothes onto the back seat of the Land Rover used by Brice for maintaining the gardens and park.

He had pretended that he was going for a weekend break at their country house in Sauny, a hamlet less than an hour and a half's drive from Saint-Cloud. And he did not give a damn that his mother had not believed a word.

He calmed down as the manor house grew smaller and smaller in the rear-view mirror. Among the cache of files he was carrying, it was Camille's that was waiting for him, but he had not yet had the nerve to open it. At Sauny, the cashier-proprietor-shopkeeper of the mini-mart remarked that they had not seen him or his family for years, and asked innocently for news of his mother and Camille. Lucas momentarily allowed himself the luxury of living in a happier imaginary world, responding that they were both extremely well.

Leaving the hamlet, he followed the private track that wound its way up a steep hill topped by the centuries-old, completely isolated Soultier family farmhouse. He parked the four-by-four in the garage, its bonnet jutting out slightly as though lying in ambush. A fine rain persuaded him to take off his coat to protect the box and computer, and he half-ran, shirt sticking to his skin, to the door of the sleeping house with closed shutters.

Some dry logs in the hearth began the task of warming the stone walls while he removed the white sheets covering the furniture in the main room like ghosts he was scaring away. By the time he finally thought to sit down, night had already engulfed the hill.

In one of the kitchen cupboards he had found a tin of soup that he had heated then left untouched on the kitchen table. He was hungry, but for something else. He settled in front of the enormous fireplace, built at a time when animals were roasted whole. The fire he had lit there looked pathetically small. In front of him he laid out the computer, the box of case files, and the dossier Monsieur Simon had drawn up on Franck Samoy before he had been thanked and paid off. The laptop needed a password and Lucas, who had a conflicted relationship with computers in general and stealing data in particular, put it to one side. Even though he could have recited them by heart, he reread Monsieur Simon's notes and those of the journalist, as this put off the moment when, like a funeral prayer, he would have to confront the raw, almost dehumanised words of the police and the pathologists.

He remembered the day when he and his mother had visited the mortuary, where, to protect the family honour, she had preferred to say nothing. The day he had discovered on Camille a tattoo he already knew. Just next to her groin.

Camille. He too had recognised her. His Camille. His almost sister. He had recognised her and remained silent. It could not be her: surely he would have known her that evening, by her

217

voice, her gestures. And if his eyes had been deceived by a different body, his heart would not have been fooled: it would have warned him, and he, Lucas, would have saved her. Yes, he would have saved Star, the girl with the red tattoo. Saved her, not fucked her.

He stared at the photographs of her lifeless body stretched out on the metal table minutes before the autopsy. Every word the pathologist had written turned to crushed glass he had to swallow, shard by shard, slicing into his mind and destroying his mental equilibrium.

His knuckles bloody from having lashed out at the still cold stone wall, heart beating in the void, Lucas ran out of the house and fell to his knees on the muddy ground. All the muscles in his body seizing up with cramp, he gave the most despairing cry of pain, without any sound rending the night.

His tears mingled with the rain, the blood from his hands, and the earth. He felt torn apart.

He awoke the next morning on the mud-covered leather sofa, in clothes stained from the previous night. He could not remember how he had ended up there. Yet, against all expectation, his brain had swung into action during his uneasy sleep, and when he opened his eyes, his subconscious had worked out in detail what was going to happen in the days to come. He took a lengthy shower, prepared coffee, pulled a new notebook and felt-tip pen from his briefcase, and ranged them neatly in front of him. Then he calmly chose his first target.

49

Franck Samoy had long since injected into his veins everything he had got from selling his car. Like a genius alchemist, he succeeded in changing everything into heroin, even T.V. sets. And yet, in the few minutes of lucidity he had on waking, he recognised he had been really stupid to get rid of his studio apartment on wheels. Now he was reduced to begging every day for a place in an emergency hostel, as that sort of establishment did not take reservations. At least he knew how to beg, and in Aubervilliers he had identified an area no bigger than a square kilometre where there were three of them. Inside the hostels it was common to be robbed, attacked or raped, because the same rules applied as out on the streets. A night spent there consisted of huddling in a corner, clinging on to possessions stuffed in plastic bags, eyes closed, mind alert. Not exactly restful. Since Samoy's wanderings had not escaped old Simon, Lucas knew where to start his surveillance.

He would have thought that the list of things he needed would be longer; he even wondered whether he had forgotten something. A flashy rental car, a bottle of whisky, a fine wristwatch with a loud gold bracelet, a few sachets of Stilnox stolen from his mother's medicine cabinet, fifteen hundred watt electric cooking rings, and a length of metal wire. Two hundred and eighty euros well spent, the watch a fake bought surreptitiously and costing almost as little as the wire.

He had seen Samoy go into the Refuge, the hostel on rue Hamelet, at two-thirty, and was now waiting for a lack of drugs to force him out of his cover. Night had barely had time to fall on the city or for Lucas to rehearse his carefully planned role when the main door opened and three emaciated figures appeared. Some inaudible words, an invisible exchange. There was a woman among them, who burst out laughing and immediately grew angry and pushed one of the men. Then the group split up, leaving his target isolated. He rapidly identified him. Unkempt hair, jeans, denim jacket, long threadbare white woollen sweater, eyes darting around.

Lucas switched on the ignition. Whereas the Land Rover gave him the impression he was astride a buffalo, the small, responsive Audi he had just rented wanted nothing more than to fly. He drove at walking pace, overtook Samoy in a few metres, then pulled in to the kerb. Pressing the automatic window switch on the passenger side, he leaned to the right and, as Franck Samoy walked past, prayed his voice wouldn't fail him.

"Good evening, young man."

The silhouette continued on its way. Shit, he had not come up with a proper pick-up line. He set off again, drove at the same speed alongside Samoy, and tried again.

"Excuse me, please."

The shadow slowed and turned towards him. Inspected the car. A nearly new Audi, not a patrol car. He stooped to peer inside and surveyed the driver. He looked like a juvenile lead, but Samoy didn't drop his guard. Policemen these days did not look like policemen. Anyway, he had nothing in his hands or pockets. A magician fresh out of tricks.

"What you want?"

"I was supposed to meet someone right outside the hostel, but . . ."

As Lucas laid his hand on the door sill and stretched out his arm, his watch popped from his shirtsleeve, shiny as a gold bar.

" . . . maybe there was no room for him tonight. Perhaps I should come back tomorrow. Unless you know him?"

Samoy's eyes flitted from the flashy watch to the Audi's gleaming bodywork. He told himself the night was going to be shorter than he had imagined.

"What you looking for? A cheap thrill in the suburbs? You want some shit? You don't look the type though . . ."

Lucas smiled shyly; he was playing the innocent perfectly.

"That's not what I'm looking for."

"Listen, I'll suck you off for fifty euros. Without a rubber is double."

"Get in."

Guided by his knowledgeable co-pilot, Lucas went round the porte d'Aubervilliers roundabout and took avenue de la Grande-Armée. This was a long road hidden between suburban train lines and makeshift wood and canvas shacks that was a slum by night and a ghost town by day. The day after the Arab spring, the number of migrants from Tunisia and Algeria had tripled, without any provision for welcoming or housing them. Drawn to the lights of Paris only to be immediately expelled like foreign bodies, these new migrants had as usual ended up being welcomed by the poor cousin of 93. They had driven out the Romanian prostitutes and settled in their place in this street that the police patrols studiously avoided.

Lucas switched off the engine and at Samoy's insistence also doused the headlights, leaving the car as anonymous as the line of other vehicles. Only a single nearby street lamp allowed him to make out the outline of things around him. He closed his eyes for a few seconds to create total darkness, and when he opened them again, the face of his passenger and the inside of the car were much clearer. His guest's heavy acrid smell of sweat, stale tobacco and damp enclosed rooms filled the Audi's interior.

"There's a bottle of whisky in the glove compartment. I think I'm going to need it: I'm not used to this kind of encounter."

"Yeah, I can see that."

Samoy stretched out his hand, turned the latch and the flap fell open from the weight of the bottle.

"Can I?"

It was a rhetorical question: his lips were already round the neck of the bottle and after a few mouthfuls the level had gone down by a quarter. Dosage: one 10 m.g. pill a day, to be taken last thing at night. Lucas wondered whether the dozen Stilnox tablets, even if they were diluted in a bottle of alcohol, might not kill Samoy. His passenger passed him the bottle and he pretended to drink while the other man lit a cigarette. Even though he was prepared for it, when he came into contact with the wet glass the mingling of their saliva made him shudder with disgust.

"You want to kiss me or something?"

"Er . . . no."

"So what are you after? Want me to suck you, or you to suck me?"

"I'd prefer it was you."

"You got a rubber, or do we run the risk?"

If Lucas Soultier had been a policeman, he would have known that however meticulously planned, an operation never goes entirely as expected. He had thought the sleeping pills

222

would take effect more quickly. He was going to have to wait another few minutes, and he was fearful how they were going to fill them.

"Let's run the risk."

He pretended to drink once more, then handed back the bottle. Franck Samoy threw his cigarette out of the half-open window, allowed himself another three big mouthfuls, screwed on the top, and dropped it onto the floor of the car. Turning towards his client, he wiped his lips with a vulgar sweep of his sleeve. His hands went to Lucas's flies and he calmly unzipped them. He fumbled between his legs and pulled out his sex, then began clumsily to rub it. Lucas raised his eyes to the heavens in a misplaced prayer as he felt the man's mouth close round him. His whole body stiffened: seeing Samoy's head rising and falling as he warmed to his task almost made him throw up. To go this far had not been part of the plan, nor that the addict would take it so seriously. He could feel saliva dripping from his limp sex onto his stomach. Samoy turned his head and looked up at Lucas.

"Warn me before you come, right?"

His words were already slightly slurred, Lucas thought to his relief. Samoy wasn't going to be able to resist the effects of the pills much longer. His movements slowed and eventually stopped altogether. Lucas realised he had not dared breathe while all this was going on, and finally took a deep breath. He looked around. Street, pavement, passersby, cars: they were alone. The renewed silence was broken only by a faint murmur that was reassuring, almost touching. The sound of a suckling child. In his enforced sleep, little Franck was still at his mother's breast.

Taking him by the shoulders, Lucas pulled him away with a plopping sound. He drove off.

*

The attendant at the service station confirmed that his car used lead-free petrol and as requested gave him an empty five-litre can. He had topped up the almost full tank of the car and was about to fill the can with the same petrol when another car pulled up under the dim neon lighting alongside him. At night, service stations in 93 ask customers to pay in advance in order to avoid any unfortunate forgetfulness, so the new driver headed for the cash-window. As he walked past the Audi, he saw the passenger asleep, chin slumped on his chest with a drool of spittle dangling from his mouth. He looked across at Lucas, who was staring at him, petrol can in hand. Some sort of tramp sleeping flat out in a top of the range car with a guy in a suit buying some extra petrol as if this was the last service station before the desert; the driver decided to keep his eyes down, fill up, and get out of there as quickly as possible. The "Good evening" Lucas offered with a smile, vainly trying to seem normal, only made him hasten the more.

Less than two hours later, the headlights picked out the stone walls of the farmhouse in the hamlet of Sauny. Hoisting the sleeping body onto his shoulders, Lucas entered the house. He carefully organised his guest's awakening and then sat patiently opposite him. After half an hour, he slapped him. At the sixth slap, Franck Samoy struggled to open his eyes. He understood quickly that he was no longer in a car, or in any familiar surroundings. His mind clouded by the drugs, and believing this must be a bad dream, it took him ten seconds to accept the new reality. He was sitting tied to an iron chair in the middle of a big room, hands bound behind his back, feet attached to the chair legs. He looked down to see what was producing such a strange sensation. His bare right foot was plunged into a pan full of water, his left foot in another one, and the two pans were resting on a double electric hob that was switched off. His growing fear expressed itself in a "What the fuck is this?"

At the risk of unscrewing his head entirely, he swivelled round to see where he was, to size up the place or to find some way of getting free. Lined up on the solid wood table in front of him were his mobile, his I.D. papers, a few cents and some long O.C.B. rolling papers. The sound of footsteps caught his attention. If this had been a film he could have pretended he was still groggy, ready to attack his opponent when he was least expecting it, or leap up and knock to the ground the person who had tied him there. If only it had been a film, but unfortunately . . . At the sound of the first footsteps, Samoy started howling and pissed himself.

"Good evening, Franck."

"Fuck, who are you?"

Lucas could have told him straight out: "I'm Camille's brother, and you are the first link in her downfall. I know you're the beginning, even if others are the end. You're only the first act. You initiated her and then poisoned her with drugs, until her life became nothing more than a long, interminable path to destruction where even my love no longer had a place."

But it was far too soon for sharing secrets like that.

Lucas bent down and switched on the electric hotplate. The lead had been too short, so he had plugged it into an extension attached to the wall socket.

"Tell me what you want. Tell me, I'll do whatever you want, just tell me."

"You're going to have to be patient, but don't worry, we've got a lot to talk about and I'm afraid you're not going to take me seriously at first, so we're going to start by showing you just how serious I am, alright?"

His prisoner rocked his shoulders to and fro desperately, and begged:

"No, fuck it, I don't want to, I swear I'll take you seriously straightaway."

The water heated up, at different speeds according to the size of the electric ring. Lucas decided not to say anything more, not daring to admit to himself that this position of absolute power really aroused him.

"I can see you don't need money, so what do you want? Look, I can find you young queers who get off on this kind of game, you can do whatever you like to them."

His lower jaw began to tremble uncontrollably, lending his words a terrified quake. His moans mingled with thick white saliva, flowing snot and terrified sobs.

"Fuck, you realise this is torture? Tell me what I have to do, for God's sake!"

As the water came to the boil, the pain in Samoy's left foot became unbearable. With the strength born of his suffering, he heaved and the chair he was tied to and the bonds themselves turned out to be far less solid than they had appeared. Flailing, he toppled to one side, and knocked over the two saucepans. One of his hands came free, and he fumbled behind his back to find the other knot. Lucas leaped over to the hearth and seized a heavy, still burning log. Just as he hit his guest with it in an explosion of sparks and ash, the water from the pans reached the extension lead and tripped the fuse. There was a loud bang and the entire house was plunged into darkness, the only points of light coming from a few glowing embers on the floor.

"Shit."

Lucas had a minute or two to modify his plan. The first time round it had been too complicated; now he had simplified it.

When he came to again, it took Samoy a moment to recover and understand once more where he was. Just as daylight only reaches us some time after it has been generated, reality also suffered a slight delay. One that was quickly compensated as everything came rushing back to him. Lowering his eyes, he saw his shoes were back on and the hot plate had disappeared. His jaw was aching terribly. Feeling with his tongue the spot where he had been hit, he he found he was missing some teeth. He cut himself on the sharp edge of a broken molar. A canine that had been knocked out was still in his mouth. He spat it out.

Lucas came into his field of vision. He bent down to the wall socket and plugged in the new apparatus. He had read the story of a gang of mindless, ultra-violent gypsies who, like the Droogs in *A Clockwork Orange*, had swept through neighbourhoods of villas and isolated houses. They had adopted a fairly simple M.O.: they smashed a window, woke the sleeping family up and herded them all together in one room. Then they burned the face of the mother or one of the children with their own iron. An ingenious if perverse way of avoiding having to carry a weapon on them, even if it is regarded as impolite to turn up at someone's house empty-handed. At the first touch of the iron on skin, the P.I.N. for the credit card and the whereabouts of the family jewels were quickly revealed. Lucas was only after information, and the red button on the iron showed him that the maximum temperature had been reached.

"Now what are you doing? Fuck, not that! Tell me what you want, I beg you."

"Don't wear yourself out, you've already begged."

Anticipating the horror Samoy was about to suffer, Lucas added, as if doing him a favour:

"You can yell if you like, though."

"We can come to an agreement, you don't need to do that!"

"Unfortunately for you, I do. I'd imagined a bit more of a show, but you're forcing me to be more direct. I'm going to ask you a series of questions, but first of all I want you to realise that any lie or cover-up is unacceptable. Do you understand everything I've said?"

Going over to him, Lucas pressed the flat side of the iron heated to 205 degrees Celsius on the left side of Samoy's face, from cheek to forehead. During the first quarter of a second, a time lag occurs when the brain signals it would be a good idea to pull your face away but as yet there is no pain. Samoy's "please" turned into animal yelps as his face began to burn, giving off an acrid smell of charred flesh. Black smoke poured out of the iron, and when Lucas tried to pull it away it stuck. The effect would have been exactly the same if he had pushed it against the plastic face of a mannequin. The skin from Samoy's cheek was stuck to the flat side; a bit of his eyelid hung like a piece of fried bacon. His bottom lip had turned inside out and was now stuck to his chin. The iron's aluminium surface was completely covered with grilled skin, and although Lucas had not ironed many of his own shirts, he knew about the existence of the steam button. Like a perfect housewife, he pressed it, and a cloud of white vapour emerged. By now his guest was reduced to making breathless gargling sounds, but when he ironed his right ear, they were displaced by an inhuman roar.

"Now I'm going to ask my first question. Do you remember Camille?" Lucas whispered into his left ear.

* * *

Lucas had carefully noted all the replies from this strange interview. Brahim the dealer. The first needles taking over from

228

sniffing. The constant lack of money and the tricks done to get half-price heroin. Camille's services did not even mean she got it for free. Then Samoy had told him about how she was handed over to Bébé Coulibaly, always on the lookout for fresh candidates. He had their addresses, telephone numbers and even knew their filthy habits. Samoy talked without stopping, sometimes in incomprehensible phrases, strings of words with no logic to them, or details of no interest. He was not really talking, just playing for time. The fire died down in the hearth. Lucas went behind his prisoner, tipped him up, and dragged the metal chair over to the smoking fireplace. The back legs of the chair left two irregular parallel lines on the floor tiles.

Samoy was bawling his head off, hiccoughing like a hysteri-cal child. Lucas sat on the sofa facing the hearth. He placed a lacquered wooden box on his knees and took out the Luger Po8 that had been in his family for more than seventy years. Samoy's ruined eye made it hard for him to see, but he could clearly make out the metallic glint of the gun barrel.

"I don't know what you're going to do, but let me go! I won't say a word, I don't even know who you are, I don't know you, just let me go."

"My name is Lucas Soultier," he announced, as if passing sentence.

"No, I don't want to know, dammit! I swear I won't say a word!"

Gun in hand, Lucas pushed in the clip, drew back the hammer, and inserted a round in the chamber. So far so good: he had been practising. He took three steps back, aimed, and pulled the trigger. There was a deafening plume of flame, and the bullet missed by a metre to the right, splintering some of the brickwork. Lucas felt his eardrums reverberate, and dropped the weapon. The condemned man's snotty, snivelling laugh resounded through the room. The desperate laugh of somebody who knows they're already dead. The words mangled by his mutilated mouth were still clear enough to take Lucas aback.

"Loser! You don't even know how to shoot. Go on, I'm waiting for you. Go on . . ."

The tone of his voice changed to an almost imperceptible prayer.

"Go on . . . go on . . . please . . . go on . . ."

Lucas took a step forward and fired three times, three bullets in the chest. Samoy fell backwards into the hot embers, sending up a grey cloud. Lucas pushed the chair to the back of the fireplace with his foot, then straightened Samoy up, pulling hard on his collar with both hands. He was upright now in the centre of the hearth, in his beautiful bloodstained white sweater.

Lucas left the farmhouse, and returned carrying the five-litre can of petrol.

Though he had made far too many mistakes, he had succeeded in the first part of what he had planned. His approach in the future would have to be simpler. And yet this murder had no echo beyond the isolated farmhouse. Such a cruel lack of an audience, such a lack of recognition if that had been all there was to it. But Lucas had thought beyond that; in fact, everything was already decided. Each painting was conceived as a diptych. One half dedicated to those who had led his sister down into hell. The other for the police who had tried to make her invisible. All he had to do now was to stage his show and inform the press. Nobody was going to be able to delete this folder.

The whistling sound from the four gunshots still buzzed in

his ears like a persistent mosquito. He took off Samoy's clothes and started a new fire in the hearth.

A few hours later, he wrapped the body carefully in a thick blanket and stowed it in the boot of the Audi. An abandoned villa he had located in Pré-Saint-Gervais would be the scene for what came next. He drove there with the window down. It felt uncomfortably as if the smell of burnt flesh had settled directly on his tongue.

50

For Lucas Soultier, the main problem Bébé Coulibaly presented was his size. Thanks to Franck Samoy's information, he had not been hard to locate. In fact, it was impossible to miss him, because he looked like the only grown-up in a world of children. If Lucas did not want to be crushed to a pulp, any face-to-face meeting was unthinkable. He would have to entice him somewhere, but also calculate his weight as exactly as possible so as to get the correct dosage of his pills.

He was careful to make his purchases in two different pharmacies. He rented the wheelchair from the first, and the ether in the second, even though the purchase of that needed a doctor's authorisation. Madame Margaux was an old and regular client. What with her excessive orders of sleeping pills, antidepressants, and all the other medicines that maintain a crumbling lady afloat, she could have kept both of them open and profitable. Lucas had only to invent a dog plagued with ticks and the man in the white coat had asked no more questions of the Soultier son. He smiled broadly and wished him "Good day" as he put the small blue bottle of ether on the counter.

Back in his bedroom, exhausted, he closed one of his brother Gaël's many medical manuals. Gaël Soultier had also fled the family manor as soon and as far away as possible. Following their father's death, he had been left to face his mother's stubborn silence and his little brother's impossible expectations of him. With his pharmacist's diploma in his pocket, rather than looking after those close to him he preferred strangers on another continent. It had been vital for him to leave, even if he understood that Lucas could see that as a second abandonment, a second loss. Lucas had projected that loss and grief onto Camille. He had suffocated her just as completely as if he had used a pillow. Then she in her turn quit him, taking with her all the feelings he had left, leaving him all but empty.

He put the copy of *Médicaments – Fiches synthèse* on top of another manual entitled *Pharmacie galénique – Formulation et technologie pharmaceutique.* Now he knew the dosage by heart. He put the book back in the dusty box he had found up in the loft among the things his brother had left behind. He recalled there had been a time when he wondered why he himself had not been put away up there, along with all the other useless objects.

Bébé Coulibaly received the text message on his phone as he was having dinner with his mother, brothers and sisters. Mafé chicken, okra and tiep rice: the whole of Senegal on a big, full plate.

"New girl –want to try her?"

His mother rolled her eyes and his little brother poked fun at him, calling out, "Han-la-laaa."

"No mobiles at table, Monsieur Bébé."

"Sorry, maman."

The S.M.S. was from Franck Samoy, an unimportant addict who had supplied him with some interesting candidates. Little junkies for smart porno evenings, to be sacrificed on the altar of vice. Lucas had hoped that the proposition would entice him to appear on his own for this preview. Bébé replied, tapping furtively on his mobile under the table: "At my place – Store room 55 – 23.00."

That was easy to find. Most storage spaces in the tower blocks are empty and open. Locking them is simply an invitation to be burgled. Only Number 55 had a padlock on it. Everyone knew it was used by Coulibaly, so nobody went near it. Lucas went into the cramped space behind the door marked Number 53 and waited. Through the half-open door he would be able to see if his victim was on his own. He switched on his taser to make sure it was working. With a violent discharge, a blue flash leaped across the two points of the electric pistol bought for eighty-one euros in the Gare de l'Est gun store (ladies' model also available – in pink). The salesman had pointed out that it was a high-security weapon that required official authorisation and he could not sell it to him. The hundred-euro note placed on the counter on top of the initial price saved him some saliva and brought his lecture on weapons legislation to an abrupt halt.

The taser is a unique means of defence. Starting from the principle that the stronger your adversary, the less likely you are to win, with taser guns it's the exact opposite. Its fifty thousand volts numb the central nervous system and paralyse the muscles. So the more heavily muscled your opponent is, the more vulnerable he is. The perfect weapon for this quarry.

After waiting almost an hour, Lucas Soultier was hopping from side to side to get rid of the pins and needles in his legs when the sound of the opening lift doors echoed through the basement. A massive shadow slipped past him: he thought that was what it must be like for a diver to have a great white shark swim past. His heart rate accelerated. He came up behind Bébé and unleashed the fifty thousand volts as soon as the taser touched his skin, jabbing the two metal darts into the fatty folds at the back of the giant's neck. Robbed of the use of his legs as well as all his other muscles, Bébé collapsed to the dusty earthen floor. Lucas followed him down, letting the electricity flow through his body for the five seconds maximum the instructions recommended. He waited a moment, then decided to play it safe. He pressed the two darts against Bébé's shoulder and launched the current, counting another five seconds. Now he had a few dozen seconds to act. Releasing one of the straps of his backpack, he swung it round in front of him and took a blue glass bottle from one of the side pockets. He raised the head of his unconscious victim, which flopped backwards. He unscrewed the bottle top and soaked a pad with the contents, immediately holding it under the man's nose.

Bébé had never suited his nickname more than when he was lying there, head lolling on Lucas's crossed legs as he gently fell asleep. All that was missing was someone to sing a soft lullaby. Lucas pulled away the pad, by now almost dry due to the ether's rapid evaporation. He tapped the sleepy face, then allowed himself to give it a resounding slap. Bébé did not wake up. Lucas stood up, went back to Unit 53 and pushed out a wheelchair. He had taken enough risks, the rest would be much more relaxed in the lonely farmhouse, waiting like an ogre for its second meal. Now he felt not only the excitement of revenge but the dizzying pride of taking justice into his own hands.

Stretched naked on his stomach, firmly tied to the table in the main farmhouse room, Bébé woke up with a searing headache in the top of his skull. At first he thought he was in a completely dark room, but then he felt the rub of cloth on his face and his own breathing coming back warmer on his skin. When the hood was removed, the light blinded him and he had to blink several times before he got used to it. All he could see was a brown-tiled floor in a big room with stone walls and wooden beams. It was warm, and when he raised his head as far as he could, he made out a huge fireplace. Lucas had no wish to talk to him, and the silence he imposed on the scene was only interrupted by his new victim's unanswered questions. Getting no reply, Bébé launched into a long stream of insults. Plunging his hands into the flesh of his open thighs, Lucas firmly gripped his penis and testicles. He wrapped strong string round the base again and again, pulling it tighter and tighter. The purple hues of Bébé's garrotted member grew darker and more disturbing. The paralysing fear of his outsize prey prostrate on the table was due more to apprehension than any real pain. Having trussed up his joint of meat, Lucas took hold of both testicles, pulled them back as hard as he could, then cut them with a single snip of his scissors. Hardly any blood flowed. Bébé screamed at death.

Thanks to his brother's manuals, Lucas had been able to make a list of what his mother's medicine cabinet contained, and calculate the correct doses. As he did so, he realised Camille should never have left the manor house to drug herself: all she needed was within reach. He had calculated the normal dose of barbiturates for someone weighing ninety-five kilos, then multiplied it by four in view of Bébé's massive frame and what he wanted to achieve.

He held up the bottle of water the barbiturates had been dissolved in. Like two similar magnetic poles pushing each other away, every time the bottle came near his lips Bébé turned his head aside. He was no longer impressive or intimidating. He was nothing more than a kid crying softly, repeating "Why?" endlessly and pointlessly.

"You've still got your prick. I can chop that off as well."

Convinced, Bébé gulped down the water.

After less than a quarter of an hour, the giant's eyes closed, and Lucas began the second half of the diptych. He pulled on the sweater with the three holes in it, then used the wheelchair to bundle the giant into the Land Rover. He headed for the disused warehouses at Pantin. Thanks to his nocturnal investigations, he had been able to verify that the security guard never left his portable T.V. set, and that his guard dog was not exactly fierce. Just in case though, he had thought of a way to keep it busy if it was too nosy. A titbit to keep it happy. A titbit he had just sliced from Bébé Coulibaly.

51

Two news flashes had been enough to bring a radical change to Monsieur Simon's life. The first was a report that combined a castration and a return to life mid-autopsy. The story in the newspaper was so incredible it amused him at first, but then he was intrigued to recognise the face of one of the people Camille had known: the black giant he had thought was an occasional acquaintance.

Three days later, while Monsieur Simon was trying hard to shave his wrinkled face without cutting himself too often, a small radio hanging from the handle of the bathroom door broadcast the early morning bulletin. He was only half listening until the presenter's voice informed him that "The mystery surrounding the identity of the man found burned to death in a villa in Pré-Saint-Gervais has finally been solved. Franck Samoy, a 31-year-old . . ."

The name stung him like an electric shock. His mind went into overdrive. Four decades spent in the same trade, paid to nose around and keep quiet, had endowed him with an ability to sniff a change in the wind. Since he was the one who had established it, he was well aware of the link between the shame-fully buried Camille, Franck Samoy and Bébé Coulibaly. The question he was now asking himself was whether this information put him in danger.

He was not a believer. The precepts of the holy book did not exactly coincide with the less rigorous ones of his profession, but he said to himself it might be time to leave and pay a visit to the city of his ancestors in the Middle East. And so he disappeared, for long enough to be forgotten.

PART FOUR

"A fine sight the two of us make, bound and gagged."
Marc Farel

52

For the pill to work more efficiently you were supposed to let it dissolve under the tongue, but Coste hated the taste and tried to disguise it with the sugary tang of orange juice. He had already taken half, and allowed himself the other half before going to bed. He needed a proper night's sleep, and if he could not manage it on his own, Lexomil would take care of it. Just before he went under, he mentally sifted through the case data, going over all the details, those already stored and the new ones he had yet to analyse. There were the two staged murders, and all those other forgotten deaths. There was his friend Mathias. There were the lies. There was the disappeared Soultier girl, whose face fitted only too well onto that of the young addict in the squat at Les Lilas. He would have to wait for the results of the exhumation and the D.N.A. test, because not until then could he trample in his muddy shoes on the velvet of the Soultier family's cushioned world.

A comical skeleton with syringes sticking out of its skull began dancing round him. Coste closed his eyes to pursue him in his dream.

The first loud bang jerked him upright in his bed. He sat in the darkness, ears pricked. Almost imperceptible murmurs. The second blow smashed down his front door. The wood splintered in the entrance, and one of the hinges pinged against the walls before crashing to the floor, spinning like a top a few seconds longer. A wave of black uniforms swept into his apartment. He was dragged out of bed, hands behind his back, head forced down. From behind his visor, one of the men yelled:

"Your gun! Where's your gun?"

Coste had always wondered what effect a six-in-the-morning raid with a battering ram would produce. Now he knew.

Seated on the edge of his living room sofa, hands still cuffed behind his back, dressed only in boxer shorts and a white T-shirt, Coste gave his colleagues time to complete their security search. Once all the rooms were declared clear, a man in plain clothes made his entrance. Coste recognised Dariush Abassian at first glance. He heard the sound of barking in the next room and turned towards the head of the I.G.S.

"The dog unit? Really, Abassian?"

The police dog unit in 93 has three functions: sniffing out explosives, maintaining law and order, and searching for drugs. Coste often used them, and with good reason. One of their Alsatians was enough to instil respect in a gang of ten threatening louts.

The dog handler, his animal pulling on its leash hard enough to choke itself, lowered his eyes in embarrassment and greeted Coste. The capitaine recognised Dominae, the Malinois cross who specialised in sniffing out drugs. Although Coste had no idea of the reasons behind this show of strength, he had enough experience to know it was best to wait to be spoken to rather than to try to understand, even if the contours of the trap were becoming clearer.

*

Coste had been waiting patiently in one of the cells of the I.G.S. at 30 rue Hénard in the XIIth for two hours. Judas had received thirty pieces of silver for betraying Christ, an invaluable mnemonic device to remember the exact address of the police's police.

The guard had brought him water and some biscuits, which he put to one side; his clenched stomach could not have digested anything. At some point in the morning he was taken to a room with beige walls and no decoration, unless the plant dying a death in one corner and a digital clock counted as decor. Abassian sat opposite him and asked for the handcuffs to be removed. On the desk in front of Coste he laid out a series of photographs showing him and Lieutenant Ronan Scaglia deep in conversation with Jordan Paulin. Abassian's voice was deep and soothing, in sharp contrast to the veiled accusations he was making.

"Three hundred grams of coke disappear from your offices . . ."

The arm wrestle between the two men had begun and Coste, still unsure just how deep was the tank of shit he found himself in, took a defensive stance.

"You're wasting your time, Abassian. I'm not in Groupes Stups."

"I know. As I was saying, three hundred grams of coke disappear from your offices, and a few hours later you're seen shooting the breeze with Monsieur Paulin alias Brahim, a small-time dealer about to move up a notch, in the heart of the Paul-Vaillant-Couturier estate with only two other policemen in attendance. Not much back-up for a spot like that, was it?"

"He has a direct link to one of my investigations. The file is on my desk. We can talk about it. Where did you get those photographs, Abassian?"

"We have our anonymous informers as well."

"When an officer gets shopped, it's usually by another one. All we were doing was talking. Listen, Lieutenant De Ritter took Paulin's statement yesterday. Get in touch with her, for Christ's sake. That's what you should have done before breaking down my door at six in the morning, isn't it?"

"That could be complicated, Coste. Last night wasn't gentle for everyone."

"Meaning?"

"I was coming to that."

53

Jordan Paulin's flat, 5 a.m. The ideal time. Any earlier, there was a risk of running into celebrating night owls; any later, the still sleepy passengers from the earliest trains and buses. Lucas placed the last dark red jar with the others in the fridge he had previously emptied. He left the door open so that the light from inside was the only illumination in the room. He was getting better at his staging: his search for perfection did not lie so much in the crime itself but in its presentation. His own personality had been swallowed up by the vengeance of which he was nothing more than a simple instrument. There was another man in Lucas now, a man he himself would not have recognised.

Removing the latex gloves, he inspected the apartment one last time, then walked over to the stereo equipment. He turned the volume up full blast, not caring about any fingerprints he might leave, and pressed play without checking either the title or the name of the band. "Voodoo People" by The Prodigy. It wouldn't have made much difference: he knew nothing about electronic music. Twelve seconds into the track, the sampled drums kicked in, making the latest-model sound system vibrate with the beat. Lucas walked out of the apartment leaving the front door wide open. The boom basses of the techno music flooded through the whole building, following him into the lift and still echoing as he left the front entrance to return to his rental car. By now he had got used to the smell of whisky and sweat, and he drove off slowly by the glow of the street lamps, his headlights off. Behind him, a series of lights began to come on around the window of the nightclub apartment.

The first neighbour who had ventured inside came out whey-faced. He ran up the stairs four at a time to call the emergency police number. A team appeared six minutes later, and the first uniform to enter Jordan Paulin's flat did not emerge looking any better. Calls to the criminal investigation unit at Bobigny police station, then to the duty magistrate. As a result, at exactly three minutes past six, Commandant M.C. Damiani of S.D.P.J. 93 groped for her mobile in the folds of her sheets. She in turn woke up Capitaine Lara Jevric of Groupe Crime 2, who sounded the alarm for her team and the forensic expert on duty. The chain of command was swiftly organised, but no more swiftly than that of the journalists, who greeted the police with a hail of flashbulbs. There were as many officers as report-ers milling about outside the building, as many patrol cars as outside broadcast vans with their parabolic disks deployed on their roofs.

Although Damiani did not look too bad, Lara Jevric had suffered from being woken up so rudely, and her face resem-bled a crumpled sheet stained with make-up, like a failed Picasso portrait.

"Commandant, I don't understand why it's not Coste and his team who . . ."

"He's busy elsewhere."

"But wait, from what I've heard, this is similar to the other murders, isn't it?"

Damiani did not hide her exasperation. She had been told the previous evening about the I.G.S's raid on Coste, and still refused to buy the idea that he could be mixed up in a sordid drugs affair. She believed it so little that she had preferred to let things run their course, waiting for the accusations to run out of steam in the first hours of the investigation. Before leaving home she had heard from her immediate superior, Commissaire Stévenin. Irritated by the idea of 93 being held hostage by a sicko with an outrageous imagination, he had ordered her to get in touch with Quai des Orfèvres with a view to handing everything over to them.

"Lara, sweetheart, everything will be alright. I'm going to bring in the Brigade criminelle. This investigation is getting out of hand, and Coste's shoulders aren't broad enough. So you and your team check the crime scene and wait to be relieved. You can do that, can't you?"

Jevric could not bear Coste. She hated his calmness. She was jealous of his team's respect for him, and the unruffled way in which he approached whatever case he was dealing with, whereas she broke into a sweat at every telephone call. And yet what she hated most of all was being taken for a fool, because despite herself she had to admit that, if anybody had shoulders broad enough for this kind of unholy mess, it was none other than Victor Coste.

"Good morning, capitaine."

Jevric turned and greeted Léa Marquant, who had also been roused in the small hours. Despite the cold, beneath her tight-fitting black woollen coat she had risked putting on a flimsy short skirt, chosen for what she thought was going to be her first meeting with Victor outside the mortuary. Jevric wondered yet again how these women managed to look as fresh as somebody who had slept all night, whereas the early morning dew insidiously rusted her heavy carcass. Even Léa's voice was clear and soft.

"I was expecting to find Coste," the pathologist said.

"Me too, I have to admit. And I'd have preferred it."

"One of your cars dropped me off here a quarter of an hour ago, but I still haven't had access to the crime scene."

"Follow me, I'll take you there. Keep your hands in your pockets – that way you won't touch anything."

The two women forced their way through the journalists, photographers and T.V. crews who immediately turned and bombarded them with a string of questions.

"Can you confirm there's been a murder? Is it linked to the previous ones? Who is the vampire? Can you confirm you're dealing with a serial killer?"

When they're called out to a case, the police never use the lift. Kids can deliberately block them, or they can break down of their own accord. Whatever the reason, it's always annoying to waste time or to call off an operation because you're too lazy to walk up three flights. So the police never take the lift – apart from Capitaine Jevric, that is. In the narrow, noisy cabin taking them to the fourteenth floor, Léa Marquant wanted to be sure of what she had heard.

"Did that journalist down there really use the word 'vampire'?"

"I'm afraid he did."

"Because?"

"Just be patient."

The fridge door had been left open. The pathologist was given permission to look inside, even to touch, provided she wore her gloves and her surgeon's mask so as not to spray the scene with D.N.A. whenever she said anything, and provided she put everything back. She wondered if she was the only one to find the array of glass jars filled with a red liquid on a cold white background very artistic. Behind his bushy beard, the head of forensics was staring at her, and nodded for her to pick one up.

"From the colour and consistency, I might be wrong but obviously I'd say it was blood."

As if she was an assistant counting the number of children on a school outing, she pointed to the jars and counted. Accustomed to all kinds of measurements, she muttered to herself:

"Two jars with seventy-five centilitres, three with fifty, and four with twenty-five. Exactly four litres. A body has five litres. Even if I count what little there might still be in the veins and organs, there's still a litre missing. Where's the body?"

The corridor leading on from the kitchen-diner was intermittently lit by a bright white light as one of the crime scene techs took photographs from every angle. Accompanied by Jevric, Léa Marquant followed the flashes leading her to the bathroom. Once again, the same combination of colours gave her a pleasant surprise. You needed to have seen your fill of shocking images to find room for aesthetic appreciation in this kind of situation. The white of the wall tiles and bathtub contrasting with the blood that had sketched gradually diminishing arabesques as the blood pressure dropped.

A violent blow had smashed the centre of the bathroom mirror. A splintered, tortured image of Léa Marquant's face was reflected in it. It occurred to her that the killer must have looked at himself in this same mirror a few hours earlier, and she felt closer to him. Almost too close.

"Sorry if I'm repeating myself, but where's the body?"

The man taking photographs pointed for her to carry on down to the end of the corridor. She walked a little further into the apartment, thinking of the *Divine Comedy*, the nine circles of Hell, and Dante's descent. "Abandon all hope, ye who enter here."

Paulin was lying in a room with blankets nailed over the windows, lit by a bare bulb in the ceiling. Stripped, his body livid, legs together and arms spread wide. Thrust deep into his chest at heart level, the broken handle of a black baseball bat. She was momentarily confused by the T.V. set on a rickety table at the foot of the bed spewing out psychedelic images from its smashed screen. The second reflective surface destroyed. The pathologist in Léa Marquant came to the fore.

"Not enough blood around the wound, especially at that level. The blow to the heart is plainly post-mortem."

Two perforations the size of a fork tine or a sharpened canine tooth were clearly visible on the side of the neck.

"Even if someone seems to want us to think so, the blood didn't come out of there either."

A red trail at groin level caught her eye. She pushed the flaccid thigh aside with her gloved hand.

"A long incision to the femoral artery. That's more like it. He must have been drained of blood in minutes – between four and seven. Skin colour pale, no sign of cyanosis."

The head of forensics had followed her into the room.

"The term you're bound to be looking for soon is hypovolemia or exsanguination."

"No, I was going to say vampirism like everybody else."

Still not recognised by the journalists, Marquant made her way through them and out of the building to find a quiet spot from where she could send her second message to Coste's mobile.

54

"That could be complicated, Coste. Last night wasn't gentle for everyone."

"Meaning?"

"I was coming to that. At half past five this morning, one of Jordan Paulin's neighbours found him dead, his body drained of blood. It had been transferred to glass jars and stored in the fridge. He has a wound in his groin, another to his heart, and two marks in his throat."

Four words danced before Coste's eyes. Zombie, spontaneous combustion, and vampire. A real video nasty. What was he doing here, held prisoner, unable to do anything? But he knew that lunatics who insist they're not mad tend to get a double dose of sedatives. There was no point him talking about a trap – Abassian had to come to that conclusion himself. He prayed the chief of the I.G.S. had his wits about him.

"What would you say about a witness who comes forward with the name of the culprit and his motives?"

Abassian was surprised Coste had decided to play the game. As if he was doing him a favour, he took him up on it.

"I think I'd be as interested in him as in the person he was accusing."

"Right. I don't like having answers handed to me on a plate either."

The office door opened and a uniform placed two coffees on the desk. Through the half-open door Coste could see a group of curious officers trying to look elsewhere and pretend they were not listening. He might not be the world's greatest policeman, but he had a good reputation in the force, and his arrest was definitely having an effect on morale in the police world.

"Do you have any sugar?"

"Sorry."

Coste was getting used to it. He drank a lukewarm mouthful of watery coffee. He said:

"First the theft from the evidence locker. Three hundred grams of coke is a worthwhile amount for selling on. Then I imagine you got an anonymous telephone call telling you to turn up at the right moment while I was talking to Paulin. Better still, and less tiring for you, you could have been sent the photographs."

Abassian did not react, inviting Coste to develop his theory.

"You organise this morning's little expedition. You bring in sniffer dogs, and at the very moment you're smashing down my door, Paulin is bleeding to death. Handcuffed, with ten officers in my apartment – that's not bad as an alibi, is it?"

"You could have delegated."

Coste guffawed. That was precisely the sort of argument he would have used if he'd been on the other side of the desk.

Despite being muffled by the walls between the two rooms, a distinctive loud voice could be heard.

"For fuck's sake, take these cuffs off, you arsehole. I'm a police officer the same as you."

Recognising the familiar voice, Coste said:

"I don't know who you've got in there with him, but let me give you a piece of advice: don't take the cuffs off Lieutenant Scaglia."

Abassian was beginning to get the bitter taste of having been manipulated. The officer sitting opposite him had an almost unblemished record, apart from one sanction for insubordination, which in itself was quite reassuring. Coste knew how to stand up for himself, and only policemen with no balls had spotless records. If he did not entirely trust the dog handlers to implicate an officer they respected, he could not seriously accuse the dogs of indulgence for not having found even a micro-gram of cocaine.

But above all there was that little man he had bumped into in the lift the previous day. Lucien Malbert. Him merely being in the vicinity made any conceivable dirty trick possible.

"So what? You were set up?"

"Don't you think so?"

"Who by?"

"I'm not going to be able to find that out with my arse stuck to this chair."

* * *

It took far more than that, however, to sway Abassian. One interview after another, the same questions repeated over and over. By early evening, Coste's arrest was lifted, and he was informed he had been suspended from duty. According to the I.G.S., this would give them time to separate true from false, and meanwhile he was to hand over his service firearm and police I.D., and was forbidden to make contact with the other members of his team or to go to his office until further notice.

He was free, but under surveillance.

55

Ronan took a cigarette out of the packet, lit it from the one he already had in his mouth, and handed it to Coste, who had emerged from the I.G.S. office more than fifteen minutes after him. In his cell Ronan had had time to think things over.

"I don't know who's fucked you, Coste, but you've caught a nasty S.T.I."

"I'm sorry, Ronan, you shouldn't be mixed up in this."

"Not mixed up in it? Go boil your head, capitaine. I'm your second-in-command, and even if that seemed to mean more to you when it was Mathias, I'm the one who guards your back now. I know you're keeping us out of this with good reason. If I'm not mistaken it's mainly to spare us getting caught up in a shitshow and, in a way I don't yet understand, to save Mathias's backside."

"Mathias?"

"Both Sam and I recognised that girl connected to Franck Samoy. She was the one in the Les Lilas town hall squat, and Mathias was in charge of that. I don't care if I'm investigating blindly – I trust you. Even in the fucking I.G.S. cells I trust you. But do you at least know what this is all about?"

A good question. Coste had thought he could keep the lid on Mathias's secrets, but now poison ivy seemed to be spreading everywhere.

Ronan had not quite finished.

"You know what I think? I think this business could blow up in our faces at any moment, and you want to be sure the team gets covered in as little shit as possible. Stupid self-sacrifice. Your own hara-kiri."

Coste threw away his cigarette and reached for another one from the packet hanging out of Ronan's leather jacket. He played for time.

"Well, anyway, we're on gardening leave now. Abassian told me that the Quai des Orfèvres is taking over everything, from the first murder to the last."

"So you can tell me what this is all about?"

"Give me a little more time. The time to understand how it all fits together."

A shiny black Mini Cooper slowed alongside them, almost invisible in the encroaching dusk. Léa Marquant sounded the horn.

They parked in the area reserved for taxis in front of the Bastille opera steps. Moments later, Coste, Ronan and Léa met Sam and De Ritter in the private room of a bar. Gathered in defiance of orders, they looked like a gang of bank robbers preparing a heist.

The bar manager plonked five glasses on the table, with a bottle of house alcohol that had no indication of strength or origin. Calling Sam by his first name, he asked if they wanted anything else, then left the room, pulling across the partition that shut them off from the rest of the bar.

Léa Marquant had sat down next to Coste. She fished a bundle of papers out of her holdall.

"Copy of the autopsy report on Jordan Paulin," she said, addressing Coste.

He flicked through the pages. The pathologist gave him a lightning summary.

"Complete exsanguination. All his blood was found in glass jars in the fridge. If you're a literature lover, it was done by a vampire. As far as forensic medicine is concerned, the blood was drained as a result of his femoral artery being severed. If you'll allow me to play detective, the care taken to stage all this corresponds perfectly to the other two murders."

De Ritter could scarcely contain her impatience.

"So is nobody bothered about why these two were banged up by the I.G.S.?"

Coste had not been sure she would come. Her probation period had hardly been uneventful. But by defying orders like the others that evening, she was claiming her right to be part of the team, and to a minimum of explanations.

"They made a hasty connection between the theft from Groupe Stups' evidence locker and our visit to Jordan Paulin. That's all there is to it. Besides, we're out now, aren't we?"

"Do you think I'm an idiot? We're forbidden to talk to one another, we can't even go into your office, we have to meet in this stinking hole. You call that nothing?"

Coste hesitated. He was touched by each of them being there, but felt guilty at the mere thought of dragging them down with him.

"I'm going to take a few days' holiday. Sam, there's one last thing you can do for me. I need the number of Farel, that journalist who tipped us off about the anonymous caller."

De Ritter scornfully puffed out her cheeks.

"Sounds like a great holiday."

He let the jibe go.

"From now on, no contact, no calls. We follow the rules."

All five picked up their glasses in unison and downed them

in one, each of them grimacing in their own way. Without bothering to be discreet, Marquant took hold of Coste's hand under the table and squeezed it gently.

He had agreed to accept a lift home, and was surprised to see Léa take the correct route without any help from him.

"You know where I live?"

"If you look at your mobile, you'll see I've been harassing you quite a bit in the past few hours. I also took the liberty of looking up the number of your landline."

"I'm not listed anymore."

She contradicted him in a whisper.

"Yes you are. Under the name of Monsieur Coste and Mademoiselle Melvine."

Coste took it on the chin.

"It's . . ."

"I know who Mademoiselle Melvine is, Victor. I know what she meant to you. I can also guess you feel responsible. So much so you're convinced you have to be there for all those you care about – Mathias, your team – whatever the risks, taking it all on to your own shoulders. So much so that you no longer dare get involved. So much so that you can't look me in the eye."

Coste's rather too open expression meant he was far from being a closed book for anyone interested; but from that to being so accurately described in a few sentences left him speechless. He knew his weakness was the Other. To hear it said was another matter.

Marquant pulled into a space below his apartment. Even after she had switched off the engine, Coste did not move. A fine rain beaded the windows, then the raindrops collected and trickled down the glass. The car interior looked like a city melting in the dark. In what might have been an awkward silence, her heart began to beat furiously. She could feel the blood pounding at her temples, and a gentle warmth spread through her stomach. If he had not kissed her in three seconds, she would make the first move.

Focused on something else entirely, Coste did not give her even that long. Catching her unawares, he thanked her, jumped out of the car, and disappeared into the rain.

Prat. She swore she would never again give him three seconds, and cursed him all the way home.

After a shower, Coste's mind was slightly clearer. He switched on his mobile. The last text message was from Sam, with Farel's details.

"In an hour?" Coste suggested to the journalist.

Farel did not sound very surprised.

"O.K., at ten. Café de la Musique, in the XIXth. Would that suit you? I've got a few demons to exorcise down there."

Coste needed to talk to someone who could offer him a fresh perspective. The journo had investigated Code 93, he had been in touch with Mathias, and yet had done nothing with his information. He was hoping Farel could blow away the fog that was clouding his brain.

56

The two men both arrived twenty minutes early for their rendezvous at the back table hidden behind the grand piano.

"You've got a policeman's habits, Farel."

"Always arrive early so you can check out the place and the people. Spot the different exits. Choose a table at the rear, and always face the entrance, never have your back to it."

"That's what we're taught."

The waiter took their orders and left them to it. Coste had no intention of staying there forever.

"I'll tell you what I know, and you try to fill in the gaps. Deal?"

"It sounds like what every journalist dreams of hearing. I couldn't ask for more."

Coste took a deep breath, as if he had to tell the whole story in one go.

"A week ago, I received an anonymous letter pointing me towards a case from almost a year earlier. A junkie found dead in a squat at the Les Lilas town hall. That same morning, I recovered the cadaver of Bébé Coulibaly in the disused warehouses out at Pantin."

"From what I've heard, he wasn't a cadaver for long."

"That's true, but it's not what's important. The next day, we discovered Franck Samoy burned to a crisp in an empty villa in Pré-Saint-Germain. At the same time, I got a second anonymous letter. This time it was about the murder of a Romanian whore found choked to death in her caravan, a rag stuffed down her throat. The two missives referred to two cases that Lieutenant Aubin had been investigating."

Coste paused, then repeated:

"Lieutenant Aubin?"

"Yes, I heard. I've met him."

"I know. He's since been transferred. So I went to see him in Annecy, and it was from him that I heard for the first time about Code 93. A statistical dodge to conceal murders of so-called socially unimportant people, the 'invisibles', simply to lower the crime rate in 93."

Farel checked that the RECORD button of the recorder in his inside pocket was pressed down.

"As easily as that? I mean, to make bodies disappear . . . ?"

"It's all bureaucratic, Farel. Lieutenant Aubin isn't so deranged he would bury stiffs for pleasure. He's nothing more than the head of a family caught by the throat."

"And that's an excuse for everything?"

Farel's remark hit home.

"Are you judging or listening?"

"The two go together."

Coste sighed, but he had no choice other than to continue, and he had no-one else to talk to.

"Subsequently we investigated Franck Samoy and found he operated round the Paul-Vaillant-Couturier estate in Bobigny. A local dealer, Jordan Paulin, recognised a photograph of him, and put us on the trail of his girlfriend, whom he identified as Camille Soultier. Wrongly, according to her family, because two months earlier neither her brother nor her adoptive mother, Margaux Soultier, had identified her in the mortuary. To complete the set, yesterday, at about five in the morning, Paulin was having the blood sucked out of him like a Transylvanian virgin. That's as far as I've got."

Coste tapped three times on the black wooden table.

"If you're going to record me, put your damned machine on the table!"

Embarrassed, Farel did as he was asked, then said:

"You've been very indiscreet about an ongoing investigation, capitaine. You give the impression of being a lone wolf who no longer knows how to get out of the hornets' nest he's blundered into. You even seem to have put yourself in danger, if we include your lightning visit to the I.G.S's cells."

"You heard about that?"

"I'd be a poor crime reporter if I missed out on info like that. I have ears in all your services, Coste."

The liquid in their glasses hadn't gone down so much as a centilitre, and the disappointed waiter turned on his heel before he had even got to them. Farel laid both hands flat on the table, fingers together, and kept his side of the bargain.

"I'm sorry for using the cliché of anonymous letters."

"I'm grateful to put a face to the person responsible."

Farel had thought this would take the policeman by surprise, but after the week Coste had been through, it would have taken more than that to shake him.

"I could have used e-mail, but there's no such thing as an anonymous e-mail – they're far too easy to trace. You were meant to uncover Lieutenant Aubin's involvement yourself. According to my information, you and he have been on the beat in 93 for ten long years; if I had turned up with my doubts and queries you'd have sent me packing."

"Probably, but you've begun at the end."

"I know. The best thing would be if you agreed to continue this discussion at my place. I have something to show you."

57

Shortly before midnight, Farel unlocked the third lock on his newly reinforced front door. As though justifying such elaborate precautions, he explained:

"Burglary, a few days ago."

He switched on the lights, threw his coat onto the white sofa in the living room, and took a bottle of whisky out of a cupboard.

"Care for a drink?"

The invitation did not reach Coste. He was standing, coat still on, facing the apartment's north wall. It was entirely covered with pinned up, scrawled on, encircled, scratched out newspaper cuttings. Added to them were photographs, pages torn out of magazines, scribbled Post-its, names and places – a mass of information linked together in a complicated spider's web.

"You worry me, Farel. It's almost an obsession."

"That's the price you pay for getting close to the truth."

Farel recorked the bottle and handed him a glass. Coste grimaced as he downed a mouthful: he did not like whisky. He turned towards Farel: his turn to confess.

"Did Lieutenant Aubin explain why Code 93 was created?" the journalist said.

"Vaguely. As far as he could tell, the aim was to artificially lower the crime figures, but to me that seems a lot of effort just to manipulate the statistics."

"Good, you're a real policeman, Coste. Trained to listen to your hierarchy without making any real attempt to understand. The opposite of a journalist, who thinks that every word he hears is a lie. Good little soldiers, putting their faith in institutions, the police, justice, government, when they're the first to bamboozle you, toy with you, and adulterate your figures."

"Figures are nothing more than an indication. Asking for a figure is simply to evaluate a task. The answer will vary according to the person you're asking. If you ask the person who did the work, it will be pushed higher. If you ask his critics, it will be lower. To rely on figures is to be certain you're going to get distorted information. Figures are only a bit of glitter to make things look pretty at the end of empty reports."

"You're wrong, Coste. Figures are everything, for precisely that reason. It's because they can be made to say anything that they are used so much. Especially those relating to delinquency and criminality, the consequences of which have repercussions at many, many levels. That's where you need the piece of the puzzle you and Lieutenant Aubin didn't have. The Greater Paris project."

"What on earth's that got to do with it?"

"Paris has been suffocating for the past twenty years. The project is to enlarge it by absorbing the immediate surrounding *départements*: 92 Hauts-de-Seine, 93 Seine-Saint-Denis, and 94 Val-de-Marne. They will create Greater Paris. The biggest property deal since Haussmann in the nineteenth century, maybe the biggest in the whole of French history. The promise of fabulous investments. An unequalled megalopolis, the breadbasket of France and virgin territory for the most audacious projects. Not to mention the necessary creation of a vast transport network, a new road infrastructure and the tens of thousands of jobs that go with it, plus the effect it would have on financial markets and stock exchanges. I've given up trying to calculate the precise value of such a project, because the amount is almost inconceivable. If you only take into account the construction of new métro and tram lines, the sum of thirty-five billion euros has been mentioned. The rest would be in the hundreds of billions. In this charming prospect, the only blot on the landscape is 93. The murder rate there is three times higher than the national average. So if you have a company, where would you choose to put it?"

"Certainly not in Seine-Saint-Denis."

"That's the problem. Because, looking at the map, your marvellous *département* ought to be part of the Greater Paris scheme, but if the crime rate isn't fixed, nobody will want to run the risk of investing there. Result: a flow of money to places all around 93, but you won't see a penny of it. An excluded region, already steeped in violence, one that will become an enclave of poverty and inequality. All of it sitting on a powder keg."

Coste had no trouble imagining it.

"We wouldn't have to wait long for the first riots."

"That and the proliferation of an underground economy. The creation of a lawless zone the size of a *département*. That idea is unthinkable to the government. Still less to the mayors, prefects, your police chief, even your commander. All their careers are at stake. Lots of bodies are going to have to be swept under the carpet if investors are to be persuaded to make Seine-Saint-Denis their new El Dorado rather than 92 and 94."

"So the political aim is to present 93 as the perfect son-in-law?"

"One can always try to sell a derelict house if the facade

looks good. Don't tell me you're surprised. Unless you are too blinkered."

Coste was following the argument in the somewhat old-fashioned position of the innocent bystander. It seemed as if the journalist could not stop.

"When certain mayors in 93 want to make sure they're re-elected, what do they do? They pay. A lot even. They shower the gang leaders on the estates with money so they stay calm for the months leading up to the vote, so that delinquency goes down artificially and they make the voters believe they're ruling their districts with an iron fist."

"I've heard the rumours."

"I've heard it, you've heard it, and so have many others. I don't believe there's any smoke without fire."

Coste resigned himself to gulping down the rest of his drink while the journalist sailed blithely on.

"Let's look a bit closer. Imagine a new shopping mall is opened. Good for the district, good for the firms who build it, and the hundreds of jobs that go with it, not to mention the backhanders for those who help promote the project. The only stumbling block is that a shopping mall in 93 is a honey pot placed right beneath a swarm of wasps. The kids and their big brothers gather there in gangs of thirty, mug the little old ladies doing their shopping and, depending on their financial needs, hold up the stores. No brand would agree to open the smallest outlet without the guarantee of a minimum of calm and public order. In cases like that, nothing easier than to falsify reality. The entrepreneur creates a budget line called 'Aid for Cultural Promotion' or 'Association for the Development of the Suburbs', anything to give the impression of a show of solidarity in daily life in the area. The local mayor is left to decide how these funds are to be used. Once again, the mayors shower money on the very same people responsible for the crimes and lack of security, in return for relative calm while the scheme is being implemented."

"What's the connection?"

"If we're already talking about fictitious budget lines, corruption and greasing of palms when it comes to nothing more than the opening of a shopping mall or re-election, imagine what can happen when it's a question of expanding Paris to three of the most densely populated *départements* in France. The project is going to generate vast profits, but your crime rate is the piece of grit that could make the whole machine seize up. As we've seen, gang leaders and their followers can be bought off, but it's more difficult with murderers. When the Greater Paris scheme saw the light of day, everyone knew it was unthinkable to clean up Seine-Saint-Denis within the projected time frame. It was predictable that one way or another you would need to make the greatest possible number of homicides disappear. Hence the choice of the 'invisibles'. Unfortunately, among them you buried Camille Soultier. No-one gives a damn about Camille, it's the name 'Soultier' that's the problem."

"But the identification of the body was negative! At least, that's what old Margaux Soultier is still insisting."

"I know you yourself don't believe it, Coste."

"It's not what I believe that matters, it's what I can explain. Lucas took upon himself the role of elder brother so enthusiastically that he was stifling Camille. According to what his mother let slip, his love for her bordered on the incestuous. I can't see him turning on his heel in the mortuary and abandoning the person he regarded as his sister, letting her rot in the cheapest available coffin, just to salvage the family's honour."

"And yet Lucas contacted Monsieur Simon to ask him to focus investigation on nobody else but that unidentified girl.

268

And it's that same girl's file that has disappeared from your archives. I personally thought that had far too bitter a taste to swallow without asking questions. I followed up the old private eye's suspicions and started to scour the newspapers and check on the deaths of persons who wouldn't make a big splash. Your 'invisibles'."

"Your lovely wall."

"Thanks. Any suspicious death in Seine-Saint-Denis ends up with one of the two Groupes Crime in S.D.P.J. 93: yours or Capitaine Jevric's. That's the usual procedure. Thanks to my contacts I followed each of those investigations and discovered that seventeen of them had disappeared from your records. It was as if those dead people had never existed. Those are the news items I've highlighted on the wall. I gathered my suspicions and went to see Lieutenant Aubin. I didn't have to pressure him very hard: I can recognise souls eaten away by remorse. A few hours later, going beyond my wildest dreams, he turned up with a box containing twenty-three cases he had carefully made vanish. I had to promise to do all I could to avoid implicating him. Him and his team, he insisted."

Coste tried to imagine his friend's double life, his daily dose of lies and secrets. Farel went on:

"It was at that point that I committed a novice's mistake. I called Soultier. Since I had the files in my possession, all I needed was his evidence, so I went in headlong. I'm not proud of it, but I lured him with the story of the suppressed deaths, and my conviction that Camille could be one of them. We arranged to meet and—"

"And while you were waiting for a guest who never showed up, you were robbed."

"That's roughly it. I got my nose busted as well, but that's neither here nor there. As I told you, a beginner's error."

"Wait a minute . . . that means . . . well, if you're correct, Lucas Soultier ended up with a copy of Camille's autopsy report? Shit! Have you read it?"

"Yes. I don't know if the medical terms soften the facts, but they're all there and in enough detail to make unbearable reading. And shortly afterwards, we have your incredible deaths: Coulibaly, Samoy and Paulin."

"Three men who in one way or another destroyed Camille."

Coste was knocked sideways. He stretched out his arm and, without asking, downed the drink Farel was offering. The journalist hammered home his conclusion:

"In getting rid of cadavers, you've woken a monster."

"At least you've got your headline, even if it's an article you'll never be able to publish. You've no real proof, no incriminating photograph, no compromising tape. You've had the files stolen, so all you have is what's pinned to your wall. You'll agree that it's not enough to bring down anyone, and the people we've been talking about aren't just anyone. At the end of the day, you're empty-handed."

"And you have a case that's been taken from you and handed over to Paris. A fine sight the two of us make, bound and gagged. What are you going to do? Turn up at the Quai des Orfèvres and ask for an audience? Tell them Aubin is a bad apple, that you've known it from the first murder, which means you too could be regarded as a bad apple, and sink your little team while you're at it?"

"I think we've left personal considerations behind a long time ago. That's not what worries me. Seeing the ramifications of this mess, I wonder if the Soultier kid will even reach court."

"You mean alive?"

"I don't know. Maybe I'm going too far."

Farel gave a mocking laugh that startled Coste. He stared blankly at the journalist.

"Yet again, Coste, you're showing that you're a born policeman, trusting your superiors and trained to believe this sort of depravity exists only in film scripts. In politics, you should start from the principle that there are no dirty tricks you can think of that haven't already been tried. Not one. Getting rid of a few dead bodies to help the creation of Greater Paris makes your Code 93 no more ambitious than a vulgar property deal. Even if it's an unprecedented one. But France cannot permit this kind of accusation. If we had more time, I'd tell you about all those people who had the good idea to die before opening their mouths, so for you to think that it's possible Lucas might not face trial is far from being a fantasy."

He stood up and turned to the wall where he had projected the contents of his mind.

"You're suspended, Coste. You've no team and no weapon, yet you're the only one who can see this through. Bring me Lucas Soultier, let him tell me his story before he tells it somewhere else. It's surely his only chance of being understood. If he agrees to talk to us, that is."

"Talk to us? He's been doing nothing else from the start. All these performances are meant for us. We try to hide dead bodies, and he offers us sensational new ones. He brings in the press, and makes it look as if we're halfwits. What he wants most of all is to talk!"

An incoming message on Farel's mobile made the glasses on the table tremble. He read the text slowly, while Coste sat at the far end of the sofa, lost in thought.

"I don't know if this is connected, but just now you mentioned the Paul-Vaillant-Couturier estate in Bobigny, didn't you?"

"Yes, it's at the centre of my investigation. It's what links Camille, Franck, Bébé and Jordan Paulin."

Farel couldn't take his eyes off the screen. Coste said:

"Another murder?"

The journalist tossed him his mobile.

"No. A massacre."

58

While Coste and Farel's deductions were bringing them closer and closer to Lucas, he had forged ahead and carried out the mission he had set himself. Exhausted and yet so wide awake. There was only one thing left for him to do, and that was the only thing sustaining him. He told himself he had to keep going a little while longer.

The black limousine purred across Paris, then took the Périphérique. His nervousness transmitted itself to the invitation card: his fingers folded it ten times in one direction, then ten times in the other, until it looked like an attempt at origami. He recognised the two canvas bags on the seat beside him. The driver began his rigmarole.

"Empty your pockets. Mobile, wallet, I.D. papers, credit cards."

Lucas replied in a flat, almost robotic voice.

"All I have with me is my invitation."

Reassured he had an experienced client on board, the driver was grateful he would not have to make conversation, and the rest of the journey took place in silence. The car came to a halt in an unlit car park at the foot of some tower blocks whose summits were lost in a thick fog. The club's organisers had recently realised that, however prestigious, hotels were too busy, with too much C.C.T.V. More than a year ago it had relocated to isolated private houses or apartments where there were no prying eyes.

"If Monsieur was used to the previous house, he needs to know the rules have been adapted to this new address."

"Which means?"

"Block F. The ground floor door is open: then the tenth floor. You shouldn't run into anyone at this time of night, but for safety's sake only put on your mask when you knock at the door of apartment 106. All the other instructions remain the same."

In the lift tagged with insults and threats, Lucas checked his weapon. The lift slowed between floors eight and nine, then the lights dimmed until it was completely dark. At the tenth, the doors opened onto total darkness. Lucas stepped out, black mask over his face, weapon in hand. Within a minute and thirty-seven seconds, he would have gunned down six people.

A few metres away, as a conscientious master of ceremonies, the man in the white mask was worried about what was happening to the girl who had been howling for a quarter of an hour or more in the back room. Mistreatment was tolerated, as it might be part of some members' requests. The goods could even be damaged, but it was strictly forbidden to smash them. This had happened once, and the consequences had all but ruined the club. Despite the size of the apartment, that bitch's moans had dampened the atmosphere, and her colleagues were spending more time looking quizzically at one another than busying themselves with the other three guests. He turned the music up and placed a metal box containing ten grams of cocaine on the living room coffee table. That should get the evening going again. Absorbed by his concerns, Monsieur Loyal did not hear the three short knocks on the front door, so he was surprised to see the bouncer backing into the room, his immense silhouette concealing the man who had thrust a gun down his throat.

A deafening roar, and the back of the man's skull lifted like a trapdoor, creating for a second the subliminal image of part of his brain. A splash of red appeared on the white mask. It was only when the bouncer collapsed to the floor that Lucas appeared. His knuckles white as he clutched his weapon, he fired another round into the organiser's throat. The man fell to his knees and groaned in a gurgle of choking blood. He vomited a spray of scarlet and slumped onto his back in a surprising limbo-dancer pose.

The sirens of the three terrified girls raised the alarm in unison. Two of the masked men cowering on the sofa managed without conferring to adopt the same courageous attitude and use their companions as shields. The third man, on his feet and not very sure of having properly understood the eight seconds that had just passed, still had a champagne glass in his hand. The round from the Luger Po8 smashed the side of the glass, turned less than once on itself in the champagne, destroyed the far side of the glass and ended its trajectory in a heart that pulsed ever more slowly, until the beats stopped altogether.

In the back room, another man was trying ridiculously to hide under a duvet after realising that this tenth floor apartment had no emergency exit. He had clearly recognised the pistol's three reports. Two more, one after the other, sealed the fate of the two remaining guests in the living room. Lucas kicked open the door. Another Camille was huddled in a corner. Terrified, one eye blackened, a swollen lip. She was trying to pull up her bloodstained pants. Urine trickled down her thighs. When she understood that the intruder was not going to shoot her, she glanced accusingly at the rolled-up writhing duvet. Lucas pointed his gun in that direction, determined to fire his last salvo. Moaning something her wounded mouth made unintelligible, the girl crawled on all fours like a wounded animal towards Lucas. Blood dripped from her lips. Clutching his trouser leg, she hauled herself up on unsteady legs. She laid her hand on Lucas's outstretched arm, moved down to his wrist, and took the firearm. He let her do it. She could be the one to kill me, he told himself. He would have liked that. She fired the gun at the bed until the clip was empty, only stopping when a metallic click told her she could do no more harm. The duvet rippled, decorated with little cottony holes, then stopped moving. The girl handed him back the pistol. Lucas ejected the clip and fitted a new one. He went over and raised the duvet. Underneath, a naked man with his bloody hand clamped across his mouth, trying not to give voice to his pain, stared at him with the glassy, horrified look of cattle in an abattoir. Lucas shot at each eye from point blank range, then threw the duvet over him again. He slipped his arm under the girl's and they walked together down the corridor back to the living room. He laid her on the long sofa in the now empty room – empty that is apart from the five bodies strewn around the floor. Searching among what was left of the man in the white mask, he found in his back pocket the only authorised mobile. Then he went to crouch down on his knees in front of the girl. He took her hands in his.

"In a minute's time you must call the police. Could you do that for me, please?"

She said nothing, but turned to him and rested her head on his shoulder. In the one minute thirty-seven seconds the attack had lasted, this for Lucas was the longest moment. The moment when, eyes closed, the warmth of a battered face pressed against

276

him, he allowed himself a respite with this other Camille. He burst into tears. She stroked the nape of his neck, and as she whispered "shhh", her breath penetrated all the way through to his lost soul.

* * *

Opening the front door of the limousine, he leaned inside, undid the seat belt, and tugged the chauffeur by his hair. The man's body slumped out onto the cold tarmac. Lucas took his place behind the wheel, started the ignition, engaged first gear. After a few metres, the absurd thought came to him that the rental car had been more responsive than this one. He switched on the headlights and accelerated. In half an hour he would be back home.

59

In the taxi, Coste went over his last exchange with Farel. Aware that in his profession he could not miss a scoop by being caught in a traffic jam, Farel didn't bother with a car. Naturally he had offered Coste a ride on his scooter. Perhaps Coste was getting a taste for theatrical effects, because he had declined the offer. He could not see himself arriving at the Soultier mansion on the back of a noisy, backfiring Mobylette. Wearing a helmet and as vulnerable as a rabbit crossing the road, he would not be able to let his mind play freely with the facts, shifting around the pieces of information and trying to fit them together. Nor would he have noticed the vehicle following them, a sort of shapeless station wagon that looked more like a barge than an automobile.

He had read several times the message that had appeared on Farel's mobile. Enough to drive newsrooms wild and send a phalanx of journalists to the address it gave. It had taken him back several days to when he had been with Mathias on the Paul-Vaillant-Couturier estate, more precisely in the immaculate tenth-floor show apartment. That was when he had made a prediction he now wished had not been so accurate.

"You do realise this is going to be one of the most fucked-up cases I've ever had to deal with?" Coste had said. If his friend had foreseen the consequences, would he have talked to him?

Would he have revealed the secret that was rotting inside him, and which occasionally meant he could not look Coste in the eye?

Before Coste left, Farel had gleaned some information and had concluded that, despite it being the same geographical location, the M.O. was incompatible with Lucas Soultier's.

"There's already quite a crowd there. As many journalists as police. Six confirmed corpses, plus one guy dead in the car park of F block on the Paul-Vaillant-Couturier estate, though there's no confirmation he's linked to the others. All shot with a handgun, make as yet undetermined. Victims men in their fifties. All wearing carnival masks, four of them found in their underwear."

Farel saw this as suggesting it had been a gay encounter, and the murderer a homophobe, but Coste was not at all convinced.

"No, I'm sure there were girls there, hostesses, but for some reason they were spared. Have the victims been identified?"

"No documents found on the bodies apart from four invitations for this evening in four different jackets. Doubtless invitations for tonight's little orgy. No theatrics, straightforward executions. You know that the people who take part in this kind of thing are rarely low-grade officials. If, as you seem to think, it's the work of Soultier, I can assure you it's going to be far from easy to get him to face trial without any hitches."

"Maybe we're wrong, and he's not aiming that high. Maybe we've just witnessed the end of it."

There was still one murky area that Farel could not explain to himself.

"Tell me, from what we know of Lucas, his three killings were carried out for revenge. What's his link with this libertine club?"

The link between an orgy and a young girl selling her body for shit? It seemed obvious to Coste.

A few hundred metres before they plunged onto the Périphérique, he addressed the taxi driver.

"I need you to do something for me."

Accustomed to strange requests from night-time customers, the driver did not mince his words.

"I drive, and that's it."

Coste skipped the pleasantries.

"I'll try again. Capitaine Coste, police detective. I really need you to do something for me."

"Can I see your I.D.?"

It's with my service revolver, probably still in the I.G.S. office, thought Coste. He placed a fifty-euro note on the front passenger seat.

"O.K., I'm not with the police. I just need to know if someone's following us."

"The Twingo right behind?"

"No, two cars further back."

"The Volvo then?"

"Probably. I know nothing about cars. Listen, you're going to jump the next red light, O.K.? Then we can see how he reacts."

"For fifty euros? Dream on. I'm not going to lose my licence for your skirt-chasing."

Just Coste's luck. Running into the only straight taxi driver in Paris. He rummaged in his wallet without success.

"Alright, alright, so at the next roundabout on the Périphérique, pretend you're taking the last exit, but go round a second time. If the car follows us, either they're lost or they're tailing us."

The driver took his eyes off the road and turned to look at Coste.

"Are you sure you're not police?"

"That's what I've been dying to tell you."

When they reached the roundabout for the Les Lilas exit, the taxi began its first circle, the indicator down to the left. At the last exit, the driver slowed a little, then, as the station wagon came up behind them, speeded up and went round a second time. In the rear-view mirror, the Volvo left the roundabout abruptly, and headed down the slip road. The taxi driver could not help crowing:

"Little bit paranoid, are we?"

"Possibly. Take the Périphérique to the Saint-Cloud exit. Thanks."

Feeling calmer, Coste allowed himself to be hypnotised by the regular glow from the street lights, which flashed by like kindly Cyclopses watching over his nocturnal race. He thought of Franck Samoy, the official boyfriend, not too jealous when it came to sharing his girl for a supply of crack cocaine. Jordan Paulin, one of the first to profit from this trade-off. And Bébé Coulibaly, who had recruited and groomed Camille, probably in storage unit no. 55, before taking her up just a few floors for more organised evening entertainment.

After that, and taking into account the autopsy report, she must have stumbled on the wrong client. Maybe even several of them. But something else entirely was troubling Coste. There were only ten floors between the storage unit and the show apartment. Ten floors between the love nest and the orgy. Given the discretion needed to set up the latter, two things puzzled him. How did Lucas Soultier know the date, and how did he get hold of the address?

As they were coming to the front gates of the Soultier mansion, he wondered whether at the start of his mission Lucas had grasped just how huge a task he was setting himself. There were those who had led Camille into the abyss. Those who had abused her when she had hit rock bottom. And those who had buried her in secret. It was as if one morning all the evil-doers in the world had got together and decided to annihilate her.

"Stop here. I'll walk the rest of the way."

60

As he strolled up the hundred or so metres of the carefully tended drive to the mansion, Coste allowed himself a cigarette. Walking almost blind in the darkness, he was guided by lights in the building still on late into the night. He arrived at the front steps, skirting a black limousine that had one front door open. Climbing the four steps, he dropped his hand to his right hip. It would take him more than a few hours to get used to not having a gun.

The door was ajar. Vestibule and corridors empty in front of him, although all the lights were on. Coste tried in vain to remember the layout of the house.

"Good evening, Monsieur Coste."

Taken by surprise, he repeated the same pointless gesture towards his missing gun. The familiarity of the face greeting him did nothing to reassure him.

"Good evening, Brice."

He stared at him, wondering how far he could trust the loyal family servant. Still a few metres away, Coste raised his hand, fingers spread, to show he did not want trouble.

"Don't run off or shout. Just tell me calmly, where is Lucas?"

"If sir would care to follow me."

A police interview involving the upper classes was very different from what Coste was used to.

After several twists and turns on thick carpeting, he was invited into the morning room, which was also adorned with heavy ornaments and ancient paintings. If he had relied on his own navigational skills, Coste would have set off in the opposite direction, and ended up in the French garden.

"Good evening, capitaine."

From the back he recognised Margaux Soultier's silver locks. She swiftly turned her wheelchair and faced him with a smile.

"Isn't it rather late for a courtesy visit?"

"Let's say then that there's nothing courteous about it."

He paused, unsure how to explain his presence. Above all, uncertain of the old lady's reaction.

"I'd like to talk to Lucas."

"Please, sit with me."

"Madame, I'm afraid the situation won't allow me to . . ."

The barrel of a handgun gave the back of his neck an icy kiss. Brice repeated the invitation, and this time Coste could find no reason to refuse. His back was covered with a thin film of sweat. He gazed at the mistress of the house with what he hoped was his calmest expression.

"I'm astonished, capitaine. By your self-assurance, your composure. Others would have been pleading with me by now."

"What do you want me to say that you don't already know? That I'm not alone, that I've alerted my team? Or should I remind you that killing a policeman is never a good idea?"

"You have nothing to fear, my dear. Firstly, because I think highly of you. And secondly, because all I'm asking is for you to sit with me for a few minutes."

She looked up at Brice standing behind Coste. He shook his head.

"And thirdly, because you're not even armed. Is that your method in Seine-Saint-Denis, arresting criminals empty-handed?'

"A criminal? Do you know something I don't?"

"There's nothing you don't know, my child," she said with a hint of irony, tapping his hand. "You're a policeman and have, what do they call it? A nose for things. And I'm a mother, despite what my children may say, and my nose is as sharp as yours."

"Meaning?"

"I lost Lucas a long time ago. First of all when his brother left, and again when Camille disappeared. I had already lost so much by then that my heart refused to suffer any further."

As the memories flooded back, it began to sound as if she were telling a story.

"And yet there's no doubt I did have a heart once. I loved my husband without wavering, utterly, so deeply I couldn't bear to see him eaten away by cancer. To hear him suffering and moaning all night long as if he were haunting the manor house while he was still alive. So I made up my mind to help him. It was out of love that I helped him go. I thought my eldest son Gaël would understand my actions, even agree with them, and face mourning alongside me, but I was wrong. He saw me as entirely responsible for his father's death, as though the cancer had nothing to do with it. Gaël could not bear to live here any longer, and ran away promising two things. That he would forget me forever, and that he wouldn't say a word to his little brother. That favour obviously wasn't for me, but for Lucas. And so I became this old lady you see before you now, shrivelled in this chair, robbed of my autonomy in a house where there is nothing but stairs and gardens. That doesn't mean I have become blind, however."

With a trembling hand she reached across the table to grasp the handle of the porcelain teapot. A wisp of steam rose from the spout. Around the teapot Coste noticed a pillbox, several ripped-open medicine boxes, and two empty blister packs.

"Some tea, capitaine?" she said, filling his cup.

In spite of the gun still pressing against the back of his head, he dared to refuse.

"I prefer coffee, with sugar rather than sleeping pills."

Unexpectedly, Margaux Soultier burst out laughing, enjoying his riposte.

"Don't be afraid, you can drink it."

Raising the cup to his lips, Coste drank a mouthful of scalding tea.

"You see, it hasn't knocked you out, has it? Where was I?"

He forced himself to swallow before replying.

"You were telling me certain things failed to escape you."

"That's right. Oh, I don't think he ever tried to be discreet either. Even though my personal pharmacy is as well stocked as that of any psychiatric hospital, I couldn't help but be aware of his regular visits to it. There was also the disappearance of a collector's weapon, a German pistol whose name I can never remember."

"The one pressed against my head?"

"Exactly. You really are a splendid fellow. Brice, would you mind?"

Taken aback at first by this polite order, the butler obeyed and showed Coste the gun.

"A Luger P08," the policeman said before it was returned to its original position.

"Yes, that name means something to me. You're a true professional as well, my dear friend. What a shame about all this ..."

She invited him to drink some more tea before continuing.

"So I was concerned by these infrequent but worrying events. I then learned from friends of my deceased husband still in post in various ministries about Lucas's prolonged and remarked absence from his office. Just think, he hasn't been ⹂ the Ministère des Finances in more than a month. When he began to take our old Land Rover from the garage, and when the keys to our country house disappeared, it seemed very clear to me that Lucas was up to something. The newspapers provided the rest."

"And you did nothing?"

"Simon Beckriche, the private detective whose services we used, had disappeared. What was I supposed to do? Stand up to my son on these glass legs of mine? Ask Brice to shut him in the attic? Call the police? For the sake of the family I left my adoptive daughter in a hole without . . . without a name, in fact. Did you think I was going to risk anything at all for the deaths of some riff-raff?"

Coste gestured with his chin at the empty medicine boxes and blister packs strewn over the table.

"So you let him go all the way, then helped him escape as well?"

"It may not be cancer, capitaine, but Lucas is sick. In my defence, even though it's all the same to me, he did not need anyone's help."

A half-smile on her lips, she looked up at Brice once more.

"Would you please stop threatening our guest and lay that gun on the table?"

He did as he was told. Coste picked it up unhurriedly, ejected the clip and slipped it into his pocket. Then he checked there was no round in the chamber, and put the weapon back on the table.

"May I go and see him?"

Margaux Soultier consulted her watch.

"Of course. Brice will accompany you."

*

They climbed the big central staircase in silence. The door was half-open. On the impeccably made-up bed lay the body of a young man, legs together, arms by his sides, head on a vomit-stained pillow.

Coste was meeting Lucas for the first time.

The invitation must have been in his left hand before he dropped it, and it lay there now against his thigh. Kneeling down by the bed, Coste used the corner of a sheet to pick it up. An engraved inscription indicated the date. Lucas was not just well informed: he had been invited.

As so often, the darkness of a man's actions was impossible to read from his face. Lucas's still childish features looked at rest, harmless. He was gone, taking with him a part of the story that Coste could only guess at. Could he have met Camille during one of those nights? Could it have been that, thanks to the masks, the unthinkable had happened? An unbearable sense of guilt that only suicide could silence, in this mansion where he could find everything he needed to put an end to his days.

Lucas had gone without facing up to himself, without answering the questions torturing him. Had he loved Camille more than a brother should? One final question must have accompanied him in his last thoughts, and if by chance God existed, he would be able to ask Camille herself, once he was on the other side: "That evening, did you know who was behind the mask?"

Coste pressed three fingers to the side of Lucas's throat, searching for a pulse. All he felt was his skin growing colder. Switching off the light, he allowed his guide to lead him down the staircase.

Back in the morning room Margaux Soultier was finishing her tea, eyes sunk in the void of a life ending badly. When she saw him, she recovered.

"Am I to expect the noisy arrival of the forces of law and order?"

"They will come when you call them. I'm not on duty tonight."

With that, he left a tired old lady in a wheelchair alone with her demons, in a mansion that was too big and too empty.

The cold of dawn swept away the warmth of the rising sun on his face. The manor house, as it was called locally, was gradually being shrouded in early morning mist. Under that grey cloak he was leaving behind a man he still could not consider a monster, a man who had punished himself for not being able to protect the one he loved. Deep down, Coste shared some of his darkness; it was no use telling himself otherwise.

An old station wagon braked beside him. Ronan pushed open the passenger door.

"Have you finished all your nonsense, Victor? Can we go home?"

"Yeah. It's finished. Who does this wreck belong to?"

"I borrowed it from Karl, Johanna's husband. There's no accounting for taste. Can you believe it, a Volvo station wagon? I've never driven anything so clapped-out, but if I'd taken one of ours you'd have recognised me and shot my tyres out."

"I don't have a gun."

"It was just an expression. Get in, it's brass monkey weather."

Ronan turned on the heating. It blew out a cold blast, so he thumped the dashboard a couple of times, which seemed to do the trick, and the car started to pump out hot air.

"Where's Sam?"

"At his computer, tracking your mobile, because you keep getting into danger without letting us play alongside you."

"Since when?"

"Since when have we been tracking you? Since you went on your little adventure to Annecy right in the middle of a murder inquiry."

"That makes sense."

"So, are you going to explain a little?"

"Find a bar that's open at half past five in the morning and I'll tell you. Where's Johanna?"

"I really like her. She wanted to come. I let her put her kids to bed, saying I was going to fill up her jalopy. I never came back. She has two kids, a husband and a full-time job that she's been in for a week now. Too much to risk for losers like us, isn't it?"

Coste rolled his eyes.

"She's not going to be pleased."

Ronan gave a resounding laugh.

"Shit, you've no idea!"

61

From the Police Judiciare armoury on the first floor of 36 Quai des Orfèvres, Coste recovered his firearm, handcuffs and police I.D. He felt as if he was dressed again. His reinstatement had come sooner than expected, thanks to an advantageous simplification of the facts that others might have called a thorough-going cover-up.

The presenter of the morning rolling news, his bleary face enthroned centre-stage on an overlit platform, had described Lucas Soultier as "an individual emotionally disturbed by the continued disappearance of his adoptive sister who had taken revenge on random marginal individuals whom he considered responsible".

But the other story, the one that had all the newsrooms holding their breath, was more spectacular. On the tenth floor of a tower block in 93, the shameful deaths in their underwear of a commercial lawyer, a police commandant, the C.E.O. of a big construction company and a state councillor were monopolising everyone's attention.

The hostesses of that private soirée, as the presenter called it, were being actively sought for their testimonies, and the silence Lucas had imposed on himself must have been a blessing for many. But dead or alive, would that have changed much? Certain strata are too high for Justice to risk any rock-climbing.

* * *

In Bobigny that same morning, a nineteen-year-old had expressed his disgruntlement at his younger brother's exclusion from the Jean-Pierre Timbaud secondary school. Carrying a bottle of hydrochloric acid sometimes used to dissolve rocks or dip steel, he had poured it over the woman teacher originally responsible for the decision. She had literally melted outside the school building without a single person reacting. Videos of the event had been posted online and had more than ten thousand views. A sordid business, perfect for the return to work of Coste's team. Things were getting back to normal.

"Sam, you look for any C.C.T.V. coverage and find the I.P. addresses of all the bloggers who put up the attack online. Ronan and Johanna, you knock on doors, in the street and at the school, and try to find any possible witnesses. I'm going to pay a visit to the Jean-Verdier hospital."

Sam was worried.

"To the victim's bedside? Oh, no! You're going to charge your empathy like a battery and when it's good and full you're going to make us work 24/7."

De Ritter joined in.

"That's preferable to seeing him working all alone in his corner, isn't it?"

Coste turned towards his friend Mathias's former desk. Or was it the desk of his *former* friend? It would take some time to clarify that. Twenty-three was still an unacceptable number. Coste took advantage of the situation to make official what was obvious.

"You're right, Johanna. I've got an empty place opposite me.

It's time you moved your things there. Well, if you still want to work with us, that is, and if you don't put pictures of your kids up everywhere."

Johanna looked from one face to another. They were all smiles.

"You mean it?"

The three words were barely audible. To be part of something. To belong to a group. Them for her and her for them. Sam whispered to Ronan:

"You think she's going to blub?"

"Probably. Girls often do that."

Johanna recovered.

"Oh, so I'm a girl now, am I?"

"I don't even know what you're talking about."

Then there were three hugs and three "welcomes". Coste had a team once more.

Alone again, Coste went out to the coffee machine. He pressed the SUGAR button several times in revenge for all the occasions he had been forced to do without, and found himself with an undrinkable Colombian concoction. There was no point lying to himself. He was only there to say good morning to Camille, a face lost among the other disappeared children on the MISSING poster. From behind, Commandant Damiani disturbed his reverie.

"How are things?"

"I wasn't away very long."

"What case are you on?"

"The schoolteacher and the acid? Initial statements point towards the brother of a kid thrown out of the school. We're looking for statements and videos before we bring him in this afternoon."

"What about De Ritter? Have you decided?"

"She's a good sort. At first she was a bit prickly, but the lads have adopted her. Besides, I think she makes them less ridiculous. Me too, no doubt."

"You have a good team, Coste, and you're back in harness a bit soon. Take the day off. Let Ronan cut his teeth on this one. I'm minded to promote him to the rank of capitaine before long. It's time for him to learn to lead a group."

"You're taking Lieutenant Scaglia from me?"

"Not immediately, Victor, not immediately. You know that a career in the police means joining one pack and then leaving it to join another one. Speaking of which, Malbert's contract hasn't been renewed."

Coste would have been surprised if it had been otherwise. Code 93 had almost come to light, and those implicated must have been sweating for a while. But he was under no illusion. For Seine-Saint-Denis to fail to become part of Greater Paris was quite simply unthinkable, and they had already shown their determination. It might take some time, but they would find a way.

Pensive, Coste turned back to the photograph of Camille.

"I never managed to work out if you were part of all that, Marie-Charlotte," he mused.

"What on earth are you talking about?"

"I'll be less subtle. Does Code 93 mean anything to you?"

It was far too late for her. Too late for her to become a defender of morality, too late for her to risk her promotion and her retirement, which thanks to her balancing act she had until now protected.

"No, nothing. And it doesn't to you either, Coste."

She headed for the door and, without turning, repeated her order.

"Take the day off, Victor."

Less than an hour later, Coste was checki.
one of the café windows. He straightened h pearance in
to smooth down a rebellious tuft of salt-and-p and tried
though it was something he had not tried to do i ir. Even
he wanted to make a good impression.   while,

"You don't intend to run away again?"

With his foot, Coste pushed back the chair opposite   n,
inviting Léa Marquant to sit down.

"I've got nothing else planned."

She sat down and took his hand without another word. She
was pressing more firmly than the last time she had dared do
that. She would not let him escape this time, and he was glad
of it.

EPILOGUE

The gardener at the Thiais cemetery allowed himself a break. Fixing his rake on the back of his dustcart he sat down on a bench. He took a cigarette paper between two fingers and laid some strands of tobacco on it. He felt guilty because he had had a break less than an hour earlier, but such an intriguing and moving spectacle made him willing to risk a reprimand.

In the absolute calm of the burial ground, a procession of twelve dark-painted vans with the same golden insignia on the side was silently advancing. The last vehicle had barely entered the cemetery gates by the time the leading vehicle was unloading the first of its bouquets of flowers. White lilies.

In the space of a few hours, four thousand bouquets were laid on four thousand tombs, and, for the first time ever, the section for the lost, the nameless and the forgotten was the scene of an unusual flowering.

Lucas had told himself that among all these bouquets of lilies at least one of them would be exactly where he wanted it to be.

NOTE ON POLICE FORCES

S.D.P.J. 93 – Saint-Denis Police Judiciaire 93: the police force responsible for France's Département 93, led by **Commissaire Stévenin** and incorporating:

Groupes Crime – the crime squads. Led by **Commandant M.C. Damiani**. This unit breaks down into Groupe Crime 1, led by **Capitaine Coste**, and Groupe Crime 2, led by **Capitaine Lara Jevric**.

Groupe Stups – the drug squad

Brigade Criminelle – central crime squad operating out of 36 Quai des Orfèvres

Brigade de protection des mineurs – child protection department operating from 2 quai de Gesvres

Brigade de répression du banditisme – organised crime squad

Brigade des moeurs – vice squad

Brigade de répression du proxénétisme de Paris – anti-prostitution squad

Inspection Général des Services (I.G.S.) – police inspectorate, led by **Commissaire Dariush Abassian**

OLIVIER NOREK served as a humanitarian aid worker in the former Yugoslavia, before embarking on a eighteen-year career in the French police, rising to the rank of capitaine in the Seine-Saint-Denis Police Judiciare. He has written six crime novels, which have sold a million copies in France and won a dozen literary prizes.

NICK CAISTOR is a British translator from French, Spanish and Portuguese. He has won the Valle-Inclán Prize for translation from the Spanish three times, most recently for *An Englishman in Madrid* by Eduardo Mendoza, published by MacLehose Press.